The Eter[n]

Rising

By Simon *f* Osborn

Author's Note

This book contains graphic violence and explicit sexual content.

It is intended for a mature audience.

Simon F Osborn Copyright House 2019

Chapter One.

A grave undertaking

7th September 1745

In the dead of night, the bright full moon glistens overhead, a carpet of mist rolls up from the river towards the old dilapidated, but occupied homes of the tightly packed streets nearby. Hidden in the shadows, a dark shape moves in a secluded doorway. A woman screams out, a heart stopping noise in the still of night, the scream rings out again. Her high pitched shrill penetrates the soul, a window shutter closes as if removing any chance of escape. There would be no help for a victim in these cruel streets at this unforgiving hour. Suddenly, much closer, the sound of two sets of footsteps nearby. One light and fast, the other, heavy and lumbering. The young woman tumbles past running into the shadowy figure standing alone in the doorway. His grasp upon an elegant walking cane becomes tighter in his hand, watching, ready to defend himself. The young woman screams again and then turns catching her breath. Her pursuer, a large heavily built man reaches out to her as she gracefully twists away from his grasp. She giggles teasing him with her smile, then she runs off turning and staring to her pursuer as if to entice him to continue to chase her. 'Come ere girl, I just wanna kiss is all.' He growls frustrated trying to catch his breath. 'Ooooh, you'll have to catch me first.' She giggled again looking wide eyed at her pursuer, completely ignoring the stranger. She turns away running off down the dark alley into the darkness. With the couple gone, the mysterious figure stood still in the doorway for a moment. He softens the grip on his walking cane, it was after all just an innocent chase. Having watched them run away he smiles and adjusts his attire as he steps out into the street from the doorway. The figure is wearing a long dark heavy coat, short felt top hat, riding boots and dark breaches. His presence is strong and proud. Strolling through the dark uninviting streets with little concern about his own safety. His hand grips the ornate silver handle on top of his cane lightly as if it was something of great value. As he walked, there was a gentle click, click, click, on the partly stoned areas closest to the houses as the tip of the cane taps the ground checking the way ahead. The beautifully crafted object in his hand seems so out of place in the dirty muddy streets of this old London alleyway. The figure reached over with his other hand, and with a gentle touch he caresses a silver signet ring crowned with a bloodstone. The ring glows in the moonlight making the tiny red spots upon the ring shine a little more brightly. He lifts the cane to the moonlight as if to salute the very night itself, with the dignity of a fine gentleman. The silvery light from the moon above hits the cane and ring making them glow with a strange but familiar blue iridescent glow. He could see tiny specs of light, barely visible to the eye, like stars appear all around him, as if floating in the night air. The strange lights begin to focus on his hand, like they were being drawn to him, and then after a moment slowly fade away. Tonight, was a magical night, a special night, every possible preparation had been made, the timing was perfect. A rough piece of paper blew across the floor in front of him and he stabbed it with the tip of his cane, stopping it from blowing away any further. Slowly he stooped down to pick it up and read the crudely printed notice. The notice was most likely once nailed to a billboard somewhere nearby, judging from the tear in each corner.

THE ROYAL LONDON THEATRE

MISS MARY SUMMERFIELD

SINGING & DANCING

SHE WILL CAST HER SPELL ON YOU

THE GREAT AL MANI

LORD OF THE DEAD

ILLUSIONIST

MYSTIC

He looked at the headline act and stroked with affection her name. Closing his eyes, he could remember every detail of her. They were lovers, meeting in secret after their performances, in her room, above the theatre where she had her lodgings. Mary straddled him, sitting high over him, her upper body completely naked. She looked so exquisite. A woman of such charm and natural beauty, her half naked upper body glistening with sweat, gently, her hips rolled back and forth against him. Her eyes closed looking upward, long luxurious red hair flowing down her back like a river of blood. She pushed down on his strong naked chest with her hands and looked suddenly down into his eyes, she smiled softly to him. He looked up to her, gently easing himself deeper and deeper inside her with each stroke she made. Her pelvic bone against his. Her mouth opened slowly sucking in air and then, she vibrated releasing her passion to him. Daydan's hands held her hips softly, caressing her with his fingers, still guiding her hips gently. Vibrating again, she fell upon him barely able to hold herself up with her hands any longer.

'Oh my lord, you are insatiable.' Her smile was so pure and full of love, her eyes sparkled from the light of a single candle that burned beside her bed. 'I am not a lord my dear Mary.' He removed his right hand from her thigh and lifted it to cradle her cheek, she looked down to him still straddling him. Although she was clearly tired, her hips still rolled gently as she rubbed herself against him, engulfing his manhood. Turning her head slightly to kiss his hand she looked into his eyes. 'Will you not give me your seed sir. I want you so much.' Again, her mouth opened and closed like a fish out of water starving for oxygen. He caressed her lips with his thumb as she pushed harder and harder into him, slowly her movements quickened. 'Is that what you want.' His left hand gripped her tightly, her lower torso was covered from his view with her simple dress, but he could feel her flesh against his body. The warmth of being deep inside her was exquisite. 'Yes. I want you. I want us, I want us to be together always. We could go to the new world, raise a family, just you and I. Please say yes. I beg of you say yes. Promise me.' He was torn between his beautiful lover and his work. His duty. Lifting his hand to her face again his thumb dipped into her open mouth, she bit gently, sucking on its tip. With a final burst of energy her hips moved gracefully again, back and forth over him, she wanted him. 'You must choose my love; I know what I want. I want you. I will always want you.' Opening his eyes, trying to clear his thoughts of the past memory, he screwed up the piece of paper and threw it onto the muddy floor of the street and continued walking. His head bowed in sadness for the memory of his lover.

The narrow tightly packed street opened up as it got closer to the river ahead. Finally, he arrived at a set of large iron gates, one side of the gates is already open, just enough to squeeze his shoulder through. He leans against the open gate and pushes it. There is a cringing squeak of metal that fills the darkness for a moment as the gap widens, he walks slowly between them. Standing quietly, he stares from the cover of the gates looking onward with a pair of soft thoughtful eyes. Shrouded in the darkness he moves deeper into what is now clearly a graveyard. Old family tomb stones, unkept graves with crudely made wooden crosses were all around. Nearby he could hear the sound of digging, the muddy crunch of a spade being driven hard into the damp wet heavy earth. He approaches cautiously and stands back watching two men hard at work digging up a recently filled grave. The small cemetery graveyard was well used and popular once upon a time. Its proximity to the river Thames meant that during the floods, which occurred often, many of the graves were submerged in water. At these times, the graves often reluctantly gave up their decaying guests to the chilling ebb and flow of the cold dirty river Thames nearby. These days it was a graveyard for those just barely wealthy enough to be able to pay for a burial. In the darkness, the sound of the spade suddenly hits wood, the numb thud rumbled in the night as it thumped against the lid of a coffin. Daydan approached the pair of robbers at the neglected grave site. He slowly walks up from behind to an old man holding an oil lamp overhead, so that the other grave robber can see a little more clearly. Again, the sound of the spade hits the lid and the grave robber slowly scrapes around it removing more dirt from the lid of the coffin. The old man suddenly jumped backwards sensing someone close by, 'What the.' Startled he stares at the gentleman behind him lifting the lamp higher so he could see his face. Daydan raised his arm and thick coat sleeve to shield himself from the light of the lamp. 'Oh, it's you.' The old man looks at their observer, the robber in the grave continued digging, caring little about the unexpected onlooker. He carefully removes more dirt from around the lid and steps back ready to open it up. 'Oi, gimme some light will ya.' The older man with the lamp obliges, he lowers it to the grave and looks around cautiously. Daydan nods acknowledging them, motioning for two grave robbers to carry on. The young grave robber removes the lid to reveal the corps of a young woman within, she is shrouded in a simple plain black peasant's dress, laying upon a large red silk sheet. She could not have been dead more than a day or two, her features still very clear, her skin, pale white against the black and red. Obviously she was a real beauty when she was alive. The young woman must have only been in her late twenties or early thirties when her life had been suddenly cut short. 'This is the one you want right guv.' Daydan nodded to the grave robber slowly pointing to the corpse of the young woman with his walking cane. There was a deep sadness in his eyes and in his movements.

The corpse of the young woman appeared to be at peace, her arms folded across her chest in the classic style. Putting the walking cane under his arm he opened up his coat and pulled out a single stem of a red rose. Slowly he stroked it across her bright red lips, coloured with some red pigment, and then carefully put the rose stem into her long thin fingers. He leaned over her cold body carefully and kissed her lips making sure not to move a single hair. '*My dear Mary. Forgive me.*' The kiss was gentle and slow. 'Cor, she was a looker, what you gonna do wiv er then.' Daydan stood up tall and pointed once more to the body of the young woman, then gestured to an old wooden barrow that was to be used to transport the body. 'It ain't nuffin to do wiv us boy, longs we get paid it ain't.' The old man growled at his naïve accomplice. The young robber huffed a little, then he tilted his head looking at the corpse in her resting state. Shuddering, he adjusted his jacket and continued with his work. Grave robbing was not uncommon these days, and it provided extra cash for many whose morals were inclined towards such opportunities. The grave robbers never did know why or what these people did with the corpses, they cared little. Sometimes the corpses would be seen floating down the Thames horribly mutilated or dismembered, days or even weeks later. Others would never be seen again, probably for the best. Any corps is not a pleasant thing to be around, whatever state it was in. The young grave digger cleared away the remaining dirt and gripped two very cleverly well-placed rope handles in the false bottom of the coffin. It made it easy to pick the young woman up out of the coffin. This robbery had been very well planned. Oddly, the grave was not deep at all, certainly it was not the recommended 6ft, perhaps a little more than 3ft at best. It did make hauling the corpse up out of the shallow grave a lot easier, and a lot faster. It explained why so many graves gave up their dead so easily to grave robbers, or during the floods.

The corpse of the young woman was lifted up completely out of the coffin with the help of the false bottom. It was carefully put onto the rickety old wooden barrow. Sliding the false bottom easily into the centre, Daydan covered her with the red sheet and put several large pieces of sack cloth that was on the barrow over her to hide her from view. In the darkness, with the full moon playing its tricks, giving a strange glistening silvery blue white reflection of light to everything. It appeared that the young woman's very spirit was trying to leave its host. A faint blue mist appeared around her body, the barely visible ghostly shape of her female form, her ethereal hand slowly reached up, her ghostly face looked sad and fearful. The faint mist of blue light that slowly formed her shape moved slowly. Daydan looked to her with a gentle smile just visible on his lips. Suppressing tears, he tipped his hat to her bowing his head politely. A single peacock feather that decorated the short black top hat upon his head caught the moonlight, which made the eye of the peacock feather shine brightly in the dim light. The eye of the feather radiated a dim light with all of the colours of the rainbow, like tiny stars of every colour imaginable, the young woman's spirit stopped moving. She was afraid, still. Daydan, with a caressing sweep of his own softly glowing hand rest it gently on her ethereal spirits chest, reassuring her, he coaxed her ghostly form back down into its corps host. His gentle touch was calming for the spirit, her spectral form relented to his caress and lay slowly back into the young woman's body, the glowing light slowly faded away. Daydan grinned happily to himself, he sighed with relief, her spirit was still within, he was not too late after all. The night was young, and tonight all things were possible. A gentle smile forms on his hidden face, the silver signet ring on his finger was glowing in the moonlight, the silver toped cane and the peacock feather on his top hat glowed softly too, catching every ray of moonlight. His hand weaving a tapestry of strange light between the softly glowing objects. It looked like a magical thing to him, these mysterious energies, but to others few even saw the gentle glow. Small wisps of light, like tiny blue fireflies or stars danced around him. They appeared to be drawn to his hand or the items he carried. The movement of the small specs of light was not random, but in some way deliberate, like a swarm of insects' drawn to him. The grave robbers were oblivious to the gentleman's display, but to him tonight was a special time, all the right elements seem to coalesce, working together to some dark eerie mysterious magic. He lifted his hand to his face, and he could see the glow, the energy, like his hand was burning in a rich blue light, it was a beautiful magical thing to behold.

The two grave robbers were unaware of the corpse's actions or that of the cloaked gentleman nearby, they quickly began filling in the open shallow grave as fast as they could. The job was done, all they cared about was covering up their crime and getting paid. The gentleman tapped the older robber on the shoulder with his cane, who turns slowly to face him. Daydan put a well-used leather purse of coins into the older robber's hand. The old man's fingers wrapped around it and paused for a moment. He nods tipping his cloth cap slightly. 'Fank ya me lord, nice doin business wiv ya.' The old robber clenched the purse of coins tightly and quickly pushed it into an inside pocket beneath his heavy coat. Daydan nods politely and begins to walk away watching over his shoulder that the older robber is following behind with the barrow. The sound of loose dirt being flung onto the refilled grave could still faintly be heard. With each spade full of dirt, the sound grows quieter. 'You finish up ere boy, I'll meet you in the tavern and we'll divvy up, I'm just gonna drop off er ladyship ere.' The younger robber pauses for a moment and nods to the older man, he spits into his hands rubbing them together for a better grip, and for some much-needed warmth as the chilling night air cuts deeply into his bones. Dark shadows close in around Daydan and the old man, as the small oil lamp lights the tiny area around them, they walk back towards the streets and dwellings. The dim light does little to hold back the thick mist from the river nearby, now gently rolling up the bank to the graveyard, as if enticing the inhabitants into the very Thames itself. The gentleman moves to the old iron gates and pushes them open wide with both hands, the tell tail slow screeching shrill of iron on iron penetrates deep into the night. With the gates now open the barrow is wheeled through and on into the shadowy streets ahead. The strange squeak of wooden wheels on the partly cobbled road eerily filling the quiet streets with a monotonous, rhythmic, hypnotic bump. The night was still cold and uninviting, the air was damp and thick with fog, but the full moon over head seemed to shine a welcome silvery blue glow lighting their way as if some magical force was watching over them. The small tightly packed homes were for the most part dark and uninviting. An odd house on their journey might have a single candle or lamp burning in a first-floor window or some other ground floor room. The old man pushing the barrow was beginning to struggle, the efforts of the night clearly not something a man of his years should be doing. The breath from his warm body soon turned to mist in the night air, adding to the fog that formed all around them. A few moments later the gentleman stopped at an alleyway, a little way down the alley there is a wooden gate just large enough for the small cart to fit through. Over the gate a wooden sign with branded letters burned neatly into a beautifully polished plank of wood overhead. *UNDERTAKER of all trades.* Just as they were about to enter the alley and leave the streets, a pair of horses approaches at the gallop. Two cavalry officers were drinking from clay earthenware bottles bickering and boasting until they see the odd scene ahead. One of the officers draws a long cavalry sword and raises it above his head and then points to the two men, he kicks his steed and lunges the animal forwards. 'Charge.' The officer swings at the two strangers, back and forth, who easily avoid his weak clumsy drunken attack and he loses balance falling unceremoniously off his horse. He first falls onto the cart, and then into a heap on the muddy ground of the street. As he fell, he hit the barrow and some of the sacking shifted and the corpses hand flopped over the side of the little cart, dropping the delicate red rose stem to the ground. Daydan reluctantly puts his large boot over the rose stem, just as the old grave robber instantly placed himself between the barrow and the other officer to hide the corpses hand from view. The mounted officer unsheathed his own sword and pointed it to Daydan, who by this time joined the older man blocking any chance of them being able to see anything other than the barrow. He turned and looked to the cavalry officer directly, but his eyes were not visible thanks to the brim of his top hat, if they had been visible, the Kings Officer might have identified the contempt in his gaze. He tucked the hand of the corpse neatly back up under the sacking cloth. 'What have you there.' The mounted officer pointed his long-curved cavalry sword to the gentleman and attempted to look around him, leaning off his steed a little to get a better look. The old robber, having seen his employer cover the corpses hand, deftly kneeled to the fallen officer and seemingly helped to assist the embarrassed man to his feet. Daydan was quick to see the old man draw a small blade, as if to slit the throat of the fallen cavalryman where he lay, but it was not to be. In a movement so fast for such an old man, he saw the grave robber cut a purse of coins from the officer's belt, quickly hiding both blade and purse within his own coat. Daydan grinned warmly at the robber's efficiency and held back a laugh. Clearly needing a distraction from the unfolding events, he slowly pulled an object from within his own heavy coat while calmly placing his elaborate walking cane under his arm. The sound of a cork popped, and he lifted a small clay bottle to his lips, then he walked to the fallen officer's horse and stroked its nose talking quietly to the animal. The horse calmed and sniffed at the bottle in his hand. The officer on the floor was being assisted by the grave robber sitting him up on the muddy ground. Daydan stroked and petted the horses, the cavalry officer laughed at him mockingly. 'A horse whisperer.' He put his sword back into its scabbard and manoeuvred his large white horse closer to him making the animal nudge him to one side. He ignored the cavalryman's rudeness and still attended to the horses, he looked up to the officer on his horse raising his bottle to his lips again in a mocking salute. The cavalryman leaned forwards on his saddle looking down at the gentleman.

'I am Captain John Atwood, of his majesties royal dragoon guards, we will meet again someday horse whisperer.' The officer tugged at the reigns of his horse to regain control of the animal that was enjoying the attention and affection from the gentleman on foot. The floored officer helped by the robber was assisted back up onto his steed next to his comrade. The night air softened for a moment, the moonlight still glistened overhead shinning rare silvery beams of light, the air once again turned to a bitter cold. The gentleman lowered his drinking flask, replaced the cork and put it back inside his coat, giving the young cavalry officer a polite yet begrudging nod. The captain kicked his steed into action and turned it grabbing the reigns of his comrades' horse who was still rather dazed from his fall, the two officers rode off slowly. As they did, the young officer looked back watching them for a moment and then turned away. Daydan and the old robber watched the cavalrymen ride away and when they were gone, the two men looked to each other in silence for a moment. The old man rolled his eyes gently tapping the bulge in his coat from the newly acquired coin purse.

'I was impressed, dunno about you guv.' The old man laughed shaking his head and turned back to the cart. With a smile and a nod Daydan turned and pointed to the gate just a little further ahead. With a slightly forceful push of effort, the barrow was moved down the alley and through the gate into a very small yard on the other side. The old man proceeded to push the cart down a small incline that gently led to the basement under the premises, a workshop of some kind. Once inside the workshop, the grave robber looked around at the dozens of strange jars and the objects within, that quite frankly turned him rather fearful. The space was once used as a blacksmiths workshop with a large furnace at one end, it had been easy to turn the space into a more useful multipurpose workshop. It now looked like something more akin to a carpenter's workshop, a smithy, an undertaker and a laboratory all in one space. The old man was thankful for the few candles and oil lamps dotted around to see by. Some of the objects looking back at him from the specimen jars were quite frightening to behold. Strange unnatural shadows were cast upon the walls around them. Daydan pointed to the door tapping the old man on his shoulder with his cane, he says nothing to him, but his gesture is enough, the old man tipped his hat and turned to leave. He paused a moment and spun on his heels and pulled out the fallen cavalry officers coin purse, attempting to split the spoils. Daydan put his hand over the coin purse, shaking his head he pushed it back into the older man's coat. The old man nodded turning without any resistance or objection, then he left the basement quickly closing the large door slowly behind himself as it creaked and clunked into place. Alone now, Daydan turned a large heavy key in the door, locking it and put a swing bar down across the door slamming it into place. Now secure and locked in, he could not be disturbed. He slowly pushed the corpse of the young woman from the cart onto an elaborate beautifully decorated wooden plinth, his bright sparkling eyes peering down to her. He slowly removed the sack cloth that covered her corpse from prying eyes. She lay there in front of him and he just watched her closely for a moment in perfect silence and stillness. Slowly, he reached for the hand of the corpses holding it gently in his own, he kissed it softly. Closing his eyes, concentrating his thoughts, once again the bloodstone ring on his hand seemed to glow very softly in the night, small specs of blue light as before floated like embers between the ring, the gentleman's hand and the corps. Slowly, a ghostly hand reached out to his own from the corpses hand, and once again the strange blue flickers of light seemed to connect between himself, the ring and the corpses now slowly awakening spirit. Her ghostly form grew slowly, steadily forming her image. Her shape, her looks, even her clothes, clearer and more detailed with every passing moment. The moonlight streaming in through a street level window above them illuminated the scene beautifully. She reluctantly and very slowly began to sit up. Fearfully, her form slowly filling with more detail every single second, her hair, the detail of her features, soon her entire form became perfectly visible in every detail in a light blue iridescent ghostly glowing haze. It was very clear that she was in life a very beautiful young woman in her time. Daydan knew her well, the time they shared in life was nothing more than the blink of an eye. Perhaps he could not have her in life like he wanted, but he could have her now in death. At least for a while.

He coaxed her apparition gently away from her corpse still holding her hand in his, she seemed reluctant at first, but slowly and carefully with ever growing confidence her apparition broke free of its previous shell. He stepped back encouraging her to leave her corpse completely and join him. He made a single step towards an open area away from her corpse. Still holding the hand of her spirit in his, she slowly joined him swinging her legs out from her sitting position over the side of the plinth. A pair of long youthful stockinged legs under a simple black dress made her look like a peasant. Yet she looked wild, graceful, free spirited and seductive. The momentary glimpse of her ethereal flesh beneath her dress at the top of her stockings remained with him like a curse. Holding his hand gently, her beautiful form now very pleasant to observe as she watched him closely. She looked a little confused as she turned to her corpse, then she looked sad and held her tummy and looked back to her body. For the first time he noticed the huge gash in the corpses throat and another in her abdomen, quite vicious wounds.

The causes of a very horrible death no doubt. Turning away from the corps he reached out to her with both hands, he coaxed her away from her corpse further. She was free now. She held his hand for a moment moving around him very slowly, parading herself, she was well aware of her presence and her own very provocative movements. She took his hand in hers and held it against the her wound on her tummy. The proximity of her corpse seemed not to bother her any longer, now was not the time for remorse, sadness or revenge, they were together again. She somehow realised she was no longer alive, but she was aware of her existence, a slight worried look took the smile from her face, it seemed that she remembered her demise. The cruel painful death blows that ended her days with the living. She closed her eyes and clenched her abdomen again and put her other hand up to her throat. Opening her eyes, she recognised the man standing before her. Mary tried to speak, but there was no sound, it was odd, but he could understand her all the same, hearing her words in his mind.

She looked away shamefully from him. Behind him was a poster, a poster of her from one of her many performances. Recognising her name, she slowly approached him and caressed his cheek in the palm of her hand. She knew him well. He took her ghostly hand in his and kissed it softly, looking up into her eyes he smiled, his bright gentle eyes seemed to relax her, she felt safe. Mary began to move around him slowly and smile still holding his hand. Taking the hem of her black dress in her other hand she danced beautifully around him. Her lovely thin stockinged thighs occasionally giving a teasing glimpse of her feminine figure beneath her simple off the shoulder dress. She knowingly teased him with her dancing, effortlessly circling around him time and time again in an ultimate tease, flashing her upper thighs to him with the occasional swish of her dress. She was enjoying his attention, her stockings rising three quarters of the way up her thin pale legs. The flesh that she revealed would have hypnotised any man, yet Daydan was clearly someone who had loved her and adored her very deeply. They remained in that basement alone for some time, enjoying each other's company. He was happy to have her with him again, even in this undead form. Her beautiful red lips, her pale skin, even as a ghost it looked whiter than white. Her long red hair, the black dress, her stockings, her simple shoes. She was a sight to behold.

Sometime later the light from the moonlight made long shafts of moonbeams spread across the basement floor and walls from the window just above street level. Daydan watched as tiny specs of light began to take shape, Marys ghostly form fearfully backed away hiding at the rear of her lover, watching from a safe distance behind him. Very slowly a vague shape gradually began forming from the tiny fragments of light, the small strange specs of light again began to dance around, forming and taking shape. When the figure was complete in its ethereal mist it moved slowly towards them, removing a three-pointed hat, the newly formed spirit made an elegant overly flamboyant bow to Mary, and remained still for a moment. He stood up straight, a well-dressed gentleman in a flamboyant heavy coat, tight riding trousers and riding boots, two flintlock pistols were holstered into his belt. Across his chest he wore a powder flask and a small pouch, a coin purse, and on his right hip a very savage, well-worn heavy cutlass. Beneath his three-corner hat he wore the white wig of a gentleman.

Daydan pointed to the wall with his cane, and as he did so, again the tell-tale forming of yet ethereal energy took shape. It was slow at first, very slow, then steadily the light coalesced more rapidly until another ghostly form stood in the basement with them. This time it was a tall half naked African looking man, in life he would have been very dark skinned, strong, and muscular in build and completely bald. His body was marked with scars of all kinds, tribal scars, wounds of all kinds, some clearly from the lash. The ghost stood tall proud and defiant. In his right hand he held a menacing dark wooden club, tribal in origin. The four figures looked to each other, a polite silent understanding exchange of glances. Daydan stepped forwards and tapped the stone floor with his cane to get everyone's attention. He smiled looking to each of his companions in turn. 'Gentlemen,' he turned to Mary, 'and lady, we have work to do.' He spoke softly as he looked towards his mysterious companions and smiled, his lips still pressed together deep in thought, but the line of his mouth clearly showing that he was more than pleased with his nights work. They watched each other for some time, Mary, was very shy and hid herself behind Daydan watching his other two companions carefully. They in turn watched the young woman, exchanging glances and nodding respectfully to their host. There was no long conversation, no social display of greeting, just mutual respect and acceptance, these were spirits tied to the present world in need of peace, for now, they were the most unlikely of companions.

Chapter Two

Am I dead

Later that night, the embers from his stoves fire burned steadily. The heat radiating from it made the space nearby a most cosy, welcoming place to sit and rest, especially to fall asleep by. A simple copper pot sits carefully on the embers and a steady trail of steam was slowly billowing from it. He reached over and poured some of the steaming water into a cup with a generous spoon full of dried tealeaves. A welcoming strong odour from the tea filled his nostrils and reminded him of a time with his father in a place much warmer than here. He took a sip of the hot drink and relaxed back into the high back chair and breathed out a long easy breath as he drank his hot tea. He lived in an amazing time, a time of science and medicine, philosophy, art. It was called the great awakening, a time when religion and reform were becoming strong, if there was any time that his work and knowledge could be passed on to the masses, it was now. His father, and his father before him, tried to pass on their craft and understanding of their wisdom before. Back then they had been outcast, expelled, beaten and stoned just for trying to tell people the truth.

Two great forces were at work in this time, the Age of Enlightenment, and The Great Awakening, you could say the forces of good and evil, of light and dark, knowledge and ignorance. Religious men would argue that one should show piety and utter devotion, whereas the enlightened would rebel against the state and all forms of control. This new way of thinking was most popular with scholars, writers and poets of the time. Reform politicians and the students embraced the age of awakening. This way of thinking brought forth some great minds in philosophy and the sciences, art and literature. They were always popular topics at any gathering, and much more interesting than religion or politics. He leaned back in his comfortable high back chair and sipped his hot cup of tea enjoying its aromas of some exotic faraway place. In his small home in the basement of an overcrowded dwelling above, in a back-street slum between the river Thames and the Kings Road in Chelsea, he lived a rather reclusive lonely life. His calling kept him immensely busy. He often dreamed of faraway places, of debating with intellectuals who were truly open minded. Were the awakened really awake, were the enlightened truly enlightened, or would this be yet another repeat of all those times that his own father and his fathers' father before him, tried to free people from their own subservience and ignorance. He closed his eyes thinking of the trials ahead and let the cup of hot tea sit lightly on his lap. His large heavy coat had served well to keep out the cold and damp, to give him the comfort and warmth of a restful night that a fire could not. His thoughts drifted back to his youth remembering back to a time when such heat was on his face, a smile gently formed across his lips and his cheeks puffed slightly. Hot intense sunshine beat down, market stalls trading spices and fabrics. He could still remember the rich smell of spices like it was yesterday. The smell of livestock and street food of all kinds was everywhere. The hustle and bustle of a large city market, it was exciting, vibrant. He had never seen so many people in one place ever before. His father walked briskly through the crowded marketplace and he followed behind carrying a large pack upon his back that was pretty much the entirety of their worldly possessions. They lived a permanent life on the road moving from city to city. His father found a spot upon a broken wall, a good vantage point from which he could be seen and heard. He clambered up and smiled to his son reassuringly then smoothed over his long beard, robes and headdress, and stamped a large staff heavily into the ground to get some attention.

'My friends'. He bellowed. Raising his hands up towards the heavens, still grasping the heavy staff in his hands, people stopped and turned to listen. Another speaker, another storyteller perhaps, it was entertainment none the less. Not as interesting as a stoning a flogging or an execution, but it passed the time. Several travellers and onlookers stopped in their tracks to listen. 'We live in a blessed land and a wonderful time of science and medicine, but did all of this come from Allah.' More people gathered, whispering began, his father continued to speak shaking his outstretched arms at the heavens. 'We are not slaves to Allah, we are immortal spirits of the universe, unending, children of the stars. We do not answer to gods.' The gathered crowd, now swelling, looked puzzled, the gathering grew a little more, and he watched his father carefully listening to his words but also watching the crowd of onlookers. 'My friends, brothers and sisters, open your eyes, open your hearts, we are one, all things are united, all that is will always be, it simply changes in form, but in essence we are immortal, everything is forever.'

Murmurings began to whisper close by, an uneasy atmosphere rippled across the gathered crowd as some of the onlookers reached to the ground putting rocks onto their sleeves. His father withdrew an ebony coloured rock, like glass, he held the object up to his face that was the size of his fist and closed his eyes. Slowly, small specs of light could be seen, dark blue and black sparks of light gently danced about the blackened glass, to the closest onlookers a face began to form, twisted and contorted. They stared in amazement at first. His father continued to focus his mind on the piece of obsidian. Suddenly from nowhere there was a woman's scream, then something hit his father's head. His father immediately shielded himself with his robed-sleeve and shook his staff at the crowd. 'Sheep.' He shook his fist at them angrily and tried to spot his attacker. A man pointed to him. 'Necromancer, blasphemer.' The man threw another rock at his father and then others joined in the impromptu stoning, rocks pummelled his father from all directions, even with his arm raised only to defend himself other rocks found their target easily.

A man in black robes raised his arms and yelled out. 'Stop, what are you doing, let him speak freely.' But no one listened to the Alim. It was to late, rocks flew at his father and unable to stand and talk freely, he shielded himself and ran away as fast as he could. He was clubbed several times from passers-by with their walking poles. Normally a weapon for defence, a tool, but here they were swung with one intent. He ducked and weaved between the blows calling out to his son before sprinting off doing his best to evade the crowd. Daydan followed his father as best as he could. He too sustained injuries from poorly aimed rocks that were likely aimed at his father. Ducking and weaving with the heavy pack on his back was not easy, but it surely protected him from a severe beating. His light youthful physique allowed him to race through the narrow streets much faster than his pursuers and he made sure to keep an eye on his father's escape route. They agreed to meet at the docks if things did not go well and to his joy, soon after losing his father for a moment he saw him standing at the jetty near a small sail boat talking to one of the crew, no doubt bartering for passage to where ever it going. When his father saw his son, he smiled and held out his arms to him in greeting. 'Come my son, I feel it is time we need to move on again, this place is not for us, the people are like children.' He nodded to his father respectfully, shifting the large heavy pack on his back. He gave his father a concerned but respectful smile. 'Yes father.' His father put his hand on his shoulder and looked deeply into his eyes. 'No matter what, our duty is to spread our knowledge. Promise me.' Daydan nodded to his father. His father shook his head.

'Promise me my son.' Daydan looked to his father, he was all he had, not brothers or sisters, no mother, no family. This was the only life he knew. He looked up to his father wanting him to be proud of him, wanting to please him. 'Yes father, I promise.' He was little more than a boy himself, almost a young man. They nursed their wounds sitting upon the deck of the small boat hiding behind some fishing nets in the hot sunshine. The small fishing boat creaked a little and made its way out into the Mediterranean Sea. Another adventure, another city, he pulled off his pack and lay back upon some of the nets closing his eyes and enjoying the heat of the sun on his face. Smelling the salty air of the sea was refreshing, he always loved being near the sea. It often meant change, starting over. He breathed deeply and reached over to his father and smiled. His father laughed nursing a large wound on his head patting his son affectionately on his broad young shoulders and smiled to him. His fathers' skin was old yet tanned and leathery.

The heat felt nice on Daydan's face; it was something that brought him peace. He sniffed the air with his eyes still closed, but it was not the sound of water lapping at the sides of the boat. He opened his eyes to darkness, his stove flickering gently warming his cheeks from the coldness and damp outside. The smell of fresh brewed tea was still rich in the air, and he took a long savouring drink of the hot beverage and relaxed himself, sitting back in his chair and getting comfortable again closing his eyes for a good night's sleep.

Later, returning from sleep he felt a presence close by and slowly turned towards it without opening his eyes, he sniffed the air for the tell-tale signs of sweat. The scent of a thief or burglar, an intruder, but there was none. He opened his eyes slowly and looked towards the presence he felt before him. Mary's ghost who he just returned from the dead, her spirit, was standing in front of him. She gazed into his face with her hands behind her back twisting slowly from side to side. He smiled to her; she was indeed a pretty thing. Even in this form her beauty and charm radiated from her apparition in the dark room. She looked to him and although her lips did not move and no sound came from her mouth, he could hear her thoughts as if she spoke them to him. 'Am I dead?' He looked to her and nodded plainly. 'I don't understand.' She stared deeply into his eyes, clearly needing some kind of explanation. He stood up slowly using his hands on the chairs arm rests to push himself up and approached her. 'It is not an easy thing to explain,' he frowned a little, 'but I will try.' Picking up his tea he thought for a moment then he finished the hot drink in one mouthful and put the teacup down on a handy yet simple small wooden table nearby. 'Your spirit, your energy, what makes you, is eternal, but it is not done with this life yet,' He paused and looked deeply into her eyes. 'You have something you wish to do.' She looked puzzled, he paused for a moment, how does he explain this to a woman who he predicted had very little understanding of the sciences and beyond. Even the greatest minds of the time were unable to grasp such a simple concept. Could she comprehend this fascinating science that even he was still struggling to completely understand. Mary, in life, was a witch, full of magic and ancient knowledge. She fascinated him. How does he explain this. It was a question that he hoped to answer very soon, because he was expected to speak publicly about his work to a select few of England's most powerful and influential figures. He looked to Mary and smiled trying his best to put her mind at ease amidst her confusion. 'When you die, your spirit, your essence, your energy leaves your body, and it is reborn. But sometimes, that energy remains, like you. You have something you need to do before you feel it is time to move on, to renew. You will be tied here until you feel it is time to go, just like Jin, and Angus, they too are not yet ready return to the source.'

The young woman paused for a moment as she listened to her mysterious saviours' words. She seemed to accept what he had said even though he doubted whether or not she truly understood what he was trying to tell her. 'This, person who did this to you.' he said the word person mockingly and stood up straight facing the young woman. He put his hand gently on her abdomen and looked into her eyes. 'What happened to you was wrong, it was a wicked act. They should pay dearly for that cruelty.' She put her cold ethereal hand on his and smiled weakly to him. 'You cannot undo what has been done Daydan, even you, not even you.' He lowered his eyes trying to think of what to say, something reassuring perhaps. He smiled and touched her ghostly cheek with his hand. She softly leaned into his touch with her cheek and her beautiful eyes sparkled too him. Once again, his mind wondered and he remembered his companions, the ghostly forms that he had collected, lost souls, wronged souls that wanted revenge. It was a concept that he struggled with. The universe was chaotic, yet there was a majestic order that was without doubt perfect. Good, bad, hot, cold, dark, light, one could not exist without the other. He knew that in order to achieve harmony there had to be a balance. He remembered the slave, Jin, a powerful tall man, larger than life and full of anger and hate. He was on a slave ship during a storm bound for Liverpool, then off to some other far off land. The ship was taking on water and damaged, the captain ordered that any nonessential cargo, sick or dying be thrown overboard to save the ship from sinking. It was a practice that was becoming more and more common, slaves referred to as cargo, lost at sea, were insured. When this happened on the ship Jin was incarcerated upon, word travelled fast as screaming slaves were thrown overboard still chained to the dead or sick. It would be hard enough trying to survive such an ordeal without the added encumbrance of a dead or sick body dragging them down into the depths. The healthier stronger slaves hearing the screams and some witnessing the murders rose up and began attacking their guards. Some were still chained to their bunks; others broke free and caused chaos and mayhem in an attempt to survive. When they reached the deck, expecting to see the land and a shore to swim to, their fate became obvious. Die fighting or give up. They set fires, smashed barrels and stores, tore at the sails, unlashed rigging. With the ship in flames most of the crew jumped overboard or fled in one of the two small rowing boats until finally, there was a huge explosion that ripped through the hull of the ship. The carnage was terrible, debris and bodies everywhere, with not another ship in sight, soon after it sank. Off the southwest coast of England, debris was washed up upon the shore, bodies, driftwood, the remains of a once fine ship. With such a large number of bodies in one place, it made sense for an undertaker to make the journey that took an entire day and a half by carriages from London. There were bodies of all kinds in the wreckage, broken, mangled, and bloated. But one, was floating upon a large flat piece of driftwood, a thick heavy cabin door. When Daydan leaned down to measure up the body of the deceased slave for a simple wooden box coffin. The moment he touched the body the spirit of the slave began to form in front of his eyes. He was overcome with excitement and wonder, the slaves form ebbed, between the spirit world and the source. To return to a world between the living and the dead. His hand glowed gently with a mysterious blue hue, he pushed down upon the slave's chest forcing his spirit back into his broken battered body. The silver bloodstone ring on his finger pulsed and all he could do was laugh. Laugh out loud. Realising that for the first time, he could bring back the spirits of the dead. The slave was the first spirit he ever resurrected, to that state of consciousness between life and death. Because they were conscious, they knew of their past, they were aware of their present. He found this limbo state fascinating and believed that it held the true secrets of the universe, the source of all knowledge and understanding. There are only two ways a spirit can cause harm upon the living, through fear, or through the viewers own submission. Often the wronged would give up their pursuit for revenge, because the recipient simply did not care, or they were oblivious. He returned from his memory and looked back to Mary for a moment. She had no anger, no desire for revenge, he sensed that she was a gentle soul, so why did she come back so easily. Why could Mary not move on. Was there something that he was missing. She moved closer and put her arms around him in her ethereal form and rest her head upon his chest holding him tightly.

As she held him, he turned his thoughts for a moment to the other companion he befriended. Angus Turin was a Jacobite outlaw. Captured and imprisoned and executed for crimes against the crown, namely highway robbery. Stealing, rabble rousing and horse theft. He spoke out against the crimes against the Scott's. He targeted officers, soldiers and dignitaries between York, Leeds and

London, until the time he was captured and beaten. His execution in London at the city gates was an elaborate affair. In his day he was a flamboyant gentleman and womaniser. His fighting prowess was second to none with a very obvious military background. He was half Scott and half French noble, an unlucky combination in such a turbulent time. He was the victor of many private duels. And the breaker of many women's hearts. It was Daydan's job to supply cheap coffins for pauper burials after public executions. The position was given him to provide the necessary service. Angus Turin on the other hand, although his body was broken and mutilated, was not done yet. When his battered body was laying on the table in his workshop, Angus's form rose up. The stories he told, the skill with which he could fight were lessons for survival. In a quiet dark basement hidden from prying eyes, the spirit of a notorious highwayman and a gentleman could duel and talk undisturbed. Thanks to the highwayman, Daydan's prowess with a foil or his cane were a joy to behold, thanks to the tutoring of military gentleman long since dead. It was this ability to reclaim knowledge and experience from the dead that made Daydan realise how precious his ability was. He returned his attention to Mary and held her close comforting her, until her spirit faded from view.

He spent the next day alone, preparing coffins, smoothing the wood by hand, a slow time-consuming task. There was something about the smell of fresh planed wood that felt comfortable. Carpentry was one of many skills he had to learn, but it was one that gave him great pleasure. Working with wood, iron as a blacksmith, ingredients as an apothecary, studying bodies and anatomy as an undertaker or physician. It was this access to knowledge that gave him a very different view of the world. He performed a respectful right to the dead as he burned Mary's body down completely, in the old way. In the end, all that remained was the ash from her bones, which he made sure was ground to a fine powder. Between his work schedule he would bring Mary back in her spirit form. In their own way they talked and conversed, she danced for him and was attentive and caring. He in turn watched her, listened to her songs in his mind and remembered how much he enjoyed watching her on the stage. How much he loved being with her in life. Maybe she was dead, but there was a part of him that felt like she was special, that they had a connection. Perhaps in a different time they would be together again, even lovers. Her smile felt like sunshine, and he would stop from his labours and awaken her from her ethereal slumber to spend time with her. The minutes were irrelevant, hours turned by unnoticed. He had his companions, his strange other worldly life. Studying the undead, the source, bringing them back to an unlife state, a necromancer learning his art in secrecy. Learning the secret of the universe. He studied hard, night or day it did not matter. By daylight, candlelight or oil lamp, a corner to work was more than enough. Learning how materials behaved in different states. How life reacted to different things, how death transformed itself from something useless into something new. Eventually everything returned to the source, to be reborn, renewed, something else. The only thing that had a true beginning and end was the transition from one life to the next, awareness, consciousness, that was the mystery that he wanted to understand. Jin was so full of anger and hate. Angus just wanted to fight his fight and frighten people to death for revenge. But Mary, she was different. Her thirst for revenge was non-existent, how was she able to stay and not transition to the source of the universe. It was necessary to work, small jobs trickled in, a coffin, a box, a repair, a cabinet, gate irons, hinges and nails. Quick easy jobs that paid enough to keep him in food and rent. Enough to enable him to study, research, experiment, write down notes. A strange life indeed for a simple man of the mid-18th century. His evenings were much the same, a hot drink in-front of an open fire. His adoring companion huddled up around his feet looking into the flames, she would look up and hold him closing her eyes and smiling. It was like she was keeping a beautiful secret from him, knowingly waiting for the right moment. He watched her sometimes and drifted off into a dream thinking about a life that could have been. She held his leg and leaned her face upon his knee looking into the hot embers of the stove close by. 'Did you ever want a family, a wife perhaps, children, babies.' She laughed and seemed to kiss his knee hugging him closer. He cleared his throat and took a puff from a clay pipe and coughed, smoking tobacco was supposed to be the fashionable thing to do these days, but he found it quite distasteful, and the smell was rather intoxicating, perhaps that was the attraction. He coughed and put the clay pipe down by the fire. 'Maybe, my lifestyle would not suit most women, and my beliefs I feel would frighten most away, wouldn't you agree.' He looked around the workshop at the handmade coffins, jars of chemicals and anatomy. Folding his arms across his chest he grinned waiting for her confirmation and response. 'Maybe you could change.' He laughed as her voice flooded his mind, she seemed to roll her cheek across his knee, her head of hair hung like water over her shoulders and she had a presence that was gentle and alluring. 'Maybe.' He replied slowly; his hand reached to her head even though his physical body penetrated her ethereal body. His hand gently caressed her hair and the shape of her head, she turned to look up to him and tilted her head seductively looking into his eyes from her lower position at his feet. 'Would you change for me my lord.' He looked to her beautiful apparition; he felt his heart skip a beat. It was not just her simple beauty that he found alluring, there was something else, something deeper that he could not explain. It was like she knew him better than he knew himself. He felt vulnerable, before, there was just himself and his father. After his father passed away all he had to care about was himself, his studies and work interfered with any thoughts of having a normal life. He stroked her head and rest his hand on his knee as she stretched her neck a little to seemingly kiss his fingers. Was this possible, the feelings he was having. He leaned back in his chair and closed his eyes. 'I am no lord; I am just a simple man.' She didn't move, but the voice she put in his head felt like she was just humouring him. 'As you wish my love.'

He must have fallen asleep; he awoke jumping a little and when he opened his eyes his lovely ghostly companion was sitting sideways across his lap. Mary had wrapped her arms around his neck laying her head on his chest. He leaned back his head trying to see if she was awake, she seemed to just be holding him, when he moved, she turned to him and sat up on his lap looking into his face and smiling. 'Did you sleep well.' She asked with a cheeky grin, her head tilted slightly allowing her long hair to cascade over her shoulders and down her back. He remembered her hair from seeing her on stage, a lovely copper red colour that reflected the light beautifully making it shine with a healthy glow. In her ghostly form her hair was light blue and transparent, a shadow of light and depth. His memory remembered her mostly for how she was. He started to move, and she shifted herself to stand up and folded her arms across her chest watching him closely. 'I did. But now we have things to do.' He quickly gathered his things together and washed his face to wake himself up a little, then he dried himself off quickly. He looked around his dark lodgings, the few scattered candles and oil lamps did little to keep out the darkness of the night. The embers of his stove glowed with a gentle red and orange giving off a little heat, doing its very best to dry the damp air that was very normal in London this time of the year.

Chapter Three

It is time

The next day, after having spent several hours working on a simple coffin for a client. He made the necessary arrangements, leaving the coffin at the client's home, and setting the corpse in state for a wake and then for a burial the day after. On his travels he picked up many skills and studied hard to make the best of every opportunity. He enjoyed broadening his understanding of the sciences and the natural world. Learning different trades. His constant search, trying to understand the calling he was set upon, by his father, and a grandfather whom he never met. Trying to find the long-lost secrets that would enable him to bridge that gap between life, and the metaphysical world. The age-old secret of what happens when we die. The sad thing was, for many who dabbled in this field, it was not a subject that many could understand or tolerate. In order to continue his research, he must tread a very delicate path. His only real companions were the few restless souls of the dead he met on his adventures. Right now, those very souls were more real to him than the living.

Tonight, there was work to do, cleansing London of a cruel murderer. The idea and the act always left him feeling at odds. Was he doing the right thing. What right did he have. Slowly he walked over to a table and poured some water from a jug into a wash bowl and swilled his face, the clean cold water felt good on his skin and he removed his shirt, continuing to strip wash the upper half of his body. When he finished, he sat down in his high back chair and stoked the embers of his fire, putting some coal and wood on it to bring the stove back to life. He always made sure that there was hot water on the stove, making full use of the heat. A hot brew always made him feel good while keeping warm by his fire. The wisps of steam soon appeared from the pot on the stove and his heavy eyes watched eagerly for signs of the boiling water. Using some of the boiled water for a cup of coffee and the remainder to shave with. Refreshed, he felt ready to face whatever trials would come to him this night. No matter what happened, at least he would look like a gentleman, and not some common criminal. His handy yet sharp straight razor was one item that any real gentleman should never be without. His, was one of his most prized possessions. He used it to shave carefully, listening intently to the sound of the blade cutting across his neck and cheeks, slicing through the stubble that grew on his face with ease. An everyday reminder that time did not wait for any man. He looked up into his mirror as he shaved and saw the instantly recognisable ghostly shape of Mary forming in its reflection. He watched carefully as he finished his shave and turned to her closing the razor, careful not to cut himself, he put it down on the wash table next to a large porcelain bowl and jug.

When her form was clearly visible, he watched as she checked herself smoothing down her dress. Combing her fingers through her hair, she approached him slowly but confidently. Watching her, he remained still as she moved closer. Less than an arm reach away she stood in front of him and looked up into his bright sparkling eyes and smiled, he bowed his head politely smiling back to her. He took her hand in his helping her stand. 'I think, if you will allow me, I will still call you my Mary.' She giggled. He treated her with such kindness, so unlike other gentleman she met in her past life. He truly was kind and thoughtful. She tilted her head watching him. 'As you wish my lord.' He bowed flamboyantly to her making her laugh. She covered her mouth shyly watching him as he followed her every move with his eyes. There was a beautiful affection between them, an instant chemistry, they would watch each other intently. When their eyes met, they would helplessly smile to each other. He studied her so carefully, the way she proudly held herself, confident but shy, yet intoxicatingly alluring. After a long silence as they looked to each other he finally turned away from her gaze. He tucked his shirt in doing up the cuffs of his sleeves and made himself presentable and ready for the night ahead. He removed his heavy coat from a wooden peg on the wall and picked up his hat and cane from a nearby table. From his dresser he tucked an ornately made ivory handled dagger into his boot, then taking a strand of black silk he formed a neat tie about his neck and pointed to the door with his cane. 'You must show me the place where you were.' He pointed to her abdomen and stroked her neck with the back of his fingers. 'I mean to put things right for you, so you can rest.' She looked nervously to him and then downwards to the floor avoiding his eyes.

'Why do this.' Mary watched him as he gently rubbed the blood stone silver ring on his finger. He looked to her and tapped his cane to his top had and smiled. 'I feel it is the right thing to do, like I am being drawn.' Mary frowned slightly, she didn't understand his ways, his words were strange and confusing sometimes. Mary's world was a much simpler place, at least it was in life. She had no real desire for revenge. All she wanted was to be free and happy. She was not a real woman anymore, just a shadow of what she once was. A horrible reminder of a wasted life. She felt ashamed, angry, cheated. Her ghostly form looked around the room for something different to focus upon. With a deep sigh she turned back to face him adjusting the folds of her dress. Adjusting it to show her plain pale shoulders and to show off her long flowing hair. She wanted to look as pleasing as possible for him in her unlife state.

Looking up to him with her head bowed slightly, trying to avoid direct eye contact with him. She walked to the door and passed effortlessly through it as if the door was not there. He followed her opening the heavy door and closing it securely behind himself locking it with a large key, hiding the key into a deep dark hole in the wall nearby. Once again at last, he was in a realm that he understood, the night and the streets. Outside the stars were over head in their thousands with a large bright half-moon. Somehow, for whatever reason, he felt like that was where he belonged, where his soul craved to be, in the heavens. Free of his body, free of his earthly form. Perhaps one day, he would reach the heavens and be truly free.

He gave a long sigh as he walked and let the tap of his cane mark his progress. Daydan followed Mary carefully as her apparition danced gracefully through the alleyways, skipping with ease over mud and grime. He watched her move gracefully through the streets leading the way, for whatever reason he was the only one who could see her. This was Marys wish for now, it appeared to him that the spirits could only be seen by those to whom they wished to be seen by. They walked for some time and he noticed how the styles and grandeur of the houses changed considerably, from the shabby wooden homes of the slums and tightly packed homes where he lived, to the grand homes of wealthy merchants and politicians. Even at night, horse drawn carriages, gentlemen riding their horses, large finely built homes in stone. It was a world where he felt utterly out of place, but where he was able to easily pass for one of their own. Eventually, Mary stopped at a gate supported by two stone pillars. The house beyond was strange, masterfully built in brick, very new, modern and grand. It was some distance away from the other houses, alone on the king's road, number II. Not the English numeral, but roman, cut into the stone at the top of the front door was a warning, five symbols watched over the doorway, a spiral carved into the stone, then a daemons head also cut into a stone, then again a spiral, a head and another spiral. The spiral circles Daydan knew to represent Saturn, an ancient symbol that most understood to mean the devil, Satan. He knew better, the circles represent law and order, or rather lack of, its meaning was simple, 'unto his own,' the proprietor recognises only their own law and authority. The demonic faces represented fearlessness, again, not representing evil or demon worship, simply that they feared nothing. A warning. The house was named clearly as Argyll house and was rather grand indeed, but not overly so. Over the door was a name carved into the stone which he guessed to be the family name. Atwood. Whatever trouble Mary had been in with this family, the signs were very real, they would be ruthless in their response. Mary pointed to the iron latch on the gate and waited for her escort to enter.

When he moved closer, she pointed to another entrance to the side of the house off another street. He looked around cautiously thankful for the darkness and the cover of night. He could have easily been mistaken for a common criminal or murderer lurking around these streets hiding in the shadows from view. The side of the house did not look as elegant as the front of house entrance. Mary pointed to the servants entrance of the house, the service entrance gate opened easily and he made his way to the door down a small step, then he tried the door slowly, it clicked open and he could see the light from within, slowly he pushed it open. A few small flagstones led directly to a large wide door down a couple of large stone steps, he listened carefully pointing his ear to the door and paused, Mary turned to face him for a moment. 'Whatever happens inside, please, do not be disappointed with me, it was not my fault.' She turned away, he could see that she had a sadness in her eyes that he had not seen before until now, regret perhaps, no matter. He followed her and put his questions to the back of his mind for now. He watched her and followed closely behind as best he could careful to not make any noise.

Mary walked in her ghostly form through the door to the other side where upon a woman screamed in terror and then the sound of a muffled thump on the floor. Mary appeared once more with half of her upper body and her head fully through the large door. She gave him a playful smile and motioned for him to follow her. With a forceful nudge it opened easily, and he pushed it carefully to one side to see the mass of cloth and a body beneath. An elderly woman in simple servants' garb was laying on the stone floor. He dropped to one knee and put his hand across her neck from one side to the other to feel her blood pumping rapidly, he concluded that she had just fainted from shock and he stood up looking to Mary once more. 'I hope you are pleased with yourself.' He whispered softly to Mary grinning to her as he stood back up. 'Meah.' She giggled playfully to herself and smiled shrugging her shoulders. 'It was fun.'

They made their way through a service entrance into the main house, through a well-stocked kitchen, the woman on the floor had been preparing food for the next day. In the rest of the house and all around not a sound was heard. He proceeded through the house behind Mary moving slowly and quietly as he did so. In the hallway they climbed up two flights of wide-open stairs and into the heart of a rather grand house, fine pieces of art hung on the walls, old family heirlooms filled cabinets and dark corners. A large chandelier hung from the ceiling with candles long since burned out. It was a fine house when seen from the grand entrance hall below. Daydan admired the style of the house, the art and finery, but it was not something that he desired or even aspired to for himself, he preferred a much simpler less materialistic lifestyle. At the top of the stairs there was a room with the main door slightly open, Mary stopped for a moment. She stood still clenching her fists tightly by her sides and then held her abdomen with her right hand. Daydan put his cane into his hand and held it so it hung straight down in a nonmenacing way and used his free hand to slowly push open the door. The room inside was primarily dark, the only light coming from a well-stocked fire and a candle on a table by a tall chair. He could see a figure clothed in a black dress and veil sitting in the chair. An old woman of considerable years, she lifted her head and looked up as if she was expecting him. She was completely unafraid, almost relieved to see the stranger standing before her, she stood slowly to her feet shaking a little with age and instability but defiant and proud. Her long silver hair cascaded down her back covered with a small veil of black lace, he found himself smile slightly to the old woman feeling oddly mixed about the task he set himself. Mary appeared to the old woman at which the old woman stood up straighter and raised her walking cane taking a swipe at Mary and watched in torment as it slashed through Marys ghostly form without effect. Clearly, for whatever reason Mary wanted the old woman to see her. 'Whore.' The old woman shrieked out, her voice cracking under her laboured breath. Mary approached her and slapped the old woman across the face, Marys ghostly hand sweeping effortlessly through the old woman's face who turned to Mary and then to Daydan. Although the old woman could not hear Marys voice she had responded with a scream of murderer, which he heard very clearly even if the old woman did not. From another chair a huge man awoke, he wore an old overly whitened wig and several layers of clothing. He grunted at being awoken so abruptly and tried to stand, but he was so large it was only due to quite an effort that he could stand at all. 'What is the meaning of this. Thief.' The old woman shushed him abruptly. 'Shut up you old fool.' Turning away from the fat man she focused her attention back to Mary. She looked to her attacker and then to the mysterious man standing before her steadying herself. 'This woman is a whore, a seducer of young men.' She stumbled back into her chair and sat exhausted for a moment. Mary looked to Daydan and cradled her stomach and stared tearfully into his eyes. He looked wide eyed to her, was this all a mistake, he had always admired her beauty, her grace and her elegance, her purity. Yet she was wild and untamed and that was so exciting. Daydan turned to the old woman and approached her slowly, she bowed her head as if ready to accept a death blow. 'The boy you speak of.' The old woman clenched her walking cane tightly, her already pale hand turning a deathly white. 'Twenty-five years.' She narrowed her old weary eyes and looked to him angrily. 'My John is just a boy, easy prey for this, harlot.' She pointed to Mary with a long thin crooked finger. The old man thumped a heavy club like walking stick on the floor diverting the attention to himself. 'What in God's name is going on here, I demand an explanation sir.' Both Daydan and the old woman uttered very similar words to the large old man. 'Shut up you old fool.' He sat back down and slumped unceremoniously into his chair mumbling to himself. The old woman looked him deeply in the eyes, as she spoke her words spat out with anger. 'My son told me of this woman, he was drunk, they were both drunk, fornicating at some party, she seduced him, can't you see, look at her.' She spat to her side. 'Whore.' Mary mocked the old woman knowing full well that no matter what, she could not hurt her now, not anymore. 'I am not a whore, I have only ever willingly lay with one man.' She raised her index finger and pointed to Daydan. 'Only one. I swear it.' She lifted her finger to the old woman gesturing to her angrily. The old woman took a swipe at her with her stick again from her sitting position and hissed angrily when she missed. 'Once a night whore.' Daydan removed his hat carefully fingering the inner rim looking to the old woman. 'You murdered her for laying with your son.' The old woman pondered his words for a moment, then she reached for a letter knife with two blades, she held it in front of her face and sighed. 'She came to my house in the night and said my son raped her, she threatened to tell the authorities. I refused and summoned my son, he confessed to me, that they were drunk, and they lay together one time.' The old woman lowered her eyes. 'I later found that he was, not himself that night. He has a sickness to opium. He is just a boy, and she, look at her. She looks like a witch.' Daydan knew Mary well, her dress style, always in white, red or black, mostly in a simple peasant's dress, off the shoulders. Tight at the waist accentuating her hips and curves, stockinged legs and light flat shoes. Her hair was always free and flowing. She looked different from the other women of her time, but very beautiful non the less. The old woman clenched her fist and rotated the letter opener in her hand gripping it tightly like a weapon. 'I sent my son away, and when she came closer to me, I offered to pay for her silence, but I didn't give her a penny. I took this knife and I cut that unborn out of her womb and threw it on the floor in front of her, then I slit her throat as she watched her unborn on the floor. At first, I was glad of my efforts, but.' The old woman bowed her head. Mary grit her teeth angrily clenching her fists, tears fell from her eyes. She dropped tearfully to the old woman's feet. Mary put her cold ethereal hand upon the hand of the old woman and when she slowly looked into the face of the younger woman the old woman seemed to breathe out a sigh of relief. 'You are a strange girl indeed Mary Summerfield.' She looked back to Daydan and flashed a beautiful smile to him. 'It was our child, yours and mine, her son raped me. I swear to you that is the truth.' Daydan looked down to Mary and then to the old woman. 'The child was mine, ours, nothing to do with your son.' The old woman had indeed murdered this beautiful woman and her unborn child. Their child. He moved deliberately closer to the old woman and put his left hand on her shoulder as she held her cane, she looked up slowly. 'I am ready for death, I am tormented by my guilt and this, woman, did not deserve my wrath, I beg you to free me from this and my shame.' The fat old man stood up slowly, he thumped the heavy clubbed walking stick on the floor. 'I will not stay silent,' He pointed the club stick to the old woman. 'You are a murderer, a serial murderer, of the innocent, neither had done any wrong, you should repent, donate your possessions to my church and prey for forgiveness.' He pointed his stick to Daydan. 'And you sir.' The old woman looked to the large fat old man and frowned. She pointed her bony finger to him. Mary stood up and starred at the ongoing drama with interest. 'You sir, Bishop of London, were at the same party were you not, that could have been you, not my John.' The old man blurted out a cough covering his mouth and adjusting his robes. Mary stood up and visibly shuddered reeling from the large man retreating into Daydan's embrace. 'How dare you.' The old woman laughed for a moment seeing the disgust on the younger woman's face. 'I am weary and tired, tired of life, tired of trying to steer my family to fortune, yet they squander and make rash decisions.' She let out a sigh and pointed to Mary. 'Name your price.' Mary frowned and stared at the old woman. 'What good is wealth to me old woman, can you not see. I have lost everything, the man I love, a future in a far-off land away from here. My child.' It was strange, but the woman appeared to hear Marys words. She pointed her cane to Daydan and looked sideways to him. 'This gentleman, he is your man, your husband.' Mary blushed and shook her head. 'No, sadly, we were unmarried.' The old woman frowned for a moment and looked to Daydan; the way Mary held herself close to him for protection as well as comfort. Daydan watched the old woman, she had an air of wisdom about her. The silence was broken only when the old woman spoke again. 'I have an idea, that I hope will please us all, and you bishop, will remain silent.' The bishop huffed and sat back heavily into his large chair with an awkward grunt. Mary stood up next to her gentleman and smoothed over her attire and combed her fingers through her hair looking as nice as she possibly could as if she was about to receive some high honour from the king himself.

Chapter Four

The shame

Part of him felt sorry for the old woman, trying to guide her wayward son wisely to protect her family name, a son that no doubt was enjoying the advantages of privilege. His family wealth and status as so many in the same position would do, twisted his morality. Nevertheless, she murdered Mary in cold blood, and that of her unborn child, cruelly. She now had to live with that guilt, if she did indeed feel any guilt at all. Or was she just trying to protect her family's reputation. With a slight frown on his brow he felt slightly ashamed, Mary meant everything to him. She was after all now a spirit of her former self, and she appeared not to be terribly troubled by her mysterious ethereal state, she mostly appeared rather joyful, often oblivious that she was no longer alive. When the time was right, he felt there was more to this story, but this was not the time, it could wait. The night had begun with him determined to put an end to a wicked person, however, revenge for revenge sake was not his way, but something did not feel right. The noble and proud lady slowly stood up. She pointed to a table and some rolled up papers next to a burning red candle, she then took a few steps forward and steadied herself on her walking cane holding the top in both hands, turning slightly but not looking directly at him she gestured towards the papers with a nod of her head and spoke very clearly.. 'I have been expecting a caller in the night, the spirit of death himself perhaps, my guilt is obvious, as is my shame, so I have prepared some papers, something which has in the past caused me nothing but grief and distress, perhaps this is what was meant to be, and in some small way it will make up for what I have done.' She pointed to the papers with her cane and steadied herself again. 'There are documents, certificates and a transfer letter for my shares in the Honourable East India Company and the new Bank of England, at this time the share value of two percent each.' She coughed clearing her throat, 'My father Josiah will leave me with nothing on his death, I married my second husband against my father's wishes, and he disowned me. I have no regrets, my husband is a good man and cares little for my father, so, you will take my shares, sign and they are yours, and then you must leave me and my family in peace or do your deed now.' She hit the papers with her cane.

'They have been a curse and brought me nothing but trouble, I am glad to be rid of it.' She turned to face him looking him directly in the eyes. 'Do we have an agreement.'

A little puzzled all he could do was stare at the woman for a moment, was this a bribe, was it even legal, he walked over to the desk and looked over the papers, it did indeed look all in order. If it was a ploy it was an elaborate one, he read the papers and saw that there was a letter of transfer detailing the certificates, a letter to her solicitor detailing the transfer and a joint letter of consent. With the old woman's signature at the top, her husbands' signature as a witness and her solicitors, it looked all in order as she indicated. All Daydan had to do was sign, there was even a quill and ink ready for use, and a family seal, it all felt far too easy. He poured through the documents for a moment and then turned to the old woman and then back to Mary who was still visible and understandably, seemingly a little confused by the old woman's change of heart.

'Bishop, you too will sign as a witness to the transaction.' The bishop stood up slowly and grumbled angrily, he pointed his heavy walking stick to the intruder and growled. 'This man is a common criminal, and you, you should confess your sins to God and repent, these shares should be a gift to the church for the redemption of your soul.' He growled under his breath breathing heavily with the effort of standing up. The old woman struck out at the large fat man with her stick and shouted at him. 'You, eat my food, drink my husband's brandy, give not a penny in appreciation and take donations from this family frequently, how dare you accuse anyone of a crime.' She pointed a bony finger to him. 'Of Gods seven deadly sins, which are you *NOT* guilty of. Bishop.' She hit the papers and pointed her walking cane to the certificate and glared to him. '*SIGN*. This gentleman is my guest. Sign it and let me have some peace you old fool.' The bishop was silenced immediately and coughed clearing his throat, the old woman was easily half his size if not less, but she had a presence that was undeniable. The bishop stroked his face and a slight resentful smile crossing his lips. He mumbled under his breath and slowly moved forwards adjusting his robes and poking a large chubby hand through the sleeves of his house coat. 'As you wish.' He slowly signed the papers and nodded both to her and begrudgingly to her guest.

A part of him felt like he was betraying Mary, he wanted revenge for her, but it did not feel right somehow, he looked towards her ghostly form, then he looked deeply into her eyes as she stared back to him with a puzzled look on her face. 'Will this give you peace.' Waiting for her answer he looked to the old woman, she was frail and weak, yet clearly very proud. Strong willed, but her shame for killing Mary it seemed was very genuine indeed. For her murder, and of her unborn childs. With her head bowed a little he heard Mary speak to him in his thoughts. 'I do not wish her dead, just her regret.' He paused for a moment and looked to Mary. 'I think that it is obvious she regrets what she has done.' he looked over to the old woman and approached the papers taking the quill into his hand and dipping it into the ink carefully to remove the excess ink from the nib. 'What is your name sir.' The old woman spoke softly. 'Daydan.' He replied simply. She frowned a little holding her walking cane steadily in front of her. 'Daydan what.' She tapped the floor with her cane. 'Are you Catholic, a Protestant' He looked up to her and shook his head. She looked suspiciously to him as if she was looking into his soul. 'You are a foreigner, tell me, what is your last name.' He cleared his throat for a moment and stood up tall. 'I don't really have one, but, I suppose, my father gave me the name Al Mani.' The old woman blew through her lips shaking her head. 'No no no.' You must be an Englishman, that name will not do. Think of another.' He was a little shocked, what did his name matter, why was that so important, and what was wrong with the name his father gave him, he was after all, The Eternal Hand, the protector. He turned to Mary as she remained for the most part behind him in silence, keeping him, between herself, the old woman and the bishop. 'Mary, what was your last name.' Mary held his arm as he spoke, she looked up into his face and smiled a little. 'My stage name, is, was Butterfield, but my family name is Taboate.' He smiled from one side of his face as he heard her voice in his head, clearly this name would be equally displeasing to the Atwood woman. He coughed a little trying to cover the silent pause for a moment. 'What does that mean, Taboate.' Mary smiled and blushed a little as she held his arm with both of hers holding onto him tightly. 'It sort of means, naughty, an outlaw, you know, Taboo. Things you should not do.' He smiled softly to her and grinned. 'What you do,' She bit her lip and looked away slightly. 'That is Taboo, is it not.' He hadn't really thought of his craft and his skills as Taboo, but in truth, it was. Almost everything about him and his way of life brought him close to the edge of right and wrong, in his eyes he was doing what was right, what was best for all, what brought peace and balance. He thought deeply for a moment, Mary had a point, but the name was like a wake-up call, he was most definitely on the edge, constantly. He turned to the old woman and stood up as tall as he could proudly looking the Atwood woman straight in the eyes. 'My name madam, is Daydan Taboo.' When he spoke his new name, there was a deep resonance in his voice, it felt right, and even the sound it made was like the hum of eternity itself. He nodded to the old woman and tried to acknowledge the Bishop who had returned to his large armchair by the fire and was already pouring himself another brandy. Daydan checked his attire and smartly began to sign his new name to the parchment. 'Then It is agreed.' The old woman nodded and moved uncharacteristically quickly to his side and prodded him with her cane hard. 'There is one more condition I demand of you that I will trust you to keep as you are a gentleman of your word sir, are you not.' With pen in hand he paused. 'What is that.' She looked up coldly into his eyes. 'You will leave my John be, it was my mistake, not his, and I do believe that he did feel something for this woman, maybe.' She scoffed as she turned and looked at Mary. He also faced Mary who listened thoughtfully to the woman's words, she shrugged her shoulders and frowned nodding back to him. He looked back to the old woman. 'Agreed.' The old woman let out a long sigh and slowly returned to her high back chair and sat slumping down deep within it in clear relief as if a huge weight had been lifted from her shoulders. He signed the papers and slowly turned to the old woman, Mary walked up to her and stood over her looking down at her with a little sadness in her stance, like she wanted to hold the woman but kept her distance. The old woman put her head back into the chair and opened her eyes. 'Take the certificates and letters of transfer on the desk, I will speak with my solicitor first thing in the morning. You will have to see him yourself within the next week to finalise, but the deal is done, there will be no problems, I give you my word, and I trust that you are a gentleman of your word sir.' He frowned to the old woman, what she was asking. It would be difficult to come face to face with her son and not want to kill him for what he did to Mary. She tapped the floor with her walking stick to get his attention. 'My son is not well; he has a sickness.' Daydan stood in silence listening to the old woman with his hand gripping his cane tightly. 'He has a sickness that is killing him. I know the cause, and I would have you eliminate that cause. If you are interested, we could perhaps come to an agreement.'

His hand relaxed a little on his walking cane. Mary stood at his side but slightly behind him holding his arm in hers. The old woman took a long breath and looked up to him, her cold old eyes looked misty and indifferent. 'There is a menace, the judge, in the prison on the hill, he is untouchable to most, but to you. He is the source of the midnight oil and opium that comes here from the east.' She tapped her cane on the floor. 'I would have you kill him, and all of his associates, I will pay you handsomely, when the deed is done.' He was a little shocked to hear such a request, she was asking him to murder someone. A master criminal, running a drugs empire from within one of his majesty's prisons, and his minions. He nodded reluctantly to her and put the papers in his heavy coat and tipped his hat to the old woman, he never said another word as she closed her eyes, and let her body relax visibly into her chair. Her grip on her walking cane subsided as it fell gently to her thigh, still held softly in her thin frail bony fingers. The bishop watched him closely, sipping slowly from his large glass of brandy. Daydan watched them both in silence for a moment before moving, the woman looked to be in a restful sleep, a picture of age, wisdom and dignity. He felt a little admiration for the old woman as he again bowed his head to her, and the bishop, in polite acknowledgement. They made his way out of the room. Taking the exact same route as before, down the stairs and out through the small kitchen where they first entered. The servant who collapsed earlier began to stir and was on all fours trying to get up onto her knees, she stared wide eyed as he moved quickly towards her and then straight past without even a look, then to her horror, Mary's ghostly form danced around her smiling and mocking her with her graceful movements. The servant screamed out again in horror and collapsed to the floor in shock again.

Outside, he looked to Mary who seemed rather happy with herself, unfazed by what just happened, he half expected her to bid her farewells after putting to rest her unfinished affairs. Mary remained in her ethereal form, happy, dancing, cheerful. Back out in the streets again the air seemed thick with fog, damp, but not so cold as to feel uncomfortable. His companion gracefully danced through the street singing to herself and dancing along ahead as if she had not a care in the world, he couldn't help smiling as he watched her, she was so carefree. Mary seemed so innocent and so naïve about the world, yet there was something very mysterious about her. For a while he followed her at a good steady pace at the speed of a brisk walk, he could see her form dancing up ahead for a while until she disappeared from his view completely, he was sure they would meet again. She still seemed to be hanging on for some reason, this state between life, death and renewal. Her murderer made some small amends, it was as if revenge was not the reason, she was still present here. His journey back to his residence was at a much slower pace as his mind ran over recent events trying to make sense of what just happened. Had he sold Mary out, was the bribe of wealth a good enough reason to betray his promise to Mary, there was a degree of guilt in his mind as he slowly made his way through dark streets and open parks. The city of London at this time was crowded, there were indeed many slum areas, but also vast open areas of land used for farming and agriculture, public parks and the new age of iron and steel, the docks were always busy with trade coming from all over the world. The empire was growing, and London was growing with it. When he returned to his home, he picked up a note nailed to his front door for more work which at this time did not seem at the fore front of his mind. So much has happened, so many thoughts going through his mind, he entered his dwelling as he always did through the side entrance careful to lock up behind him as he did so. Inside he placed the note on a table and removed his heavy coat. He stoked the dwindling coals in his fireplace. The embers were still hot, and he knew that with a little kindling and some coal it would soon lift the fire back into warmth and life again.

Daydan prepared a pot of water for boiling and sat in his favourite chair by the fire and began to look over the papers the old woman had given to him. It all looked very official and in order, but these papers were rather unfamiliar to him, he knew nothing about shares, bonds, certificates. The old woman seemed genuinely glad to be rid of them. Were they cursed, was that even possible. He lay them out on a table and studied them carefully. As he was reading, Mary's face began to form in front of him, then the rest of her body. Her long dark red hair cascaded beautifully over her shoulders and she was leaning her elbows on the table with her chin resting on her hands looking rather happy with herself, her eyes looked deeply into his. 'What.' He looked to her with a small smile on his lips as he spoke, just being near her was a celebration of joy for him, he knew she was just a spirit, a shade of her former self, but there was something about her. She smiled to him and shrugged her shoulders still watching him and resting her chin on her hands. 'I like it when you smile.' She said softly. She slowly stood up watching him and smoothed over her dress and adjusted herself moving around in front of him. 'What do you like about me Daydan.' He smiled to her as she watched him, had she been alive, things would have been very different. His performances at the theatre were only recent. Mary on the other hand was a resident in the theatre and performed for a full house almost every night apart from Sunday. They met as lovers secretly and it was beautiful. Mary knew he was in love with her. She enjoyed that knowledge making herself even more appealing for him every chance she got. She had many admirers, and he was by no means the most obvious choice.

He felt rather vulnerable, his feelings for her, for a ghost, an apparition, it was not normal, then again, he was not a normal man, and Mary, was not a normal woman. He shifted slightly contemplating whether or not to take a puff from his pipe, or to forgo the embarrassment of choking in front of Mary again and try to change the subject. He cleared his throat calmly. 'What happened, the night you were, murdered, what happened before, you said something about a party.' Mary began to look at her feet and then put her hands behind her back, she looked a little embarrassed as he watched her sway from left to right a little trying to think of how she would explain what happened. 'It was a special night, the theatre was packed with dignitaries, even the King was there, politicians, military men, lots of important people, we were all told to be on our best behaviour and to be, 'nice.' She smoothed her dress nervously behind herself and sat down, as she sat she lowered her eyes avoiding his. 'There was lots of food and drink and other things too, you know. I ate the food, it was wonderful and plentiful, but I did not drink much, just a glass of wine. The girls were being shuffled off between the guests, they didn't seem to mind. It was that kind of party. But I did not want to do that. I entertained our guests and I sang some songs. I danced for them; it was fun. We laughed allot.' She started to play with her fingers in her lap. 'An old cavalry officer, and a younger officer approached me, he said he wanted someone special for his friend, of course I said no, I was not that sort of girl. I offered to sing a song for them instead, and they agreed. Then we talked, we laughed, and I sang another song for them, I sat on his lap and sang to him a funny song. We laughed so much, and then the older officer gave me a drink and poured some black liquid into it, he also poured some into his own glass, and the young officer, he said it would sweeten the wine. They said it was Molasses. It smelled like molasses, so I waited for him to drink it first. He downed it in one, then the young officer drank his, so I drank mine, just like that. It was all very funny at the time, innocent. I had to be sure that they drank some first though right, I mean, it could have been poison or something bad.' She blushed nervously and breathed softly looking away shamefully into space trying not to catch his eyes. 'When I woke, I was in such pain, so much pain.' She held her breasts and pulled her legs up into a foetal position, holding her knees. 'The young officer was laughing at me, he was sitting on the edge of a bed, I was partly undressed, my clothes were torn, my body was scratched bruised and bleeding, and I remember I was crying, but I.' Tears began to form in her eyes. 'He laughed at me and threw some coins on the bedside table. He said I was worthless and should be grateful.' She pulled herself into a tighter foetal position as she hid her face, he could hear her sob softly.

'I don't remember, after the drink and singing, I woke up in that bed, I knew what had happened, I was so ashamed, I was in so much pain and I wanted to kill him. All I could think about was you, if you would forgive me. When I told the other girls, they teased me and laughed. They said I should have charged him more, that was what mostly happens at those kinds of parties.' She looked up to him with tears running down her cheeks, all he could do was look on intently to her to let her finish her story, but inside he could feel her sadness, her anger and her shame. 'Why.' He stood up and walked over to her and put his hand on her arm, rubbing her gently. Then he slowly stroked her hair and caressed her cheek softly and smiled to her. 'Because you are beautiful, and beyond the reach of any man.' She looked up to him and rest her cheek against his hand. 'You mock me sir!' He just smiled to her and shook his head, he breathed a long sigh of regret and sadness, there was so much more to this woman than met the eye. There was such joy in her, of course that was appealing, but she also had a very natural beauty about her. She was gentle and kind, but vulnerable. And maybe sometimes a little naïve. She sat up fully adjusting herself and wiping her eyes and started to smile a little. He put his arms around her and comforted her as best he could. 'You can rest in peace now Mary, it's over.' There was a long pause as he held her, she held him tightly, her ethereal form embracing his living form. Her ghostly presence shimmered in the dim light and seemed to brighten to a more vibrant blue white light. 'Not quite.' She replied. 'I want to stay with you a little longer.' She stood up and smoothed over her dress and adjusted the dress off her shoulders. Her soft pale shoulders remained visible, then taking the hem of her dress, she started to dance around him again, but this time much more slowly, and much more seductively. 'You didn't answer my question sir; will you not tell me.' He looked to her puzzled. 'What question.' She looked to him and smiled turning her body away from him but looking back to him over her naked shoulder. 'What do you like about me.' He chuckled to himself and folded his arms across his chest and smiled to her. He shook his head slightly. 'Oh, that. Well, you are persistent.' His chuckle continued. 'And you are always happy, you make me smile, you are carefree. And, I think there is allot more to you than meets the eye Miss Butterfield. Or should I call you miss Taboate.' He held out his hand to her and she took it, she started to dance around him twirling beautifully, making her dress spin outward showing her ankles and legs and letting her hair fly freely. She was the classic character of a Gypsy girl, happy, healthy, carefree and full of spirit, but there was a very seductive side to her, he liked that unpredictability. Mary stopped and stood in front of him looking into his face. 'Why have you never married.' He cleared his throat as she looked deeply into his eyes as if searching for the answer within his gaze. With a slight shift of his weight he stepped back a little and visibly pondered the question for a moment. 'Things in my life are, complicated. And she would have to be a very extraordinary woman to want to share her life with me, and I with her.' He smiled to her. 'And I am yet to meet such a woman.' Mary let out a laugh and circled him dancing and twirling youthfully around him. 'Am I not extraordinary my lord.' She teased him with her eyes and smile pouting playfully, using her arms to add to her graceful seductive movements. He sat on the edge of his work bench and smiled with his arms folded across his chest again, he watched her smiling back to him as she danced. 'Yes, you are Mary, but.' Mary stopped dancing, she put her hands on her hips and gave him a stern look. 'There is a but.' She walked closer to him right up to his face, their noses and lips almost touching. There was a long pause as she watched him, he still had a slight smile on his lips trying to think of his response. Clearly Mary wanted to know the answer to her question, and she was not going to be satisfied until she had it. 'I think you are lovely, beautiful, feminine, healthy, funny.' He stopped talking, Mary was looking into his eyes still face to face with him. 'But.' He looked closely into her eyes. 'I should have said yes that day. But I also made another promise Mary, to my father.' She pulled back slightly wetting her lips as if preparing for a long deep kiss. 'You are not your father; you have your own life to live.' She reached out to him putting her arms around his neck and slowly leaned forwards and kissed him deeply. Of course, he was kissing a spirit, an apparition, but he could feel something, a sensation that felt right, his lips tingled, and his body felt a carefree weightlessness that was a pure delight. Mary kissed him intently and he returned the kiss as if he was kissing a living woman, he cradled her in his arms gently and embraced her lovingly. The kiss lasted for some time and was very passionate and of an intensity that he had never before shared with any woman, ever. When Mary slowly pulled away, she stared up into his eyes waiting for him to speak. Slowly and gently she licked her lips again and softly combed her fingers through her hair. 'Oh my.' She closed her eyes and as she did so her pale blue ethereal light radiated more brightly around her lips and face. Her expression changed from a blank confused look to one of joy, she smiled stroking her lips and watched him looking for his response.

There were no more words spoken, just a long silent pause of two people looking to each other with deep affection in their eyes. As he watched, her ghostly form faded and vanished slowly away. Eventually he turned away from where she was standing, he looked around for his things and watched the light coming from the street level window overhead and welcomed the early morning light. He picked up his coat and put it on, then picked up his cane and hat and walked up from the basement workshop. He walked out of the large door and up the small incline to the gate and the side ally to the street. His head was spinning with the evening's events. With Mary, with the bribe, with the papers he had be given, he needed some time to try and make sense of it all. A nice early morning walk would surely do the trick, a chance to clear his mind. A chance to put everything into perspective and to decide on his next move. Putting his top hat on to his head he stroked his lips with his forefinger. He could still taste Mary, the sensations he felt, the deep bottomless look in her eyes as they kissed, it was a strange situation indeed. He tried to convince himself that it was wrong, but it did not feel wrong. He always felt that he knew the difference between right and wrong. He believed he was a moral person with good intentions, trying through his own efforts to keep a balance between good and evil, right and wrong. It seemed especially in these times, that the potential for man as a species was so incredible. The pull for most was towards selfishness and greed. It was easier. He understood very well that sometimes bad things could come from genuinely good intentions, and also good could come from something quite unthinkable. In his mind and in his experience, there was a balance, and in most situations good things happened to bad people and bad things could happen to good people. In general, the experiences of one life would always bring things back to an equilibrium. If you had the clarity to see. When bad things happen, you push through and move forward, when good things happen you enjoy and flourish. Taking the bribe of the Honourable East India Company shares from the old woman seemed wrong to him. Mary appeared indifferent, she was no longer alive, her murderer was regretful, the real guilty party in this story was the young officer. The image in his imagination sent a rage through his body as he clenched his walking cane tightly. He shook his head desperately and tried to think of something else, anything to take his mind off what he was feeling, what his mind was taunting himself with. He looked at his bloodstone ring and was a little relieved that it was not glistening brightly showing that there were none of his spirit energies nearby. All he could feel as he walked briskly from his small abode to the park was shame and guilt, like he had sold Mary out to greed. As he walked, ahead of him he remembered Hyde park and prepared himself for a long hearty stroll. As he walked, he remembered reading about the east India company in news sheets and a very popular new idea called a magazine of the time which showed illustrations aimed at gentleman of means.

The era of print had come along in leaps and bounds, and news from the colonies and all over the world could be brought to the homes of most city folk. For a small fee of course. Books were becoming more and more common as printing began to take on a more industrial scale. Trade from the company seemed to be mostly around the East Indies, reaching out as far as Asia and across the Atlantic to the new world. The most common trade cargo was tea, silk, spices, saltpetre, slaves, indigo and of course the largest profit-making cargo, opium. The trade of opium had traversed the entire globe, black oil, midnight sun. He felt a knot in his stomach as he thought about Mary, helpless, unconscious. He turned slightly looking up to the blue sky over head and watched a flock of starlings dancing and weaving an acrobatic dance in the sky. He smiled slightly grateful for the distraction, trying to come to terms with the conflict in his mind. This was imperialism, this was capitalism, this was the norm for any conquering power throughout time, going back as far as records showed. He pondered a question that became the guiding factor for his current predicament and conscious torment.

Where can I be free. The answer was clear and simple. His pace eased slightly, he stopped and removed his hat and pulled a handkerchief from his pocket and wiped the sweat from the inner rim of his hat, he took a long slow breath and exhaled as if releasing the conflict that was within his body, mind and soul. He knew now the task at hand, the what and the why, but not the how. He smiled to himself and thought about his strange companions for a moment, and then of course his thoughts turned to Mary. He taped the ground lightly with his cane as he walked through the park, politely acknowledging the ladies and gentlemen who walked the park or rode in the carriages or upon their beautiful horses. He closed his eyes as he walked from time to time taking in the smells and letting the sun warm his face. Now, at last, he knew his way ahead, and in a way, it made perfect sense, indeed, he felt like life was guiding him gently toward a goal. What will be will be, taking the hard times and learning from them, embracing the good times. In the end there would be a balance, some kind of equilibrium that gave one peace.

Chapter Five

The push

The events of the night left him in a slight torment with himself, previously it was his intention to get revenge for Mary. The stroll in the park was meant to ease his mind, he pondered the bribe that he felt Mary wanted him to take for her murder, and the murder of their unborn child. It left a bitter taste in his mouth, the idea that the perpetrator of Mary's death was free and cared little for his selfish consequences. Could he really look him in the eyes and not want revenge. He paused in his tracks finding himself in a clearing with a large stone horse trough and a pillory near the park gates, there was a young man locked into the pillory mumbling to himself. Around him ware fragments of rotten food, often thrown at the prisoner for the ritual humiliation of its captive. The unexpected scene was a welcome release from the battle that was raging in his mind, he approached with a little caution at first. 'Water, please sir, some water if you will.' He was going to walk right past the captive had he not spoken, but while this person was here for a punishment, for others it was entertainment, it seemed odd that the discomfort of one was so entertaining to others. His own understanding of being at peace and the way things worked, this seemed to be at odds. What he understood of the way one should live their life. Do unto others. Lessons were everywhere in life, if only people could open their eyes and see them. He pulled a clean handkerchief from his pocket and cleared the surface of the water from the horse trough and dipped the cloth into the water, then he lightly removed it and carefully rang it out so that most of excess water ran away. Enough remained to provide something to drink and rehydrate the young man. He approached him and began to hold the cloth to his lips which prisoner sucked at for its welcome drink.

'Thank you sir.' Nodding to him he wiped his face clean with the moist cloth a little. The young man lifted his head and gazed back at him with the most incredible blue eyes. It was still rather dark so making out much of his face was difficult, yet his blue eyes were very clear indeed. He smiled warmly back to the young man on one side of his face and began to wipe his face more, cleaning him up as best he could. Rather than get up and leave he sat upon the pillory and tapped his cane on the stone floor near to the captive's head, the chink of the silver tip on stone made a crisp clicking sound.

'So.' He spoke softly but swiftly, 'What have you been up to. Are you a debtor.' He looked down towards the young man who twisted his head ninety degrees so he could look up to him. He smiled a little and spoke with a rather feminine tone. 'I impersonated a woman.' He frowned slightly at the prisoner's response, unsure as to the meaning of what he had just said. 'To what end.' He replied cautiously, had he just befriended a dangerous criminal. The prisoner looked down to the ground no longer wishing to make eye contact with the generous soul who just showed him such kindness and compassion. 'So that I may lay with a man, for love and money.' There was a long silence between them, even the tap of his cane on the stone floor stopped for a moment. Eventually the rhythm, yet slightly slower continued again. 'And what was your sentence for such a despicable crime.' There was an odd tone of mockery in his voice, but not for the prisoner, more for the system which labelled it a crime. The young man turned his head to look at him again slightly but did not turn up to meet the speaker's eyes. 'Thirty days of prison and three of the pillory.' Again, there was a slight pause, but the tap of his cane continued in its gentle click, click, rhythm. 'And have you learned your lesson young man.' He asked with an air of authority in his tone. The young gentleman looked up to meet his eyes and almost smiled. 'Probably not.' The young man laughed softly and was surprised to hear his companion also laugh, which infectiously grew for a moment. Daydan stood up and tapped his cane right in front of the young man's face on the floor ahead of him, as if pointing to the dirt. 'I wish you well young sir.' he said as he turned and began to head off to enjoy the rest of his walk and his morning stroll in the park. Before he cleared another dozen steps the young man's voice rang out in the early morning light, it was strong, yet still rather feminine. 'Go in peace my lord.' It made him pause for a moment, the words had great meaning, whether or not the prisoner fully understood them or indeed meant them. He focused on those words for some time, then he bowed his head for a moment and put his walking cane over his shoulder as he moved onward. His stride was long, deliberate and fast. The birds of the early hours were already singing away ready to meet the warm sunlight breaking through a rare cloudless sky. A fine day was beginning. A day of change and opportunity. 'Go in peace,' still those words filled his mind, is that what the old woman wanted. Was that what Mary wanted. Was that what everyone wanted. Peace, in his world, the world of understanding, the ebb and flow of all things, and that of the ghostly world of his companions. Peace was an odd word to use, what did that mean exactly, being in harmony, avoiding resistance, to not hate but to embrace, balance, calm, contentment.

When he was still, completely still, it felt like there was a tone in his mind, a soft hum, a rhythm of life, a gentle peaceful tone, it always made him feel at peace. Everyday life was often in chaos, the sounds, the hustle and bustle of life, the struggle to survive. But when one stopped, there was tranquillity and peace. When one really listened to that inner rhythm, the same rhythm that was all around and in all things. He shook his head, did anyone else sense these things, was he alone, how was that even possible. He could hear it and feel it. His entire life was about doing what felt right, not what felt right for personal gain, but what felt right for him, his conscience, his soul. His inner voice always seemed to guide him along the right path, that path was sometimes not the easiest, but it was always a path that felt like it was the right thing to do. When he did that, the results were always favourable. It felt right to take the bribe, it felt right to live the way he did, it felt right to help those lost souls, it felt right to have these strange feelings for a girl who was no longer living. It felt right to be alive. And it felt right to follow the path that he felt drawn to all his life, until now. We have an instinct to survive, an instinct to flourish, that should be embraced.

He sat on a park bench for a moment watching the people go about their business. Some going to work no doubt, some like he, just enjoying the luxury of being able to take a morning stroll. His cane tapped the stone floor again near the bench giving him a sense of security. He thought about Mary and what happened to her, her loss. The evening at the party where that young soldier drugged and raped her. The old woman murdering her and their unborn child. It was all rather horrific. He coughed uneasily to himself thinking about everything Mary had gone through, yet she was not seeking revenge. Just the knowledge that her attackers were sorry for what they did. Was that enough. Was the young officer sorry for what he did, unlikely, was the old woman sorry she murdered Mary, unlikely. Did she know what her son had done that night. Did she even care. She was using her wealth and position to bribe her way out of not one but many crimes. Maybe the bishop was right, maybe she should be punished for her crimes under the law, but with her wealth and connections, was it likely that she would be punished. The Bishop clearly had eyes on her wealth, for whatever reason or purpose her confession would only benefit the church.

He knew Mary was naïve, she was a very sweet and kindly soul and she was not driven by revenge, hate greed or selfishness at all. It was as if she wanted him to take the bribe. He stood up adjusting his attire, wrapping himself up against the slight chill of the morning, a fine misty fog hung low on the ground which the sunlight would soon warm and chase away. He breathed softly looking up to the sky in awe. It was an amazing time to be alive. Science, medicine, technology, transportation, discovery, adventure. The only thing stopping one from doing anything was one's own imagination and desire. His desire for understanding and knowledge were no different, now was the time, this was his time. He grinned to himself feeling a sense of excitement wash over him. He made his decision, it felt like the right thing to do, not because of the opportunities it would afford him, because it surely would be advantageous, but because it felt like Mary wanted him to do it. He felt like he had to keep his promise to Mary, even if it meant breaking his promise to his father. A flyer rolled across the ground in front of him which he stopped with his foot and read the heading. *HANGING*. The daily press news sheets, most of the news was printed now, the type was simple and the process although faster than writing was still labour some, yet to read something in print rather than handwriting was becoming much more common, and preferred. The flyer reminded him of where he first met Angus Turin, the Jacobite highwayman. He was to be hanged in public for his crime. The criminal was given the chance to say a few words before his hanging, the entire time he spoke out against the crown for their crimes against the Scottish, and the Irish clans, he loathed the royal aristocracy in France and here. It seemed odd to him that Angus had such a clear view of right and wrong. The crowds gathered and people came from near and far to hear his last words, and to see him dance on the end of a rope. His hanging made national news sheets across London, and to the other major cities of England and Scotland. When the day finally arrived, quite a crowd gathered to watch him swing from the gallows. A high stand was erected to give the wealthy spectators a more advantageous view from which to see the spectacle, at a premium price of course. When the heavy trap door fell from beneath his feet dropping the man some six feet straight down yanking his head cleanly to one side and instantly breaking his neck, the crowd stood cooing like mindless pigeons. The hanging man kicked and struggled helplessly and then all of a sudden, the tall spectators stand collapsed. Having refused the hangman's hood, it was probably the last thing Angus saw, the stand crashing to the floor and several of the spectators being killed instantly and many others dying days later from their agonising injuries. People close to the gallows said that they heard the highwayman laughing before he finally died. Supporters of the Jacobite cause said that Angus died laughing, opposition to the Jacobite cause said that Angus had cursed the spectators and any such Jacobite's should be executed also. It was a strange day indeed. The memory brought a wry smile to his face. What kind of people relish in the suffering of others, in a way it was poetic justice and it was a scene that he would always remember, with a smile. He was the undertaker assigned to dispose of the bodies of such things in the proper way. When he took Angus's body to give him the proper burial rights that he deserved, it was Angus's spirit that needed so little coaxing to remain with the living.

When his spirit rose from his corpse, he was laughing to himself and checking himself for wounds. He had a very different character than that of Jin. The slave was full of hate and anger, Angus on the other hand had a very practical, simple, nonmaterialistic view of life. He felt that each spirit he connected with taught him lessons that he would otherwise never have learned for himself. In everyday life, knowledge and information was shared by and with a very privileged few. Only those with the time to sit and study had the opportunity to broaden their knowledge. Most of society had to work hard long hours just to survive. Meeting these souls, these extraordinary people, he was able to see things differently, more clearly.

Life was indeed a brief moment of time, enjoying that life was everything. Every moment is precious and should be enjoyed. He thought about the time and opportunities he wasted trying to live his fathers and his grandfather's dream. He thought about the opportunity that just come his way, if he went ahead, he would be given the chance to really study his art. To have the time and means to pursue it with all the focus and passion that it needed. Mary had endured so much; she had been through such torment and pain. Her attention and her desires recently always seemed to be upon him. To be upon his future happiness, her life had been one of such unselfishness. Enjoying her life without causing any harm or discomfort to anyone around her. That was an incredible achievement, she had every right to be happy.

His pace began to quicken slightly as he walked through the park in a large circular route. Daydan started to make his way back towards his small workshop that was his home. He had a calling that he had been set upon before he was even born, it was something that he spent hours, days and nights studying. With this strange unexpected twist of fate, he could really devote his time to understanding the threshold between life and death. The existence of all things. He believed that everything was connected. He felt he had a very personal connection and relationship with death, but that held the true secret. The strange yet undeniable forces around him. The smile on his face as he realised the incredible opportunity that had fallen into his lap was like a moment of clarity. He had indeed been lucky, lucky beyond his wildest dreams.

A feeling of excitement and euphoria washed over him like a hot cleansing bath washing away any doubt. He was almost running the last few streets as he recognised the area he was in, the buildings, some of the traders already set up their stalls. The shops and businesses along the street opened their doors for the day, a bakery was already putting out delicious smells of fresh bread and buns. Daydan was still deep in thought. 'go in peace.' The lesson of his own life experiences always seems to point out one clear rule, to go with what feels right. Your instincts will never let you down, the head will sometimes guide you to selfishness, in most cases, but the heart, the soul, that will almost always guide you well. Balance, often the difference between right and wrong can be little more than personal perspective.

By the time he reached the front door of his premises, he came to terms with what transpired earlier with Mary and the old Atwood woman. Once home he put the large heavy key into the door lock that he took from its hiding place in the small hole by the door. He felt that what he decided upon, was the right thing to do. There was great comfort in that decision. The answer was simply, revenge served no purpose, at least not in this instance. It served no purpose for Mary, and it seemed Mary wanted him to take the documents and start a new life in the new world, just like he promised her. Entering his abode, he closed and locked the door behind himself and walked over to his favourite high back chair and sat down.

The fire long since burned out, the oil lamp was still on with a very low glowing light that illuminated the small area around his chair and the cold embers of the fireplace. The room was cold and damp and only the early morning sunlight light cracked through the street window high up near the basement ceiling. He let out a sigh and closed his eyes, as he lay back his head into his chair a peaceful content smile took hold of his lips. He stilled his mind and drifted off into a very welcome peaceful and restful sleep.

Chapter 6

The road to Bedlam

The next day he was faced with a very different challenge. A visit to Bedlam, it was the nickname given to the prison on the hill, one of several very overcrowded prisons dotted around the city. But this one had more than its fair share of the most violent and evil prisoners. Residents nearby often told of hearing screaming from the prison all night long.

For many of the prisoners they were there for petty crime, stealing food or begging in the wrong street. One could easily be sentenced to some minor crime, be imprisoned there, and never be seen or heard of again. If a prisoner was sent to one of the colonies to work off their debt, they should consider themselves lucky. Many were murdered by a fellow prisoner for a few scraps of food, or just for the sheer pleasure of it. It was a place so cruel it turned your blood to ice as you made your way through the dark ominous foreboding front gates. The chill of death was everywhere.

His job in Bedlam prison was simple, if the deceased had the means, a simple coffin and a Christian burial, if not, taken out to sea on one of the Thames barges and tossed over the side, neither of which was a desirable end. When possible, corpses were burned, but burning corpses required fuel, and fuel, be that coal of wood cost money. He would be employed to dispose of the bodies properly. He also had another useful role to play, in that the prison itself could become very overcrowded. Sometimes the inmates needed to be thinned out a little, he had found a way to free the tormented chaotic souls and release them from their terrors. The prison authorities turned a blind eye to the process and denied all knowledge, yet it was what it was.

Bedlam prison, as it was nicknamed, was perched upon a hill in view of Hyde Park. A large open expanse of green fields close to orchards and parkland in the Center of the city of London. It had an eerie presence about it, and always seemed to be a dark menacing place, tonight was no exception. Very soon after starting his walk from Chelsea, the skies clouded over, dark black storm clouds filled the night sky blocking out the stars and the moon. He could feel the night air charged with static energy, a big storm was brewing, a really big one. The odd thing was, he actually enjoyed a storm, the power and majesty of nature always filled him with such energy and excitement. It was a strange sensation that he found difficult to explain, but he often felt a special harmony with life, with everything around him, like they were connected, maybe someday he would understand why or how that could be.

Turning his attention from the sky and back to the prison, he pulled his heavy coat around himself and hunched his shoulders pulling his head deep down into the collar of his coat. The first drops of rain began to patter onto the floor around him until gradually the drops soon gave way to a downpour, then the air cracked, as lightning and then thunder streaked and rumbled across the sky. A loud crack of thunder rumbled, vibrating the very ground beneath his feet, each flash of lightning lit up his way, then another and another. He paused for a moment and took in a very long deep breath. The air smelled slightly musky, yet the rain would soon make it fresh and clean, oddly the rain was rather warm, and he looked up into the sky letting the rain drops splash heavily onto his face. He loved to feel the seasons on his skin, hot cold wet dry it mattered not. It was a refreshing feeling, before long, his arms were outstretched and his coat opening up to reveal the smartly dressed gentleman's attire. With his top hat still upon his head and his walking cane clenched in his right hand, he almost danced up the hill to the summit where the horrors of Bedlam prison awaited.

He loved the energy of a rainstorm, thunder and lightning, made it all the more exciting and powerful. Finally, at the top of the hill he extended his arms out wide and turned slowly on the spot as if to embrace the rain itself, closing his eyes he could feel and imagine the energy being absorbed into him. It made him feel invincible, as he closed his eyes radiant tiny blue specs of light from all around him began to dance in the night air, the peacock feather on his top had glowed with a rainbow of colours, his blood stone ring glowed brightly, the small red specs pulsing. His cane felt surprisingly heavier in his hand and he clenched it tightly, something was happening, something he could not explain but something real and breath-taking. The energy in the air all around him seemed to converge on him, like he was able to absorb it, the very source of all things so freely available for anyone open minded enough to see it, he breathed deeply feeling it recharge his soul. It felt so good to be alive, to be aware, especially on nights like this. He made his way slowly up the short lane to the prison virtually unhindered by the raging storm and rain. Once at the main gates he tapped on the large tall door with his cane. A small hatch cut into, yet another small door suddenly moved. The gentle tap of his cane alerted a guard who opened the spy hatch sharply, glaring at the smartly dressed man. 'Oh, it's you, come to round up more lost souls have ya.' He stood looking back at the scruffily dressed attendant. The guard closed the spy hatch swiftly and opened the inner gate to let him in. He returned a small nod of acknowledgement to the guard. Then he proceeded to the inner courtyard and then to a small door at the far end, where light was seen coming from under the door. Behind the door the sound of men laughing. He tapped on the door with his cane and waited. He was regarded rather mysteriously by the guards, but they never questioned him or challenged him. He carried himself with confidence at all times. More often than not it saw him through most situations unchallenged.

The door opened slowly, squeaking on its old heavy hinges and then stopped to almost halfway open. He waited a moment, then he pushed the door open the rest of the way and stepped inside cautiously. One could not be too careful in this place; the guards were every bit as dangerous if not more so than the prisoners. He held his cane tightly in his hand feeling somewhat safer, knowing that he was ready to meet whatever threat might come his way, he calmed his breathing and cleared his mind ready for the task ahead.

Once inside he shook his heavy coat letting a good amount of rainwater splash around him onto the quarry stone floor. 'You need any elp.' He turned to the guard and shook his head, He started to walk down the tight narrow corridor. 'Mind if we watch.' He turned and peered deeply through his cold bright eyes to the man. 'This is not something one should enjoy, it is simply a necessary evil, to cleanse the corrupted and misled.' He frowned slightly and prepared himself, gripping his walking cane firmly in his hand. His breathing eased to a soft deliberate relaxed inhale and exhale of breath. 'You make it look fun.' The guard said smiling nervously. He adjusted his top hat upon his head for a moment and turned to the man again. 'It is not.' He turned and pointed to the door opposite and gestured to the prison guard. 'I am ready.'

The guard put a large heavy key into the lock and slowly turned it, after a heavy cluck the door slowly opened squeaking on heavy hinges. The prison guard carefully pushed it open making sure that the mysterious gentleman was between him, and the open space on the other side of the door. Daydan walked slowly inside, the guard quickly slammed the door closed behind him and locked it. As he stood still, he could sense the occupants within, a cold chilling feeling of pure hate. The smell of death was all around him, it felt unnatural somehow, out of place. He looked ahead at the dark corridor in front of him and noticed the ground tilted upward slightly. There were no stairs or steps, the walls were stone, thick and cold, and the floor too. He took a breath and slowly walked ahead griping his cane tightly ready to fend off an attack in an instant. His skills with a blade and foil were self-taught, his father was not a fighting man, he was however a very good horseman, and he passed on many skills to his son, they seemed to have a way with animals, especially horses. He picked up some skills from the highwayman who did have military training and was very proficient with a pistol, not that it was a weapon he himself favoured. He always carried a dagger in his boot, partly for self-defence, but mostly as a tool. His mastery with a foil, which he easily transferred to his elaborate cane made his movements and skill look masterful and effortless, most of the time just a quick display would put off many unprepared attacker, but on occasion, desperation gave way to intelligence and a foolish cutthroat lay convulsing at his feet.

The prison was a foreboding place, very dark, little in the way of light penetrated into the halls and passageways of the prison, there was little point of lighting as it required fuel, and someone to tend to it, most of the time, during daylight, high windows would let in just enough light to see by, but at night, most were huddled into their tiny corner in the hope of getting some undisturbed sleep and not having their throat slit in the darkness, or a fate even worse than death to befall them. It was a horrible place, for many a living hell, but for others, a paradise to indulge in their twisted desires with no possible fear of retribution, not that is, until the gentleman undertaker came to purge the souls of the wicked and bring his own justice to the evil masters, who set themselves up as twisted depraved kings of the underworld. There were oil lamps where the guards attended the door into the prison, but something like that would just be too obvious a sign to any of the inmates within. Such a clear indication that someone from outside was foolish enough to enter. A chance that the visitor had something of use to use on the inside, to trade or possibly to eat.

Whenever he entered this place, he could not help feeling a paralysing sense of dread and helplessness, he always made sure that he was as prepared as he could be, speed, skill and utter terror were his allies, and he used them well.

Amid the screams and shouting coming from the very depths of the prison, there was the constant sound of water dripping from the ceilings, especially at the lower levels, one preferred to think of the liquid that dripped endlessly from above to be water rather than anything else, the smell however seemed to avail to anyone of what it really was. It was obvious, that if the liquid dripping from the ceilings was one thing, the layer of sludge in dark corners and the walls that seemed to move were obviously something quite unthinkable. He tried to turn his head away from the acrid stink that filled the air and slightly burned the moist sensory canal in his nostrils, but it was impossible. He moved slowly, trying to pick a clear line across the floor that was not covered in filth, but it was impossible, the guards would sometimes throw a bucket of water across the floor to try and clean an area, but water was in short supply, even hauling water from the Thames just to throw across a floor to be returned to the dirty river down the drains seemed like a pointless task. The only reprieve for such a despicable place was to try and keep down the number of inmates, that was where the skills and service of the gentleman undertaker came into play, any inspection of corpses left by the gentleman undertaker rarely left signs of foul play from him, often, just a look of terror, the look of a corpse who just had a frightening or terrifying heart attack, wide open mouth, and wide open eyes, pale and clammy like their life had been sucked right out of them in an instant.

Sometimes however, the look on the faces of his dead victims seemed to be a look of relief, of euphoria. Perhaps the escape of death was a welcome escape from the situation they were currently in. For some, death can be a welcome escape from a living misery, or a state which the soul finds abhorrent. The gentleman undertaker had seen many corpses, witnessed many last moments of life, but for him, he could see that death was not the end, simply a transition between one state of being and another. This was his dilemma, knowing this secret, understanding this strange phenomenon, how does it change man's understanding of life, what does it mean. He understood that everything that was, would always be, perhaps not in its current form or state, but certainly in its source. All things were connected, everything, without exception, but as a scientist, a physician, a scholar, how did this work. What was more exciting for him was, if he understood its secrets, could he control it, was it possible to control the very essence of life, the source of all things.

He was just a man, a man with knowledge, dangerous knowledge, a man with a very unique skill, a man who saw opportunity, challenge and adventure in everything, every skill he studied, he would strive for perfection. He enjoyed being alive, the search for knowledge, the search for understanding. When he mastered his sword play, every movement, every thrust and slash, every cut, it was like painting a masterpiece with movement, a masterpiece in time. The art of killing had become a dance of skill, a pleasure to behold, his victims, often in awe of his movements as he made the ordeal look effortless.

He didn't see his task as murder, evil, cruel or criminal, it was like a cleansing, of rebalancing the source, even the air seemed to be cleaner after he finished his work, a sense of calm that had taken hold after such chaos, it felt right. The calm before the storm found him close his mind, removing all doubt and interference from the task at hand, one wrong move, one unpredictable distraction and he could be the victim of someone else's rage or cunning, if that was to be, he would have to accept that fate. He often contemplated that time was not linear, that the past present and future was all set, and no matter what man did it could not be changed. He pondered such theories and happily concluded that there was free will, but sometimes, the past present and future could converge. Déjà vu. It would be sad to think that one's life has already been planned out, that your failures and successes were already decided. That your sadness and happiness were set and no matter what, you must suffer in silence. Clearly, some people seemed to have a life set by sadness, where others had an easy life of ease and happiness, if this was fate, then balance was irrelevant because life, and everything was already in balance. Perhaps what he was doing was upsetting the balance, if that was the case, so be it, he did not like the idea that he should suffer endlessly, some suffering with some success, he could handle, in fact, it felt fair, it felt right, and provided he could live his own life in balance and harmony, he would do his utmost to enjoy it trying his very best, to live by his own moral code to do no harm, or to ensure that others could not. A contradiction perhaps, but if others could not protect themselves from harm, was it not then right for the sake of balance, that other forces be allowed to intervene, after all, in order for balance and harmony to prevail, a process of realignment must take place.

Chaos can reset the forces that exist all around us, change is inevitable, and with change, eventually comes calm. He challenged his ideals, his morals and his desires in his own mind. It helped him to focus on the task at hand, a task that was not easy, but one that he felt was necessary. He could feel the energies of the night penetrate his body, the storm outside still raged. The lightning flashed through the few high windows above him, the thunder roared like a defiant beast overhead, the rain clattered against the thick windowpanes above and the storm in all its majesty invigorated him, it made him feel strong. But was possible that his adversaries felt the same way, were they also ready for this reckoning. He looked at his finger, the light of the lightning struck the silver ring on his finger, the blood stone in the centre glistened, the tiny red spots on the bloodstone ring began to brighten, the colours that he could see were unlike anything else in this world, they were vibrant, bright, magnificent and mesmerising, they had a hypnotic presence that was other worldly, unlike anything he had seen before, this strange power he had, this gift, this curse, it brought him joy, a glimpse into a world of possibilities, a world of adventure and mystery, and for him mystery was intoxicatingly exciting. He moved slowly at first up the dark stone passageway, the sounds of blood chilling screams echoed through the corridors like a warning, the helpless cries of fear, terror and agonising pain. His imagination added to the torment of the victims of those screams were probably worse than the reality, or then again, maybe not. His breathing was beginning to quicken, and he tried to calm himself as best he could. He knew exactly what the night would bring. Torment, suffering, but for some, relief and escape. The sound of the heavy door that closed behind him earlier reminded him just how much the world wanted to shut this place away, this dark world of horrors. As much as it hurt to see the things, he knew he would experience this night, the task at hand was a necessary one, the most cruel and vile of people existed and flourished in this realm of twisted madness and death. With each step the ground became slippery with muck, the air was thick with an acrid musk, and the sounds of agonising despair sent chills down his spine. He adjusted his heavy coat over his shoulders, trying to look like a gentleman in this place seemed to be a pointless endeavour, the only real thought in his mind was survival, and to make it through the night unharmed.

Chapter 7
Bedlam prison

The stench was incredible, a mixture of all manner of expelled bodily fluids dribbled along the stone floor like a river of mud, he pulled a black handkerchief from the top breast pocket of his waist coat beneath his heavy jacket, then held it to his nose tying it around the back of his head trying desperately to filter away some of the putrid smells.. Bedlam prison was a hive of criminality in its most base and wicked forms, evil reigned here. Amongst debauchery of every imaginable kind was abuse, burglary, rape, torture and murder, some of the most depraved criminals in London were right here. What was more bizarre was that some of the people here were here at their own request, preferring to live this way rather than in normal society. Perhaps the idea of the local justices was to keep all of the criminals and twisted minds in one place under lock and key, better that than to have them on the streets. It smelled of death here, death and pain, a gag reflexing putrid filth, filled the air, it tasted like cruelty, and hate had found a home. The idea that a thriving opium empire was being run from within these walls was hard to believe, but according to the Atwood woman, it was.

He tried hard not to retch, covering his nose and mouth even tighter with the perfumed handkerchief that he always kept in his pocket. He was a figure very much out of place in this environment. He was suddenly distracted by a cripple, crawling along the floor on his stomach and elbows. He was making good use of the wet muddy slippery floor, to propel himself at a rather impressive speed by sliding along through the slime. He laughed with a high pitch cackle that sounded more like the shrill of an old woman than the laughter of an emaciated, crippled and deformed old man. The cripple reached out slapping several rats away from a blobby mass on the floor which at first looked like a large pile of rags. When Daydan looked closer over the crippled worm, he realised that the rats were gnawing on the remains of a corpse, the carcass of which must have been dead for some time. When the rats had been frightened away the old crippled man helped himself to what was left of the pickings, deliberately cracking open the bones to get at the nourishing bone marrow within. Daydan turned away at once and again felt himself retch, covering his mouth and nose even tighter with his hand and handkerchief. The crippled man laughed with delight as he held up a piece of bone with a chunk of putrid flesh hanging from it, he began sucking at it cracking it in two with a satisfying snap. The cripple sucked at the contents devouring every last morsel. His rat like eyes glared at Daydan as if ready to defend the find with his life, but also ready to slither off and escape his wrath at a moment notice. More screams began to come from the dark corners of the prison cells and the sound of someone being beaten close by, he steadied himself and gripped his cane tightly at the top with his hands at the ready. Daydan gave the handle of the cane a slight twist and pulled near to the silver knob at the head of the cane and closed his eyes. Slowly and steadily as he pulled his hands apart sliding one down the shaft a little and the other holding the handle until a thin narrow blade could be seen with a radiant blue light in a straight line forming a long thin stiletto blade. The light and blade were in the form of something similar to that of an old-style rapier sword, he seemed to rejoice at its creation and smiled. The blade glowed in front of his eyes while being pulled out completely from the protective wooden shaft in his left hand. He swished the glowing blade through the air slowly, using it like a seasoned master. Daydan stood with a posture of a man who had been very well trained and knew exactly how to use the weapon to its best effect, he practiced briefly with a combination of lunges, swipes and slashes finishing with an elegant on-guard pose. Holding the illuminated blue blade against his face pointing upward he peered eagerly from under his top hat and his handkerchief mask and then composed himself. Closing his eyes once more to prepare himself for the task ahead, the peacock feather on his top hat began to glow giving off a faint light in the darkness, radiating a beautiful rainbow of colours. His silver signet ring with the blood stone began to glow, each barely visible in the darkness, but visible they were, all three items together betrayed him, glowing warmly giving away his whereabouts. Here was a man with something otherworldly at his disposal, his handkerchief covered his identity, his polished boots muddied in the filth that festered everywhere. He looked very much out of place here. Smartly dressed like a gentleman out for a midday stroll in the park with his lady, but alas that was very far from the truth this day. The smell was no longer an issue, the screams, the beatings, the depravity, it no longer seemed to matter, he was here for a reason, and that was the end of it, this madness had to stop. Although even he knew that sometimes a little chaos was necessary to get things done, this level of depravity certainly was not. He swished his blade through the air down to his side remembering the weight and ease at which he could wield this beautiful weapon.

With his silver blood stone ring glowing gently, behind him he saw the forms of his companions, the two spirits that accompanied him so many times in the past on his adventures, the slave and the highwayman. The slaves face was full of hate, he swung his ebony club to and fro and nodded to his new master. The highwayman pulled out his pistols and pointed them upwards cocking back the flint lock hammers and grinned. Daydan smiled and gave them an affirming nod, each seemed to rejoice at the chance to reap out some vengeance for the victims of the criminals within these walls. No sooner had they nodded to him in acknowledgement he looked up to them and smiled. 'We have work to do my friends.' They grinned back to him and ran ahead up the dark dimly lit passageway; the faint light being given off by their ethereal energy was just enough to see them in the darkness. After they vanished from his view, he could hear screams and running with the muffled cries of panic. As spirits, they would be unseen, except if they chose to be seen, and their goal this night was to strike fear and terror into these inmates, a reaction that they appeared to be performing very well indeed. Daydan grinned as he imagined the look of fear on their foes as they floated effortlessly through the darkness running with rage in their eyes and with their weapons drawn to reap out their bloody revenge. Swiftly, he moved through the narrow corridors looking left and right for threats, a scream, and then an attacker hurled himself through the air at him slashing at him with some crudely made weapon. Daydan skilfully dodged his attackers strikes, first one and then another, he twisted and turned dodging blows with such ease and precision. His long wide sweeps with his otherworldly blade slashed through the air seemingly to cut his attacker in two. The thrust of the thin blade into a weak spot, neck, throat, eye socket, heart, groin or other vital organ. The strange dark eerie blue light of the blade penetrated through the darkness plunging deeply into his attacker's torso. With a strange sense of relief his attacker seemed to relish in the precise skilful nature of his wounds, the victim falling to the floor like a rag doll in a motionless heap. With a quick salute to his fallen enemy he proceeded to make his way to the heart of the prison, and the ever-growing cacophony of screams, most likely perpetuated by his loyal companions ahead.

More laughter and screams were coming from a nearby cell as he slowly made his way forward, he moved to the doorway carefully, making sure to be ready with his weapon in case of a surprise attack and looked inside. A woman was being mauled violently, being pushed too and fro between three large men, one man stood in front of her blocking her escape from the cell tugging at her clothing a tearing at her dress. Another was behind her trying to get a hold on her, but she would have none of it, even outnumbered as she was, she fought bravely to defend her honour. What these depraved murderers had in mind was glaringly obvious, she was swinging a broken length of chain over her head sending it repeatedly crashing down on the skulls and shoulders of her attackers with as much force as she could muster. Her defiance only seemed to antagonise them, making the prize of her humiliation even more desirable. Another man stood nearby, clearly excited by the poor woman's impending plight. When she saw Daydan in the shadows of the dark doorway she screamed again, a desperate scream for help or a scream of utter fear that yet another attacker had come to join in her humiliation. Immediately and without a sound he lunged forwards thrusting the blade through the back of the man that was facing her so that the blade could be seen bursting through his chest. The victim grinned for a moment and then slumped down towards the woman, withdrawing the blade slowly the victim's soul seemed to be drawn out of the body by the blade and with a twist of his wrist he flicked the ghostly form to the floor nearby. Within moments the spirits misty blue apparition quickly dissolved into tiny specs of light that swirled effortlessly up into the darkness like smoke from a fire. Next he repeated yet another skilful lunge swiftly forcing it through the back of the other man who was watching, when the blade was withdrawn it seemed to pull yet another ghostly soul from the individual out of its body, then slowly dissipate right before his eyes. His victims seemed to relish in the swift painless end as its lifeless corpse fell to the floor. The spirit looked at his own self for a moment before its light could be seen visibly breaking up and vanishing completely. The woman now stared wide eyed at him and let out a scream and now began to kick back in terror at what she had just seen. She was trying desperately to get away from the man who was holding her from behind. Seeing the strange blue blade of Daydan's weapon he let go of the woman and stared at his companions laying motionless on the floor. He then lunged forwards with his hands trying to grab his attacker around the throat but it was to late, Daydan quickly recovered the blade from one victim and began another strike straight through the throat of the last of the three men, in seconds all three bodies were little more than a mass of rags and lifeless corpses on the floor. The woman hissed at him still screaming trying to make sense of what just happened, clearly still very much in fear of her life. When Daydan waved his hand over the bodies of the men in a slow respectful horizontal motion, his silver blood-stone ring glowed gently. With each wave, tiny specs of light floated up into the air from the corpses. The departing energy from each corpse formed a strange effortless rotating spiral pattern of light flowing upwards to the ceiling and then away out of sight. It was a rather calming tranquil sight, but not something that the unaware would be able to explain, the souls and metaphysical energies of the dead returning to their eternal, original source. The woman stood up panting heavily, her chest heaving breathlessly as she did her best to cover herself while tearfully kicking the corpse of one of her attackers. She glared up at the man who just saved her from a fate worse than death, unsure of his intentions, she moved cautiously a safe distance away but putting herself behind the mysterious gentleman. With muddy matted hair and ragged clothes, they did little to enhance her femininity, not that she cared. She looked up at him and nodded fearfully trying in her own way to acknowledge his unexpected act of kindness. He returned the gesture to her with a smile and nodded politely back to the woman tapping his top hat with his cane. With a swish of his glowing blade back and forth in his right hand, he made his way to the doorway of the cell intent on delivering more justice to the chaotic souls of this vile pit of cruelty and insanity. In his left hand he carried the outer shaft of his walking cane and used it to parry, deflect or poke weak points of his attackers, a dual wielding assault on any aggressor that came too near.

Somehow, others could sense the violent but sudden ends to several of their comrade prisoners, shouts could be heard, retaliation. Someone was organising them into a defence, or more likely a frenzied attack. Daydan once again began readying himself. Each floor became more difficult, they were much more organised as the levels rose. He adjusted his posture and ever the gentleman, he smiled as he prepared to launch himself into the fray. 'Wait.' The woman shouted at him and adjusted her dress looking around on the floor for her weapon, she picked up her length of chain. She held it firmly in her right hand and shrugged her shoulders desperately. Daydan nodded back politely and smiled, the chain may not be a sturdy blade, but it would certainly deliver a painful blow. He turned his back to her and exited the doorway, deliberately keeping himself between her and any attacker in front of them. Listening quietly, he could hear the panicked yet hungry for revenge prisoners vying for blood, coming ever nearer to where he was, he turned to the woman standing terrified behind him trembling with the length of chain held tightly in her hand. Daydan had little hope that she would be of any use if the fighting got really intense, but he admired her spirit, she was a fighter, a survivor. Even terrified as she was, she was tough and would not go down without a fight. He admired that about her. Ahead the corridor turned sharply right, the large tall square building was of a very simple design. Corridors around the outside with slit windows to let in the light, off the corridors were cells crammed with fighting squabbling prisoners. As one ascended up higher the environment was a little cleaner, yet the depravity was considerably worse. His progress through the prison was slow, yet each attacker was dispatched with skill and precise strikes to incapacitate the victims with such perfect precision and expertise, the entire process moved like clockwork, a skilful dance of swordsmanship as one after another of his attackers were slain. Any prisoner that did not try to fight him he left alone. He looked over to his new companion who looked expectedly terrified, yet she was ready with her heavy chain, looking to inflict as much pain as possible on anyone who dared come to close. The corridor to the next level was one of a constant yet steady climb, no stairs were seen anywhere, just the obvious elevation in the floor indicating that they were slowly rising, it somehow made sense. All of the spillage from the floors above would flow down to ground level one way or another, and then from there into the sewers beneath the prison which eventually made their way into the river Thames. He proceeded slowly and carefully up the passageway. Daydan held his blade down and slightly to his side, like a seasoned warrior. The eerie blue iridescent glow of his blade was just visible in the low lighting of the corridor, yet its low soft blue light became brighter whenever the light of the moon and stars was able to shine upon it. It took very little time as thugs of all kinds began to lunge at the couple from the shadows, the crack of heavy chain on skulls and bone. The cries of relief and escape as he buried his blade deeply into his attackers, *one less murderer, one less twisted mind, one less rapist.* As they climbed higher and higher up the floors to the top levels, the attacks were more organised. Someone seemed to be in charge. It made no difference to him what was at the end of this cull, each attacker was dispatched with skill and effortless swordsmanship, much to the relief of the young woman. She took advantage of the opportunity to hide behind him when their aggressors became to violent or to overwhelming for her to handle herself. She relished the chance to swing her chain and land an opportunistic kick at an unsuspecting attacker. Even through the hellish ordeal, she would glance to her fighting companion and give a toothy smile of satisfaction when, yet another foe had been slain. When they reached the upper floor, the young woman was exhausted, matted with mud, blood and grime. It was difficult to recognise anything about the young woman, only that she was wearing a dress that had been ripped and soaked in all manner of things. He finally stopped in his tracks for a moment and put his arm across the young woman's path, forcing her to stand behind him. Ahead of them was a large doorway, blocking their way was a huge giant of a man standing in front of a crudely built barricade, at the top of the barricade sat a man in a judge's wig and robes. He held in his right hand a large crudely made sceptre, he slammed it into the ground and growled. 'I will see him dead, DEAD.' He pointed the crudely made sceptre to the mysterious visitor with the strange blue glowing blade. The giant edged forwards and began to run at him lumbering clumsily towards him as fast as he could. Again, he ensured the young woman was behind him, then he also charged forwards, his heavy coat almost airborne as he sprinted towards the giant. The roar from the giant grew louder and louder. 'Deeeeaaaad,' a deep rumbling laughter gutturally filled the air, accentuated by the cheers of the judge and some depraved looking villains close by, vying for blood and pain.

In a moment of pure perfection, he stooped and lowered himself to the floor sliding across the ground, rolling over completely and rising again just in time to strike the giant with his blade right up through his groin. The giant howled as he saw him slowly remove the blade from him pulling out strands of his soul like tearing flesh from carrion. Without pause or hesitation he then circled slashing with a precise movement at the giant skilfully making his way around him, out of reach from his counter strikes. Again, and again from left and right, his strange ethereal blade passed through the fleshy mass of the giant like a hot knife through butter, then a single final thrust putting the blade deep into the giant's heart. Daydan paused for a moment to let the giant's realisation of impending death sink in, then he slowly retracted the blade extracting the remnants of the giant's soul. Once again, he held the weapon to his side and bowed his head flicking the finely hand-crafted weapon to his side. Small specs of light floated upwards, freed from their deprived hosts body at last. The giant's life force energy faded from an unrecognisable form to that of pure energy. They watched the strange light drifting upwards into the darkness and through the solid ceiling of the prison and up into the night. To their attacker it was a happy sight, the eternal energies of the universe in a constant cycle of renewal.

The judge stood up tall, towering over everyone from his elevated position on the top of the barricade, with a single look he assembled more of his twisted militia. Slowly, one by one they descended down to floor level from the barricade. They faced their enemy and his terrified sidekick, she glared at them, still shaking yet steadfast, teeth clenched tightly with her lips rolled back, her hand gripped the chain so tightly that her knuckles had turned white.

'The Law cannot be challenged.' The judge pointed his sceptre to him. 'You fool, you cannot defeat me.' He pointed with his sceptre to the dozens of corpses that had clearly been horrifically tortured, mutilated and crucified, nailed to the doors of the cells and overhead ceiling beams. Some bodies were strung up between the window frames, leaving a clear silhouette of their forms against the light of the moon. The bodies over the large windows prevented much of the daylight from penetrating within. Staring back at the judge he paused and stood up tall holding his head up, his back was straight and his posture sharp. He pointed his mysterious blade to the gathered villains and looked at each one in turn. 'I am no sacrifice, this evil cannot be, I will not allow it.' A small voice from somewhere behind him spoke nervously but determined. 'Me either.' He smiled to himself, she certainly had grit this young woman, he looked back to her briefly and smiled giving her a wink admiring her bravery. Suddenly the barricade was smashed open, the Judge bellowed at his depraved gang of murderers and made ready to watch the feast of violence as it was about to unfold. 'I will see him dead. NOW.' There was roar of voices, several men charged towards Daydan, swinging wildly with all sorts of different weapons. Large sword like blades to a length of iron or chain, a wooden club, a scythe, a length from a broken piece of prison furniture. Swipe after swipe they lashed out at their attacker, blow after blow found its mark. Daydan fought on, unfazed by his injuries, defending as best he could the young woman behind him from any savage blows. He himself felt several hard hits land against his body, but without the luxury of being able to check himself for wounds, he continued on. Slowly, one by one his skill and swordsmanship dispatched enemy after enemy until only the judge and his more cowardly follower and a snivelling sycophant remained. The judge joyfully paraded himself in front of him like a self-appointed emperor. He acted like he was completely untouchable, and God like. On the throne where the judge stood, was a large bowl full of a fine white powder, the judge would reach in from time to time with his hand, pull out a hand full of the powder and splash it into his face. Daydan knew that this had to be the opium that was coming into the city via the judge and his contacts. The quantity of opium around the room was jaw dropping, it was in the air, on the floor, many of his minions had the same splash of white powder on their noses. The judge opened his robes pointing his chest to them both and shouted as loudly as he could. 'YOU, cannot harm me, I am the Law, and you will obey, or suffer the consequences.' All Daydan could feel was an overwhelming anger, wanting to get revenge for his Mary. The judge pointed his sceptre towards the large windows around the top floor letting in just enough light to see by. One by one the sycophant pulled a sheet from the window to reveal a figure hanging like a crucifix in the light, silhouetted against the window. Sheet after bloody sheet was removed, disembowelled, dismembered torsos, horribly mutilated bodies. Eight corpses decorated the windows in an almost artful display of torture and pain behind the judge, these poor wretches had obviously endured unimaginable torture, until the grateful release of their death had come. '*BILLY...*' The young woman charged forwards staring up at one of the figures hanging in the moonlight, she sobbed and burst into tears and then screamed. With a strength gathered from some hidden reservoir of energy she charged at the judge, her heavy chain swinging wildly over her head. With her left hand, she pulled up her dress from her feet enough so as not to get them tangled as she ran. Daydan smiled, humbled by her desire for revenge, then suddenly the slimy sycophant, kicked out tripping her up. The young woman sprawled across the floor sliding in a heap to the feet of the judge, her heavy piece of chain clanking and jingling across the floor to a halt just a few feet away. She looked up to the judge crying in utter despair defiantly showing her anger and hate. Gritting her teeth her tear-filled eyes were so desperate for revenge or release from her pain. She sobbed as tears streamed down her dirty face. With no sense of mercy or remorse the judge pulled back his crudely made sceptre with both hands and smashed the foot of it squarely into her upturned face, again and again he lifted his sceptre and brought it crashing down upon her helpless form for good measure. His senseless violence was completely unnecessary as he smashed it into her body, over and over again. She slumped down to the ground motionless.

Daydan's mouth dropped open, stunned by the judge's cruelty, and utter disregard for life or mercy. He looked at the young woman's still corpse and then looked to the judge. 'Why.' He pulled his blade to his side ready to strike watching the snivelling sycophant out of the corner of his eye as he tried to move around to his flank for yet another sneaky attack. Daydan's heart had never before felt so much anger and hatred for someone before this night. The judge looked at him with an uncaring defiant pose that seemed to mock him. 'Because I can.' He shook his head. 'Just because you have the power to do such, you should know better, as a better man would.' Daydan replied calmly yet with a tone of sadness in his voice that betrayed his emotions. The judge laughed and pointed his sceptre to him. 'What gives you the right to judge me.' He curled back his lips gritting his teeth like a rabid dog. 'Weak fool.' Daydan shook his head defiantly, he looked again to the corpse of the young woman and to the dead bodies that were scattered on the ground and above. He took in a deep gentle breathe and slowly walked towards the judge, the man looked him in the eyes and rather than resist, he once again pointed his chest out to him godlike. He made ready and pulled back his blade and thrust it forwards in one motion deep into the chest of the judge right through his heart and held it so that the judge could stare in disbelief seeing himself impaled on such a beautifully crafted weapon. The judge's soul began to ooze onto the blade, Daydan slowly pulled the blade from the judge's chest and watched the small glowing specs begin to fall from his body forming into small stars of light that began mysteriously spiralling upwards to the moonlight. The judges body fell suddenly to the floor. It was an anti-climax to such a self-important figure, perhaps a troubled soul whose relief in death was his only salvation.

Daydan visibly shrunk for a moment, the exertions of the night clearly catching up with him, then a voice rippled behind him. 'Don't kill me, he made me do it.' He turned swiftly, but he was to late, a large ethereal figure lunged towards the slimy sycophant with his arms stretched high above to bring down a large ebony club onto the skull of the coward. Before he could, the sycophant screamed out and fell to the floor clutching his heart with his hands, dying in a moment of pure terror, his body spasmed in its death throws and moments later he was still and motionless, the large open room was silent. The slave looked around for more targets, the highwayman entered his view and prodded at the corpses with his rather barbaric looking blade and his boot. It was over, not a soul was left alive, Daydan slumped onto some of the barricade and pulled open his heavy coat and lifted his torn shirt to reveal a large multi coloured bruise down his entire right side. He was hit many times and although none of the wounds had drawn blood, they caused large bruising indicating internal damage. Broken ribs perhaps, but luckily none with a blade, he carefully touched the wounds, flinching with the pain. As an experienced physician he knew the anatomy and biology of the human body better than most, he also knew how resilient it could be and how given the proper care it could heal and renew itself.

Finally, being able to catch his breath he made himself as presentable as he could, he trucked in his torn shirt into his breaches and carefully adjusted his waistcoat and made sure he looked as good as he possibly could. He knelt down by the young woman's corpse and placed his hand softly on her chest. Closing his eyes, he looked as if he was saying a prayer over her, after a moment he stood up slowly still holding his hand towards her. The ring on his finger glowed softly, then with a gentle motion, he waved his hand to and fro over her body, as if he was caressing her form. Slowly, small star like specs of light were seen, then more and more until her ethereal spirit formed above her corpse, it was the young woman, she looked at herself, her hands were clean, her dress perfect, here hair looked like it had just been prepared and her face looked radiant and beautiful. She looked too Daydan confused but grateful. A most beautiful smile formed across her lips, he then looked up to the corpse in the large window and pointed his hand to her Billy. Slowly, similar small lights appeared, tiny sparks of blue, and then more and more until his spiritual form could be recognised. It seemed that her Billy was once a handsome strapping young man, most likely a seaman or land worker. When he saw the young woman, his spirit descended down to her and they embraced. Daydan smiled happily feeling a lump form in his throat, he was happy for the spirits who were very clearly lovers in life and now free of their earthly bonds to be in love again. He thought about Mary and his promise to her. The ethereal spirits of Billy and the young woman embraced for what seemed like several minutes, looking into each other's eyes and then embracing again. It was obvious they were deeply in love; it was also a beautiful sight to see, especially tonight. After all of this pain and suffering, even he found it difficult to hide his own joyful emotions.   There was a moment when their bodies were intertwined that their light seemed to shine ever more brightly, their forms merging into one brilliant radiant light, like a star. Slowly their light ascended upwards until it penetrated through the dark wooden beamed ceiling of the building, once again the huge room felt cold and dark, empty, his own loneliness became so very clear.

He paused for some time, looking around. The task was done, there was barely a soul left alive, he stood up and looked to his companions still searching for enemies. 'Our work here is done.' He nodded to them each in turn, and with a likened response his companions faded and vanished from his view. He walked back alone, slowly down the slope of the building descending through its floors to the exit. Only this time there was almost perfect silence, the screams were gone, the cold uninviting atmosphere that welcomed him only moments earlier had been replaced by quiet. There was still the ever-present steady dripping of water from the floors above. On his way, every now and again stepping over a slain body. He held his abdomen on his right side still suffering from the pain of the huge bruise and wounds that had been inflicted upon him, he was sure a good soak in a nice hot bath would make him feel much better, being able to wash away this evil foulness, and to remove the putrid smell from his nostrils would make him feel much better. Especially for a man so self-disciplined about his own cleanliness. As he descended very slowly down the passageway towards the exit, he made a mental count of the bodies and corpses, all in all he counted eighty-nine. He would receive a small payment for each body that he disposed of in the proper way, either burial or burning. It was a strange arrangement indeed, an unofficial arrangement none the less. Not only that, but the old woman would surely be pleased with his nights work, the judge and his empire was gone. Daydan was the person responsible for disposing of the dead from the prison, and with that horrible task came opportunity. The industry of law it seemed was a business just like any other, and a clever man could find ways of making a living from the strangest of circumstances.

He was very relieved when up ahead he saw the large prison door leading out to the guard room, keeping himself slightly out of view for a moment he took some time to ponder over what just happened. This time he had been lucky, very lucky, his skill as a swordsman was not ever in question, but the unpredictable situation that he just thrust himself into could have spelled his demise very easily. In the future, he would have to be a lot more careful. He was going to make a small fortune from this night's activities. Did that justify the danger he had put himself into. Was it just business, or had he learned some valuable lesson that he could take with him to somehow enrich his life a little more or was it all just about the accumulation of wealth at any cost.

Walking down towards the prisons exit he remembered the body count and pictured some of the final moments of the dead that he remembered, but there was one individual whose body was not accounted for. The old wretch he saw when he first entered slithering through the muck and feeding on the carcasses of the dead. As he walked, he looked around and listened for the eerie cackle of that crippled wretch. The young couple he reunited in death, he envied them, but he also felt a sense of happiness for them too. Perhaps there was a lesson in that. He cleared his throat and walked around the corner to the guard's door and tapped upon it with his cane, he replaced the sword back into its cane shaft and gave a delicate twist on its hilt securing it closed once again. It made it look as innocent as any other gentleman's walking cane. When the security shutter in the door opened, he gave a polite smile to the guard and tapped his top hat with his cane in a greeting.

'I fought it was quiet. You done sir.' He looked around behind him as best he could double checking that it was safe to open the large solid wooden door, strengthened with its sturdy iron supports. With a clunk the guard opened a lever at the top and bottom of the door and used a large key to open the lock. As it opened, the door squeaked heavily on its hinges and was held ready to be closed again the moment the stranger was safely through. The door closed with a heavy clunk and the levers pushed into their locks for some much-needed added security. Daydan smiled slightly mocking him. Not that the guard cared much, he was safe on this side of the door, of that he was certain.

Chapter 8

The bath house

The night air was cold and damp, a slightly brisk wind blew up the hill where the prison was situated. Daydan walked slowly, still feeling the pain from the blows he received from some of the prisoners within. From his attire he looked unmarked, but beneath his shirt his body was battered and bruised. Walking up to the large heavy wooden gates of the prison yard, the guard gave him a smile as Daydan turned to give him the agreed payment of coins. The guard tipped his cap as he tossed the purse of coins up into the air and caught it again several times. A simple deal for the guard, and at-least a month's wages, he didn't even have to lift a finger, all he had to do was turn a blind eye. Daydan began walking toward home, he calculated the cost of coffins, materials and disposal, he would turn a tidy profit. Not to mention whatever the Atwood woman would do to keep her end of the bargain. He made his way steadily with a slight awkwardness, leaning more to one side trying to take as much pressure off his wounds as he could. As best he could he stood as upright and proud trying to look like a gentleman. As it turned out, tonight had been a very good nights work indeed and hopefully in some small way a little dark side of humanity was swept away to make way for some good. Thankfully the night was coming to a close and the morning light was starting to show on the horizon.

The storm from earlier long since subsided and the birds were out foraging for insects and scraps of food lured by the early light of the dawn. The small track was the only way for carts and carriages to get to the prison, it also made for a very easy walk from the prison to the open parkland nearby. The early morning workforce of ragged men and women, slowly began to emerge from their tiny little homes, down the hill in the much poorer areas of the city. They would start long before wealthier folk even stirred in their beds and would most likely still be working late into the night. Daydan knew of a good bathhouse nearby, a chance for a soak in hot water to wash away the filth of the night seemed like a perfect idea. It would make for a pleasant stop and a chance to clean up, a chance to pick up on the latest gossip. A small smile began to form on his lips and a positive outlook for the day ahead, helped him to forget about the searing pain he could feel in his side. His pace quickened again having settled his mind on a nice long soak in a hot bath. His leisurely walk continued, despite the pain he felt, he was relieved to be once again among the houses and streets of the city. London was growing fast, as a centre for commerce as it had been for many centuries. As a centre for the modern world, its growing population, trade, education, science and culture, it was all happening here, if anywhere had to be the right place to bring about a new age surely this was it. Walking up a smart set of steps to a sturdy door he used the silver top of his walking cane on the solid door. He announced his arrival to the attendant with a solid tap on the door, the sound of his cane had a dignified rhythm about it. Moments later a small peep hatch opened up and a face appeared. He looked to be rather shocked to see a patron at such an early hour. 'Wot, d'ya want.' The rather gruff voice seemed reluctant to be polite at all. He stooped slightly, just enough to make eye contact. 'I should like to bathe sir, and a new shirt if you would be so kind.' 'A new shirt is it, hmm.' The man stroked his stubbled chin and frowned looking away for a moment, he looked Daydan up and down assessing if he was the sort of gentleman to carry extra coin. A good opportunity to add a little extra income would make all the difference. The latch on the peep hole clicked shut, as the attendant shut the spy hatch, a much louder clunk sounded as a heavy latch allowed the attendant to slowly open the main door, he stood back ushering in his guest pointing the way. This was no mere novelty for Daydan, a bath house was something he frequented whenever he could. It was a lot less work attending such a place that always had ample hot water on the boil. So much easier than having to do the task yourself. The attendant walked a short way into a doorway, he pulled a simple heavy curtain to one side which opened the way to a large room that had been sectioned off into smaller areas. Each small area had its own private bath, for people to bathe surrounded by curtains hanging from an elaborate array of pulleys and ropes, to give as much privacy to the bathers as possible. The man clapped his hands and pointed to a tub that was already half full of steaming hot clean water. Wasting no time, he began to remove his garments, carefully trying not to hurt himself and avoiding putting any undue pressure on his injuries. He removed his shirt just as a young woman dashed in with a large jug of steaming hot water and poured it into the bath. She nodded and smiled to the gentleman and curtsied to him as if he was royalty or something. He let out an appreciative chuckle and slowly with a slight wince of pain had completely pulled off his shirt, his entire side was a rainbow of colours. Although the idea of a really nice hot bath was a welcome one, he knew that what he really needed was an ice-cold bath, to help stop any bleeding. He turned to the attendant and handed him his torn dirty and slightly blooded shirt. 'My good man, a replacement shirt if you please, and, no more hot water, cold, as cold as the Thames herself. Please.' The man looked oddly to him but did not question his request, he simply gave a polite nod and took the shirt out of his customers hand and closed the curtain behind himself, to give his latest customer some privacy. He stood half naked and stripped off the rest of his clothes and folded them up into a neat pile ready to be put back on. As Daydan lowered himself slowly into the hot bathtub surrounded by curtains, he could hear other bathers nearby, some talking to themselves, some talking to each other, it all seemed very noble, but social. In a way it reminded him of a roman bathhouse of the old empire. He listened in silence to the conversations nearby relaxing as best he could in the soothing waters of the bath. It was a favoured meeting place for gentleman to talk about the topics of the day, and reasonable to assume that a good many business deals were being done here too. As he listens further, he happened upon a conversation that caught his attention, he was just about to introduce himself when the young woman opened the curtain quickly and poured a large jug of very cold water into his bath. It felt uncomfortable at first, the cold water was so cold that he really wanted to get out of the bath. Seeing the large bruise on his side he knew that the best treatment would be to keep it cold, the colder the better. A patron cleared his throat and began to mumble nearby in an adjoining section behind an adjoining curtain. Amid the sounds of chatter and bathing, the tell-tale sounds of other bodily functions could be heard, it sounded funny to him but no doubt not the sort of behaviour that a gentleman should participate in. Although the sound of someone passing wind under the bath water made him laugh to himself. 'Just like that, she signed over shares of the company to a stranger no less, a stranger.' His ears were already focussed on the voice as he heard its tone, dull and an almost inaudible mumble. He spoke up tapping on the curtain out of politeness. 'You disapprove sir.' He smiled to himself as if he knew that it would most certainly cause a reaction. The old man coughed again and opened the nearby curtain still sitting in his bathtub, he was old, rather ugly with a large pitted nose and a thin head of sparse grey hair. 'But a foreigner Sir.' The large man continued to mumble as he just watched him. 'They are a nuisance, they disrupt the economy, chase our fine ladies and cause trouble, there is a conspiracy a foot.' He stood up in his bath peering over the curtain and stared at the man, realising who he was. He put his hands on his hips displaying himself. 'Sir, I am no different to you, I do not have horns or a tail, I am a hard-working man of science. Judge me for my actions, not for my country and land of my birth, do that and perhaps you will learn something not only of me but of yourself too.'

The man looked him up and down several times, he looked healthy and clean, save for one or two scars here and there, he also sported an extremely large and ugly looking bruise covering almost one sixth of his body, obviously from some confrontation or another. The old man cleared his throat mumbling while looking him over. 'I have heard of you Sir. You are the illusionist, the magician, the mystic, the one with the pallor tricks. Yes yes, I have heard the stories.'

'Stories.' Daydan was quick to defend his art and his life's work. The fat man stroked his stubbled fat chin and squinted his eyes to give the man a more accurate look up and down. He finally introduced himself as a solicitor and judge, he cleared the snot from his nose putting a finger on each nostril snuffing out any debris from within. 'So, it is you, Lady Atwood spoke of you, I suppose she knows what she is doing, she is a very astute and ruthless businesswoman. If this is her wish I shall see it done, she pays fairly and always on time.' He nodded to the fat man and slowly lowered himself back down into his tepid yet refreshing bath water now warmed to the same temperature as his body. He leaned back and let the water cover his shoulders, then he leaned back further and completely submerged himself under the water for some time before re-emerging again. The fat man cleared his throat and mumbled. 'Very well, you shall attend my residence on the day after the morrow. I will have your papers and documents ready. All will be legally recorded, in return for my fee. Your fee shall be to astound my friends in a private show. Though I warn you, we are not fools, any trickery and you will be dealt with severely. Are we in agreement sir.' He was slightly puzzled, what trickery was he referring to, this was not some traveling side show con. The fat man seemed rather adamant that there was something underhanded about his performance. At first it appeared to be an offer to good to refuse. In the years to come the shares he acquired could become rather valuable, indeed even now they would make a wealthy man smile. The now tepid water he was bathing in found him slightly shuddering but already feeling the benefits of the numbing cold. He felt clean at last, and the smells of the prison well and truly washed away.

'We are Sir, I will attend your residence as you wish in return for your legal services, it would be an honour.'

'Ha-ha, would it indeed, we shall see showman, we shall see.' He could hear the fat old man slump in his tub as he continued to bathe, the splash of water and the constant throat clearing was disconcerting to say the least. He sounded incredibly sick and unhealthy, however, he continued to bathe nearby as best he could. By now the water was cold, and he could feel his fingers numbing and going almost a white shade of blue.

He closed his eyes and relaxed himself for a while, the young woman returned with a few more jugs of cold water. Daydan held his hand up in submission. He stood up and looked around for his clothes, spotting them on the nearby chair he slowly stepped out of the cold bath and moved over to his clothes. At that very moment the young woman returned with his new shirt, over her shoulder she held some cotton cloth and began to rub him down gently, at first, he was rather shocked by her boldness. But he was cold and the young woman's help was gravely appreciated. Her touch was gentle on his bruises which he appreciated. He moved and turned slowly to assist her as best he could, she looked to be enjoying herself as she looked him up and down several times glancing a sideways look to his eyes and smiling. He sucked in a soft breath as she dried between in legs looking up into his eyes, he tried not to look embarrassed as if this was a common occurrence, perhaps it was for her, but for him having a woman close, especially this close. It was not a situation that he often found himself in. He tensed slightly as once again her hand and the cotton towel rubbed briskly against his strong powerful thighs. He clenched his buttocks trying to control his base feelings. 'The water was very cold.' She began to calmly pat him down drying him off expertly. She stared at him and seemed to take great pleasure in tracing the lines of his body. 'We shall soon have you warmed up my lord.' He looked into her eyes deeply, she had the loveliest eyes he had ever seen, so blue, a deep blue, and hair as red as blood. 'Do I know you miss.' He tilted his head over her slightly to try and get a different angle of her that may jog his memory. She smiled and rubbed him down vigorously as he stood in front of her. He felt very self-conscious being completely naked in front of her but realised that this was something she was very accustomed to. He was a rather average looking man, slim, firm of build, his posture and manner was always sharp, and he stood up straight making himself look much taller than he really was. The young woman seemed to enjoy rubbing him down as much as he enjoyed having her closeness to his body. She looked into his eyes often and smiled beautifully to him and she appeared to take rather more time attending to drying his more intimate areas than was necessary. From behind him she rubbed his back and legs hard and then carefully dried off his buttocks. She dried over his bruises carefully and looked with interest at his hands and fingers as she dried them slowly one by one. It was like she was studying him as she carefully attended to him. The entire time he felt he wanted to reach out to her and touch her, sometimes his hand would caress the air near her, but he held firm and resisted the desire to do anything to compromise her. 'Here girl, do me.' Shouted the old fat man as he pulled open the curtain to his bath and slowly stepped out of the tub giving a rather unsightly display of his poorly kept obese body. The girl winced at the sight of him and curtsied tearing off some linen to assist the old fat man. With the girl gone he began to slowly dress himself, happy for the clean new shirt and glad to be back in his clothes again. The last thing on was his riding boots and his short top hat, he grabbed his cane and tapped the top of his hat to ensure it was on straight, then he reached into his waistcoat and pulled out a large silver coin, he flicked it through the air to the young woman making it spin in a slow smooth arch. The young woman reached out and snatched it from the air easily and tucked it down her dress into her cleavage, she smiled to him and returned to the old man. As Daydan headed for the door the young woman glanced back to him and caught his eye before he was out of sight. She looked so familiar, but he could not think why. At the front door the attendant unbolted it and stood in front of him looking up into his face. 'I shall send a boy with your bill sir.' He nodded and stepped past the man through the doorway and tapped his hat with his cane, 'As you wish my man, as you wish.' He smiled to him. 'Thank you, and good morning to you sir.' The attendant huffed and closed the door behind him carefully sliding the latch into place behind the door. He was glad to be clean again, free from the smells of that nightmarish prison. Once outside again, the morning had changed much, the dark dingy vulgar memory of last night had been on his mind, yet today, the sun was now shining brightly, he felt a renewed lightness in his step, it was a good day to be alive. Despite the pain in his ribs from the efforts of the night, he enjoyed the walk to his home, a gentlemanly stroll through the park and streets, observing the inhabitants of one of London's lesser known boroughs as they went about their business. He was an astute observer of people and their behaviour, their interactions with both the people around them and their environment. It was interesting how simple geography could influence everyday life. He watched the market traders and the patrons who would attend their stalls, the shops along the street and the people who would enter. Others who would walk past gazing wishfully into the window or at the stales in the street displaying the wares on offer. The only difference separating the two was one simple thing, wealth. He sat on a bench for a moment to observe in more detail and watched two gentlemen and a lady riding three beautiful horses through Hyde Park towards Knightsbridge. One of the gentlemen tipped his hat to him, he politely returned the gesture with a smile, the lady riding side saddle bowed her head politely and again he returned the gesture. It was after all very proper and noble, and it was a beautiful sunny morning and a perfect day for a ride in the warm morning air. One horse suddenly reared up flailing with its front hove's at two ragged workmen, most likely from one of the workhouses nearby. The gentleman on the rearing horse lashed out with his riding crop at the two men, then he slowly pulled back on his reigns as he calmed his horse and then scoffed at the two men and rode onward. The two workers narrowly escaped without injury but clearly felt that they were to blame submissively cowering and running quickly away so as to not cause a scene. He stood still for a moment remembering every detail about the scene and then began to walk down the hill towards the Kings Road about a half mile away. As he did so he remembered the scene in the park and wondered why the two workmen felt they were at fault, everyone had an equal right to be in the park, the lane through the park was for everyone to enjoy. A public highway, no one had right over any other, yet status alone, gave one the opinion that they were more entitled. The riders made no assumption that he was anything but a gentleman because of his attire and the way he presented himself, yet the ragged workmen were given no quarter. In fact, quite the opposite. The walk home presented him with a question. With such primitive inbuilt ideas about status, how could society evolve enough to realise that everyone was equal or were they. Was there something else that set one human being apart from another, or one class from another, other than wealth. Recognising his local area, he smiled to himself at the idea that the day could have been very different indeed, he felt a sense of happiness and relief, albeit a little battered and bruised. The rewards for his efforts would soon pay off, and he felt a sense of accomplishment that some of those depraved twisted criminals would never again see the light of day. The Judge was no more. He was very happy and relieved to be on his way home to his dwelling, the thought of his bed or his favourite comfortable chair, was a welcoming reward for his slightly quickened pace in a hurry to rest himself. His route home was relatively direct, but he did make his way back through the market streets where vendors had a rather good supply of fresh or relatively fresh produce, always in great supply were potatoes and rice. Some items were very easy to acquire, often due to the proximity of the Thames and the many traders that would sell their wares and produce heading into London. They would set up a stall near the river as a precaution, it meant that the more perishable items like carrots, cabbages and other vegetables although very rare were sold quickly. A very standard diet for most of the counties inhabitants especially the working class lived on a meagre diet. If one was lucky, perhaps some red meat, poultry or fish. Although fish was a common food source it was sold very quickly. He personally had a love of eggs and fruit. Fruit was not so common to the poor or working classes, but it was obtainable. The Royal Orchards were often robbed, scrumped for the very best apples, or their other more exotic fruits. Eggs on the other hand were versatile, an easy to prepare food that had so many uses. His favourite method of eating was to simply take his dagger and prick each end and then suck out the contents. It was usually very obvious soon after pricking the egg if it was rotten or bad which was very rapidly disposed of. When he got to the market, he browsed the produce and carefully looked at the vegetables for sale. It was a mix of selecting the best of the produce, whatever was left over or unsold would most likely be returned to a farm and given to the livestock. It made perfect sense. The trader loaded items into a sack for him and he gladly paid for the items and started to head home. The last stall in the market was a brewer of beer. Ale was drunk more than water even though relatively good drinking water was in plentiful supply. The brewing of beer in England has seen the country through many disasters and plagues in the past, so it was very normal for people to drink beer all the time. For the poor or for everyday drinking a cheap version of beer was always easy to obtain, soft beer, and was often sold from a barrel by the jug. A glass of wine would obviously be preferred by a gentleman, or perhaps even something stronger, but a jug of soft beer would cost no more than a penny and was very refreshing. Buying beer made him feel slightly indulgent. With his sack over his shoulder and a jug of soft beer in hand he put his cane under his arm and was happily enjoying his stroll home. Maybe next time he would be lucky enough to get some fish or meat, but tonight, he would just have to make do with potatoes, cabbage and some oats, and wash it all down with some beer. When Daydan finally reached the street that led to his dwelling, the thoughts of the night were put to the back of his mind. Now all he wanted was to shut the door behind him and find some comfort in the small basement workshop where he spent so much time. Working on his experiments or running one of his many business opportunities. He knew that very soon he would be inundated with work; the income would prove extremely valuable and provide him with some new opportunities. His meeting with the judge would be an interesting one. He was excited about the future, the opportunities that had come his way would give him options, and he thought about how to make the best use of his newfound wealth.

When he reached his home he pulled the large key from it's hiding place and put it into the lock, he loved that satisfying sound of the simple lock mechanism opening and he pushed open the door, once inside he closed it behind himself and locked the door behind him and walked over to his high back chair and slumped down with relief. After giving himself a moment to relax he stood up, removed his heavy overcoat and put away his hat and cane, then he poured some water into a pot and began to boil it on his stove. He quickly cleaned and prepared the vegetables and put them into the pot and placed an iron lid upon it. The cooking would take some time, more than enough time to relax and put his feet up and enjoy a nap. He stoked up the fire and put some more wood on his stove and settled back into his chair. Closing his eyes, he leaned back and let out a long-satisfied breath, soon after, his mind turned to more pleasant thoughts, the girl in the bath house, he smiled to himself and breathed in softly. 'I didn't even ask her name.'

Chapter Nine

The Alchemist

It was a relief to be back in his own surroundings again, the strange dwelling where he lived. It was an odd building, the dwelling started life initially a large hole dug into the chalky ground and was lined with clay and stone. A forge was built within the lined pit. He researched as much as he could about the building and found some fragments of old records dating some one hundred years prior, it started life as just a forge. For the time, metal and iron work was common, mostly for the boat builders or carpenters and stone masons. Decades after the forge was built, the pit was surrounded with a wall and then covered with a roof. The walls were built from local stone which helped retain the heat in the forge, as did the roof. It provided a shelter for the forge workers who would spend hours, days and nights working the forge to get it up to the necessary temperature. Years later the roof was removed, and a first floor added and then a new roof. The living accommodation on the first floor overlapped the footprint of the basement. The walls were over three feet thick; its stability was never in question. The basement was large, the forge was still used regularly up until the time he was able to move in, the space seemed perfect. He added the stove and fireplace, a small living area and a small but ample sized cabin bed, a desk to one side with a large work bench and table. It looked a mixture of uses, but it worked well for him. He always kept the place looking clean and tidy, as much as one could.

Whenever he found the time, he was either studying, making something, recycling or sleeping. Everything he did, whether it was as an undertaker, carpenter, apothecary, smithy, scientist, he was able to use the offcuts or refuse of one job, to create or make something of use somewhere else. It was a big part of his own philosophy that nothing should go to waste. He believed everything was connected somehow, at its most basic level, everything was the same. He tried desperately to understand his theory, and to prove it, but he knew he still had so much more to learn. One of the less desirable tasks of his job was to bury or dispose of the dead, often it was just a matter of a private burial or cremation. Disposing of the bodies in a way that they were no longer a health risk, spreading disease, or foulness in the streets. He was paid well for the unpleasant task, so it made sense to make it as efficient as possible. Cremation was not common, but it was especially necessary here. The local authorities paid him a small sum for disposing of the bodies, so he did just that. There were other locations performing the same job, but he was much better located and equipped for the part, so he was left well alone. The job carried with it a huge phobia and fear from the general population, he found that held certain advantages, and he was left alone. Before disposing of the bodies, he would perform an autopsy, something he read about from the college of surgeons. An Italian gentleman pioneered the task able to determine the cause of death. Because he was not a fully qualified physician or surgeon he would study in other ways. This gave him access to an inexhaustible supply of bodies. Of course, this was done in secret, discovery would no doubt lead to a fate worse than death. His location afforded a very useful benefit, he could fire up the forge quickly and burn the bodies and remains. The forges bellows would ensure that he could reach such temperatures that it could burn bone down to ash. The ash could be used elsewhere. As an ingredient for so many other things, the ash could be added to other ingredients to make soap or gunpowder. Another by-product that the forge was useful for was collecting fat, the fat would drain off near the bottom of the forge and was collected in small pots for reuse. Sometimes he could use human fat, but ideally the fat of animals from burning animal carcasses. Tallow from beef and Lye from pork fat. Not only did he use the fat for making candles but also, he was able to use the fat to make his own soap.

He sometimes collected plants and herbs and tried making many different remedies. Drying them and crushing them up into a fine powder, some worked well, and others did not. The process of learning from his experiments and experience was just as important. The old village herbalists branded as witches could make a formula to cure a cold or fever. Such skills were frowned upon as witchcraft, Daydan however saw the benefits of this science. His favourite use of leftovers was making beer, wine, or vinegar, there was always a plentiful supply of corn, oats, wheat, barley, honey and potatoes that could be turned into beer. He learned how to churn better, make a home-made whisky, moonshine. His unquenchable desire and thirst to learn and to understand the secrets of science, became an obsession. He wanted to understand all the secrets of the universe and of life and death. He soon became a recluse, almost a hermit in his lifestyle, and somewhat of an outcast. It would be very easy to brand him with such taboo's as witchcraft, black magic or necromancy.

He saw the families rarely who lived above the forge and his workshop, they never bothered him, and he never bothered them. He knew they kept animals outside the city not to far away, they would spend a few days out with their animals, bring back some produce. Sometimes they would return with fresh meat that he would trade for, which meant he could trade his items with them such as ironmongery, nails, tools and beer, animal fat. And he could acquire some eggs. If he could trade rather than buy, he always did, perhaps that was why he was so hungry to learn new skills, the only problem was, with each new skill he realised how little he knew about other things. Thinking of food, he put his iron pot on his stove with some boiled water and added some chopped potatoes and cabbage leaves, he would just leave it to bubble and boil as he worked. Tonight, he would not eat as well as he would have liked, possibly his last meal here. He looked around at all of the jars of pickles and body parts lined up on shelves around the workshop, dried leaves, powdered substances for experiments or mixtures that may prove useful, sulphur, saltpetre, oils, ground charcoal dust. Fine powdered bone ash, sacks of charcoal were stacked near the forge ready to be used. Sawdust, offcuts of wood, iron filings kept to one side, anything that could be used, or reused was kept. He sat back in his chair and poured some boiling water over some crushed tea leaves, he sipped carefully the flavours of the exotic drink, then leaned back and relaxed closing his eyes and smiled a little. He knew he was close to unlocking the secrets of the universe, something connected everything else together, something the eyes could not see, he was so close. His presentation at the collage had to work, with the help of the collage he would be able to study more and uncover the secrets of life, the secrets of the universe itself. If one could understand those secrets that would indeed be a power beyond measure. He looked at the small silver ring on his hand and watched the moonlight reflect off it, leaving a slightly blueish silver glow. He smiled softly and watched intently as he could see the small specs of light begin to dance slowly around the ring from his hand. The light looked like a faint blue flame burning in his hand. He breathed in deeply and took another sip of his tea and then turned sadly to his ring as the moon light vanished in the darkness behind some clouds causing the tiny specs of light to fade and vanish away. In his familiar surroundings, he tended to his fires and they began to burn hot again, after adding some more small logs to the smouldering ashes. The cooking pot of potatoes and cabbage were soon bubbling away gently, the smell of the simple meal had a nice aroma, the gentle spirals of steam rising up in small curls from the slightly offset lid was a good sign, the meal was ready to eat. The rising steam left a slightly sweet smell in his nostrils that formed a smile on his lips as he looked forward to a simple but refreshing meal. Most folk would add sugar to their food these days, a delicacy that the country had embraced and added to almost everything, he on the other hand preferred to use any sugar that came his way for brewing or distilling. The choice seemed to be an easy one not even worth consideration.

Daydan sat quietly and watched his pot of stew bubble away for a moment, his thoughts of Mary, and his promise to her. She was right, about his promise to his father. It was his life. His father spent his entire life chasing his father's work, when he died, he had nothing, achieved nothing. Daydan looked around at his workshop and realised that if the authorities found his home strewn with fats, organs in jars, bones, and any number of questionable things that were around his workshop, they would certainly accuse him of things much worse than blasphemy. They would think him a freak, a murderer. That was not his way, but no one would believe him looking around here. He stoked up the forge once more adding the last of his coal and slowly pumping the bellows to increase the heat, he put some iron ore into a stone pot and positioned it in the heart of the fire and watched it carefully over the next few hours. He added more coals to the fire and kept the heat high as he pumped the bellows again and then tipped all of his containers into the flames. He burned everything. Human organs, body parts. He poured into the fire the fats he had stored, which again increased the heat of the flames. He pumped faster on the bellows for several hours constantly feeding the fire and eventually watched the iron ore give up its iron turning into a hot molten liquid. He was exhausted, wracked with pain from his injuries, dirty again, covered in ash and the smell of the forge, he ate his meal and drank most of his water just to keep going. The hotter the heat climbed the more impurities were burned from the iron. Any bone was easily turned into ash at these temperatures. When everything had been completely consumed in the forge and turned to a fine ash, he rested a little. Everything that he could not take with him he burned, it was a long night, and the whole of the next day. He laboured over the forge without rest, before he could be safe this had to be done correctly. Wanting nothing more than to sleep and be prepared for the next day, he knew that he had to leave no trace of his work here when he was gone. It would be better that way.

Leaving England, he would desperately miss going out into the countryside foraging for herbs, plants and berries that he could add to his diet. Drying them out for their healing or health properties, he even knew one or two very effective poisons that he would package for the right price. After everything was burned, all that was left were clean pots, ash, and a few iron ingots and his trunk and his saddlebags. He would pack these with his most precious items whenever he was traveling. By this time his shirt was off, sweating and dirty with soot, smelling of smoke and singed hair. He ate little of his meal, taking a spoon full of the plain stew and keeping it on the boil, the animal fat that he added to it made it taste like there was some meat in it, but there wasn't. After he burned everything he could, he fell into his chair filthy and exhausted, but unable to resist his need for sleep any longer. The old forge workshop was presentable at last, the heat from the forge was still roasting hot but with no more fuel to burn it would cool down fast. A sense of relief came over him that any evidence that could lead to a fate worse than death was long gone. Asleep at last his mind drifted back to his studies and experiments and with a smile on his face he recalled some of his findings.

He studied the makeup of the items he used to bring back those lost spirits. Witchcraft, black magic, all manner of long forgotten arts, from the current day to civilisations that once flourished and now long since vanished. He was trying to prove a link between certain materials and the strange ghostly realm of his undead companions, he found that some things had a connection or gained power when his spiritual entities were around or close by. He knew that he could only attract the spirits of the living or recently deceased. His ring appeared to amplify his ability to detect these spirits, but when he concentrated, he could see that energy all around him, oddly others could not. It was like he was seeing things through a filter of some kind. He found the whole experience exciting and rather intoxicating, the fights in the prison, the way he was able to see the souls of his foes and to virtually tear them from their hosts with his sword cane, did that make him evil.

Some of the things he studied at length, materials such as silver gave very good results, as did some other materials, ebony, or bone, especially antlers and claws, some feathers, the more elaborate the better, he also found success with some other materials, such as gold, copper, precious stones and other base metals. In some ways the more basic the material the better the connection, even if those materials had been worked in some way. His walking cane was a prime example. A dear antler tip, on a rich ebony shaft, topped with a silver knob. All very skilfully and beautifully worked. He tried several experiments with individuals of varying classes, the results were uneventful to say the least. Every experiment that he proved success with on a personal level became a failure when trying to introduce another person. They were time consuming experiments, and the failures were beginning to take their toll. Frustration, sometimes gave way to anger and self-doubt, causing him to dismiss his volunteers rather abruptly. Maybe this was just something he alone could do. Maybe he was cursed.

He found lots of written knowledge of the objects he acquired over the years, from the scrolls of alchemists that lived and died long before he was born. For example, the peacock feather in his short top hat was said to represent vision, spirituality, royalty, awakening and guidance. Protection and watchfulness. The most striking component of the peacock feather is the eye in the centre of the largest part of the feather. In Mythology, the Peacock tail feathers had the "eyes of the stars." Other mythologies also revered the peacock feather as a sign of immortality and resurrection. It was no surprise to him that whenever he wore his hat and any ghostly apparitions were nearby, some strange energy would cause the feather on his hat to glow slightly at the slightest proximity of spiritual energy. The spirits seemed to be drawn by the colours of feather, it seemed to calm them somehow.

Silver was an element that he studied with very particular powers to his art. Silver represented the moon in all her glory, a time when all metaphysical energy and knowledge was open and revealed. It was the balance between night and day, light and dark. It is the colour of the Greek goddess Artemis, or in her Roman form as Diana the Huntress. Symbolic of purity, clarity, focus, and feminine energy. In Alchemy it is one of the noble metals, it brings balance and clarity. As the hilt of his ghostly blade, it made perfect sense that it brings a balance between the physical and nonphysical world. Whenever he would draw his walking canes blade from its sheath, he could see those strange energies about the blade, and it would glow with an eerie soft blue light absorbing the ethereal energies of his foes. His hands were able to calm the spirits, and when the time was right their spirits would slowly fade away into a harmless mist floating up towards the sky. During his research in dusty long forgotten corners of libraries museum and storerooms, he read many documents detailing how certain items, objects and materials, were influenced by magical locations. These places and times could be used to amplify this strange energy. Just like his ring, his cane sword and his hat with the peacock feather. Although he knew he could use these items, without them he still possessed the ability to absorb or manipulate this energy, he just did not fully understand how or why. One of his favourite possessions was his Silver signet ring set with a blood stone, it was a simple piece and could easily be missed, but to him it held a special meaning. Silver has always been linked to mysterious energy, especially at night, the full moon, the stars, giving a feeling of calm, tranquillity and peace. The Blood stone, Heliotrope is often a very dark green in colour with its distinctive red spots, giving it the name Blood stone. The blood stone in legend is meant to promote healing and to reduce bleeding. The Greeks believed that the blood stone could bring about change and was often used as an amulet to protect against evil. It was a symbol of Justice. Fitting really, when he dispatched evil doers with his blade, he felt he was doing something worthwhile. The blood stone is also said to be good for circulation of both mind, body and spirit, removing blockages to improve the flow of the energy that runs through all things. Sometimes when he was still, he could almost feel the vibration of all the things around him, undeniably, he knew there was a connection, but how to prove it, and how exactly did it work. He could hardly disagree with the writings of those old scholars, he certainly felt a sense of peace, physical, mental and spiritual wellbeing when he wore his ring. Or maybe that feeling was something else, perhaps also the fact that it was a gift from his father, a very precious gift. As far as value, probably rather little, but to him it was priceless. His father would talk to him for hours pointing out the majesty of the stars and the universe, of science, of knowledge. His father emphasised so much how important education was, the right kind of education, the understanding of the natural world and of the sciences. As he drifted deeper and deeper into his sleep he dreamed about his cane. The Ebony wood of his cane and the heavy ebony club that the angry slave Jin wielded with such ferocity. It seemed to also have a unique power all of its own. It was written about in history. Ebony wood is heavy, and a very dark brown or black in colour. It was said to draw energy from the deepest levels of the mind, our most ancient and primitive energy. It was a powerful material used for defence and for dispelling dark magic or evil, as a weapon, one can imagine the advantages of such an item. Often tribal leaders would carry an ebony staff or weapon as a symbol of their authority. It combines the forces of the elements of Earth, Air, Fire and Water, and is a truly diverse tool in the physical world. It is considered to be the most powerful of all the magical woods. It is protective and non-discriminating to its user. It was very clear to him that everything somehow is connected. The earth and everything in it or upon it, the universe, life, all had energy, a vibration, even un-life. This strange misunderstood, unknown world, mysterious voids of space, that world between life death and renewal. In his mind there was no real death in the sense of the word, an ending of one's consciousness may expire, but the material that made us is reused in one way or another. The true essence of us, never dies, it is reborn over and over again. There is such a beauty in looking up to the heavens at night and seeing the millions of stars in the universe. He could feel a vibration, an endless song of the heavens, like it was calling him home. All things play in its timeless eternal symphony. He knew that he could see his companions when others could not. He knew that when he concentrated, his hands could conjure the strange energies that were all around. His eyes were able to see mysterious unexplainable energy patterns, in some of the items he now possessed. He could even draw that energy to himself, what he could not yet explain was how, and why. He awoke for a brief moment, he helped himself to a spoon full of the stew and gave the stove and his fires embers one more final good stoke up. The evening air was starting to overcome the roaring fires of the day before, poking at the burned coals, some of the last hot sparks popped from the embers and faded cooling quickly in the air. He rubbed his hands together feeling the last warmth of the fire reinvigorate his aching bruised body with some much-needed heat. Sitting back in his chair he slowly turned the contents of the cooking pot with the wooden spoon. He took a portion from the end of the spoon and removed the pot from the heat and added the last of his oats to thicken it up into a gruel. He fell back into his high back chair and put his feet up upon the stove with his boots still on and leaned back closing his eyes. He must have looked a mess, dirty sweaty and unshaven. As the early evening peeped in through the high window already, he was still very exhausted from his labours, but content that whatever remained in his humble little workshop, could not give him away. Later, he would perform his parlour tricks for the fat man and his guests from the bath house. Such a performance usually combined a good meal and good quality liquor. He smiled to himself and felt the pain of his bruising from the days before, yet he was healing steadily, his body was tired but relaxed, and for now, a little more rest was his priority.

Chapter Ten

Parlour tricks

His little nap was most welcome. When he awoke, his wound was still painful and now darkened a great deal, the area around the bruising was hard and tender to the touch. Not only that but it made him rather stiff down one side of his body. The rainbow of colourful reds blues and yellows had not spread, thankfully. Whatever the injury, it was clotting, and it was healing. Having awoken still in his dirty clothes from two days ago, he stripped himself down until he was naked and stood in front of a large ceramic bowl of clean water. He washed himself carefully and thoroughly. The bowl of cold water was so refreshing on his skin, it was nice to be able to wash away the dirt and debris of his labours. The cold water then trickled over him from his head to his toes, it felt so nice. It was good to be able to wash away the grit and grime and to feel clean once again. Using his own homemade soap always made him smile, and the fragrances of the added lemon, honey and olive oil was a bonus.

Daydan used a piece of his bed sheet to wipe away any ground dirt and to rub himself down as best he could. He shaved carefully lathering his face with the soap and using his very sharp straight razor that he always kept on his person, in a pocket inside his waistcoat. You never knew when something like that would come in handy. Putting on his clean clothes always made him feel rather special. Being clean and looking smart and gentlemanly made him feel prepared for anything. His shirt and waistcoat were perfectly tailored, his selection of cotton shirts and bright silk waistcoats of blue black and silver vertical stripes made him stand out. His Riding boots were well used, but supple and highly polished. As he dressed and looked at himself, he felt like a prince, walking out in his finest clothes. It was the norm for gentlemen and ladies to parade themselves down the Kings Road in Chelsea. His old clothes and bed sheets he just threw away, they were old, torn or beyond repair. He made a decision. No matter what happened, he was going to leave, it was time to start over. Mary was right.

Tonight, would be fun, the look on people's faces when he demonstrated his art was something he would never forget. Prepared for his evening of entertainment he made his way outside locking up after himself, hiding his key in its secret place he proceeded down the narrow streets and alleyways onto the main road that led all the way to the palace. This evening however he decided to take a different route, walking along the banks of the Thames.

Tonight, he was to put on a show, a spectacle to entertain and as always, his mind was spinning with ideas, a nice brisk walk and some fresh air was always a good tonic for a chaotic mind. On his way to his latest engagement he made his way this time along the river. It was a rather nice shortcut, plus the air was good and it certainly helped him to think of interesting ways with which he could impress his small, private, captive audience. As he walked along the river, he saw a dead bird on the floor, a pigeon of some kind. It looked to have been attacked by some animal, possibly a cat. He picked it up and wrapped it in a handkerchief he took from his pocket and put the dead bird in his top hat and placed the hat back on top of his head. Enjoying his walk, he politely acknowledged several walkers enjoying the river. Most of the river was used for trade of some kind, there were one or two ferry boats going back and forth across the river in various locations. Some of the Thames had docks where the large ocean-going sailing ships were moored. He would often dream of faraway places. Adventures in far off exotic lands. He would watch the ships and boats and look at the sailors and wonder what lands they just returned from. He leaned on a wall watching the people pass by for a moment.

A ship's captain stood on the edge of his vessel pointing and shouting at his crew. The crew dashed around loading and unloading cargo, the captain looked immaculately dressed while his crew were dressed for hard labour. Most of the crew never had shoes or boots on their feet, maybe that was how they preferred to work. The ship looked magnificent and powerful, large enough to carry tonnes of cargo. He saw the captain look his way and politely acknowledge him, he returned the gesture and took a deep breath peeling himself away from his lust for adventure. Maybe someday,

someday very soon, it would be his turn once again. He thought about the scene at the docks, how strange it was to see such a divide, the class structure was so wrong, why wasn't everyone equal. Daydan did not dislike the rich for being rich or the poor for being poor, but it made no sense. Why could everyone not live as equals, eventually, in the end, we are all equal. We all end up the same, what is important is how we live our life. These were strange times indeed and being alone with his thoughts could be as much a blessing as it was a torment.

His father warned him that his path, his destiny was a lonely one. He was different, and that set him apart from others. A part of him longed for companionship, a family of his own, but what woman would understand what he was doing. As he thought further about his situation, he realised that not even he could fully understand the course that he had been set upon. How does he explain this to anyone, it was a problem that plagued him. He wanted to study, he loved to learn about new things. Science is about gathering evidence, being able to recreate an experiment and getting the same results, was it scientific to believe that a metal can generate or absorb the energy that surrounds it, harness energy from the stars, from all things. He grinned a little two himself distracted as he watched two fishermen arguing over a catch and returned his thoughts to his love of science. He was rather relieved that the burning of witches had ceased a long time ago, but the labels were still very much alive. As he walked, he shook his head and smiled. 'Witches indeed.'

From the river he walked up a tree lined street, a small open area on one side and on the other large tall houses. He double checked the address he was given and walked up to the front door giving it a tap with the head of his cane. He repeated the process and then stepped back a little and waited. Sure enough, the door opened, and a shy housemaid asked his name. When he announced himself, she nodded and indicated for him to come inside offering to take his hat and cane, he shook his head. He followed her and looked around the hallway of the very lavish house which the entrance hall alone was bigger than his entire dwelling. Striding swiftly behind the maid whose own steps were small but quick, he was aware that she was for most of the time right under his feet. The maid knocked on a door and pushed it open with two hands and immediately turned on her heels and left him standing in the doorway. He was confronted by several large men sipping some drink, shared from a fancy glass decanter. Three women sat in large chairs staring at him through single eye pieces held up on, decorated silver rods. Their bright white wigs looked audacious and utterly extravagant; their pale skin whitened further with makeup. The room was hot, a large open fire burned intently next to a large chair. The women sat together nudging and whispering to each other. Pointing quite openly to him. The large man from the bath house approached him with a huge smile and big rosy cheeks.

'Ah good, the entertainment has arrived, please, take a drink with us, we are all looking forward to a good show tonight.' Some of the men laughed, while the women seemed to be entertained by the comment, they just smiled eyeing up their guest with their rod held monocles. The man who he recognised from the bathhouse seemed to be a man of science too. All around the room there were stuffed animals, insects in display cases, moths, butterfly's and beetles. Paintings of animals and birds, and a large array of old handwritten books. The room looked very much like a large study. He looked jealously over a selection of books that would not have looked out of place in a university library. This room alone was very impressive, surely the rest of the house would be equally so. Indeed, he would have to put on a very good display tonight. If he did, it would most likely work in his favour. He was handed a glass of a clear brown liquid. From the distinctive smell he knew it was some kind of whisky. It was not something he indulged in very often, but it was nice to sample the nicer things in life. He sniffed the liquid and swirled it in the glass watching the silky substance slide down the sides of the glass with ease. It smelled of damp heather, moss and charcoal, and when he tasted it, it burned his cheeks as he swished it around his mouth. The other older men looked on approvingly of the younger man's patience in knowing how to really enjoy the drink. With each sip he repeated the process several times, and then on the fourth time downed the remainder of the glass, putting it on the table near to his host. He moved to a point where he could see his entire audience standing in front of the fire with its heat firmly on his back. 'Thank you, sir.' He said directly to his host. Then he turned to face the room. 'Ladies and Gentlemen, I understand you are here to uncover the secrets and mysteries of life, or as you prefer, to uncover the secrets to my parlour tricks.' He laughed. 'I wish you good luck, these are not tricks, simply an understanding of science and how our universe works, energy, our energy, the energy of life.

Everything, is eternal, never ending, it can evolve, regenerate, vanish and reappear, everything around you is part of you. Embrace it.' He lifted his hands up to the heavens as if he was praying. His audience was stunned, learned men, intelligent open-minded men could not even imagine what he was trying to say to them. He was a man out of his time, his father had the same beliefs, as did his grandfather before him. The Eternal Hand has a thankless unimaginable task, to educate a species that is unaware of its own true potential. Focused on greed and power. Even now, even in this new age.

Watching his audience, he removed his hat and unfolded the handkerchief from within where the dead pigeon had resided. One of the women screamed out and fainted in her chair, another fanned her desperately trying to wake her from her shock. The entertainer, continued, he closed his eyes and slowly let his hand float over the body of the bird, he waited for some time, quietly, and minutes after, his hand with the bloodstone ring began to glow. When he opened his eyes, the small barely visible blue dots of light began to float over the bird, moment by moment more and more tiny stars appeared. The light floated, dancing, forming, like a luminescent mist, until the image of a ghostly bird stared back at everyone perfectly still. One of the old men stepped closer, and the bird suddenly looked around and flapped its ethereal wings and took off launching itself up high. The ethereal pigeon was flying around and around a large candle chandelier. The woman being fanned opened her eyes and fainted again, the other woman fanning the woman in shock huddled closer to her friend but was transfixed on the scene. One of the old men stepped backwards staring up at the ghostly bird in disbelief. Two of the other men were peering behind books and paintings and other items trying to find the secret to this mysterious spectacle suspecting some projection of light. Was it a trick, was their friend in on some elaborate parlour game to make them all look like fools. The fat man smiled to himself slightly pleased with the show that was put on for his guests. 'Bring back my Poo. ' 'What.' Daydan asked sharply. The old man pointed to a stuffed animal and looked directly at him. 'My poo, bring back my poo, please.' 'Sir I cannot, I am sorry.' He handed the old man the carcass of the dead bird. 'This is recent, and intact, your.' He scratched his head looking for the right words trying not to insult the older man. 'Your pet has been gone far too long, and stuffed, there is no spirit left, your poo has long since departed.' He stroked his chin looking as sadly as he could into the fat man's eyes. 'I am sorry, once the life force of the creature is gone, it will not come back. But I am sure it is in a much better place now.' He held the man's arm trying to be comforting. 'Wouldn't you agree.' At that moment the ghostly bird changed course from the chandelier and flew through the glass window as if it was a ghost walking through a wall, his audience looked very entertained but frustrated that they were unable to uncover his trickery. 'Impressive.'

The entertainer, mystic, illusionist, magician, whatever it was you wanted to call him, was so into his art that he wanted to show more. He put his hand out to the old man and closed his eyes, then gently put his hand on the old man's chest, he slowly pulled it away. As he did so, the ethereal form of the old man began to peel away from his body, his spirit looked around aware of its situation and being pulled from its hosts body. His ethereal image was clearly visible, he coaxed the ethereal form more, almost separating it out of its living body. Both the old man and the old mans ghost seemed to be amused at first, but they must have known that if the two were separated, even if it was just for a moment, the body would die, deprived of its physical connection.

'Do you want to live sir.' He demanded holding the ethereal form on the edge of life and death, the power he had in his hands in that moment could easily turn a lesser man to such evil. Sometimes, his anger at mankind made him think of such a thing, plucking the souls from the living and leaving a wake of carnage behind him, then people would listen. 'Yes.' The old man replied, 'Yes I want to live.' He held the forms gazing fearfully to each other, each, somehow knowing the severity of their predicament, he closed his eyes and clenched his hand slowly into a light fist. 'Enough.' Cried his host. With his eyes still closed he turned his hand from a fist and slowly opened out his fingers letting his fist relax, the ethereal spirit sank quickly back into its host like it was snapped back suddenly and was gone from view. The look of relief was clearly seen across the face of the old man who breathed heavily checking himself for injuries. Daydan turned to look the old man directly in the eyes completely expressionless. The fat old man walked into an adjoining room and picked up some papers, he pulled a quill from an ink well and signed several of the papers and placed a wax seal on each. He walked up to Daydan and handed him the papers putting his hand on his shoulder. 'The knowledge you possess sir is an incredible thing, but it will bring you trouble.

I am lost for words, truly.' With little movement and a calm demeanour, he nodded to him politely and stared up into the man's eyes. Daydan slowly took the offered papers and tucked them inside his heavy coat. Did the old man understand, was it even possible for men to understand. Daydan nodded his head respectfully and turned away making his way for the door from the study, passing the two women who were clearly overwhelmed by the display. The third woman was trying frantically to stop crying. She screamed out in fear the moment she saw him and attended more closely to her female companions even more frantically trying to fan them back to consciousness.

He returned to the table where he lay the dead bird and picked it up tossing it into the large open fire. At first, it crackled and spat but was soon consumed in the fire. Its carcass now burning left a black shadow like image in the embers, he watched the bird's corpse burn for a moment and nodded respectfully with a smile. 'I am presenting a talk at the University in a couple of days' time, you should come, I think you will find it equally entertaining. And perhaps educational.' He said focusing more generally on one particular individual, looking back to the old judge. He tipped his top hat to the gathered people and turned on his heels marching smartly out of the beautifully extravagant home. It was indeed a treat for the eyes to be able to see such a magnificent home, the decadence and luxury within seemed like it would suit royalty. It was far beyond any of his own dreams or even desires for a place to live, it looked like a magnificent palace or a museum.

The housemaid was at the door at the bottom of the stairs and showed him out, and when the door closed behind him, he breathed a sigh of relief and began to walk with a brisk but optimistic stride to his step. As he walked, he twirled his cane skilfully in his hand and fingers, heading for home, or perhaps the nearest tavern on route to celebrate. With a self-satisfied grin of a good day's work, he tapped the outside of his heavy coat feeling the neatly folded papers within. He was a much richer man now, richer than he ever dreamed he could be, but just how rich he had no idea. He tipped his hat rather flamboyantly and overly dramatic to some passers-by still feeling very happy and rather pleased with himself. It had been a long time since he had felt so much joy, after such a struggle. After so much hard work, it seemed that his luck was finally beginning to change. 'Good day gentlemen.' He tapped the brim of his hat with his cane. 'And ladies.' He made eye contact with the two ladies who were being escorted by the gentleman for a quiet evening stroll. The walkers stopped and watched him exchanging remarks to each other. 'Oh, how beautifully done, he must be French, do you think he is French sir.' The other gentleman remarked slowly watching Daydan walk away. 'I really could not say, but he definitely wasn't Welsh.'

'Uh gads no, definitely not Welsh.' They both flicked their scented handkerchiefs across their noses mumbling agreeably to each other. He had not walked far when he heard the clicking hooves of a horse on the irregular stone road, the rider kicked on his horse to a slight gallop, and within moments the animal was at his side. The rider was high up, and the saddle of the horse was above his eye level. The animal nudged him with its nose. Daydan inhaled enjoying the smell of the animal, he missed being around horses and had a good memory for each animal he met. He turned slightly and stopped in his tracks, the rider was trying to block his path with the animal, but the animal was reluctant to obey its rider which caused the rider to jab the animal with his heels. Daydan made a slow grab on the horse's bridle and patted the animal inhaling its breath and breathing gently upon the animal's nostrils remembering him well. 'What are you doing here horse whisperer, you should be cheap side.' His mind was spinning as he looked up to the rider, immediately he recognised the young man. 'Atwood.' This was the man that drugged and raped Mary, he was sure of it. He looked so weak, he wanted to pull him off his horse and tear out his soul right there and then. He avoided the officer's eyes and concentrated on petting the beautiful horse that the rider clearly had little respect for. It was a fine large animal of pure white with a nice temperament, the animal kept nudging him enjoying the closeness and a fond stroke of its nose and face. The rider leaned down skilfully from his horse closer to him and cleared his throat. 'Our paths are destined to cross it seems, to what end I wonder.' The rider sat up on his animal and pulled back on the reigns to ease the animal away from him. Daydan looked the young man in the eyes, he could feel the anger brewing up inside himself and he drew a long breath. 'Perhaps to sell me your fine animal sir.' He looked away from the officer back to the horse and stroked its rump. 'Unlikely, we have a long journey ahead of us, and I do not see this beast returning to England afterwards.' The officer kicked his animal and launched it into a gallop looking back at him turning around and leaning back on his horse to watch him as he rode off. 'John Atwood.' A name he would not forget in a hurry.

He thought of Mary and felt a sense of guilt for not killing the man where he stood, but he made a promise, not only to Mary but also to the Atwood woman, a promise that reluctantly he felt obliged to keep. He walked slowly along the simple road and decided that today he would enjoy a proper pint of Ale.

He deserved a treat. He made his way towards the docks and one of the many taverns, they were always a hive of noise and activity and he felt that being with people enjoying themselves would make him feel a little less lonely. It might stop him thinking about revenge and how much he missed his beloved Mary. It might also take his mind off the share of a very lucrative business he had just acquired. A business that he knew very little about. Although he had shares, he was to all intents and purposes nothing more than a silent partner. A silent partner that makes money without lifting a finger. A nervous smile danced across his lips as he double checked his inside pocket regularly, making sure that the documents had not fallen out. When he reached the docks, he made for one of the more popular yet cleaner establishments. The bread here was not mixed with rocks and chalk and the Ale actually tasted like ale and not something you threw on the street in the early hours of the morning. He entered a large double door and dodged a couple of sailors fighting and exchanging blows, most likely arguing over some very trivial matter. Once inside he sat alone in a corner by the window and put his cane and hat down by his side, he swept his hand slowly through his long silver hair and watched the patrons going about their business. A serving maid approached him carrying several mugs of Ale, splashing rather allot of it onto the dirty wooden floor. 'Ale.' He nodded and smiled. 'Ale, yes. And do you have some bread, cheese, pork, anything.' 'Pork is it, Pork.' She looked around at the tavern guests and then to her newest customer. 'You must be a foreigner.' She laughed. 'I'll see what I can find for you sir.' He tossed a silver coin to her and she very skilfully caught it and tucked it into a hidden pocket under her petticoats. He watched her carefully and smiled, the country was always a wash with foreigners, people came from near and far to find their fortunes. They either gave up, or were found floating down the Thames, or more often than not moved on. It was a rough city, and the population was growing all the time. Almost three quarters of a million people. As far as he was concerned, people mean business and opportunity, especially for one such as himself. After a few moments the serving maid returned with a large mug of ale. The ale mugs were simple, fired ceramics, basic, but heavy and functional, able to cope with the rough usage of a busy tavern, he gripped the handle tightly and lifted it up close to his lips. She was holding a round wooden tray up high in the air balancing it on her fingertips. Having handed over his drink she dropped the crudely made wooden tray down and gave him a hunk of bread with a small bit of butter and a piece of hard cheese. The cheese looked rather dehydrated, but it wasn't rotten, so he accepted the plate and pulled it closer. She curtsied teasingly to him and smiled. 'Sorry me lord, we're out of pork.' She turned up her nose and slapped a drunken patron who was making a grab for her backside. The slapped drunken man laughed and fell on the floor, much to the amusement of others in the tavern. Daydan laughed at the scene and grabbed the bread and tore a chunk off, placing it into the small mound of butter and took a bite. Then he took a bite of the cheese, both were hard and dry, but the taste was rather good, especially when washed down with some Ale. He sat comfortably laughing at some of the scenes and watched the merry goings on all around the tavern. The people within obviously did not care much for the goings on elsewhere, this was their world, work, drink, sleep. Probably weeks or months at sea, get paid, spend the money and then find another ship to work upon. A hard life, but a carefree one.

As he watched the other people in the tavern and ate his simple meal, a man sat at the table in front of him. The rough looking military man stuck a knife into the table. He watched Daydan closely for a reaction. He just continued to eat looking carefully at the man. 'Are you a man of the sea.' The man asked in a broken croaky voice. He remained silent eating his bread and cheese slowly. Daydan shook his head. 'You don't look like a seaman.' He leaned across the table towards him and tried to look up directly into his eyes. 'I am an undertaker, a carpenter, are you in need of my services.' He looked around the man several times from side to side and up and down as he continued to eat his bread and cheese. 'I think I have a box that would fit you perfectly.' He raised an eyebrow waiting for his response. The sailor pulled his knife from under the wooden table and began carving his initial into it, first cutting the outline and then digging into the table in a slight side to side motion to rout out the wood. 'Any ship should have a good carpenter onboard.' He smiled slightly showing a line of irregular teeth. 'But today I need sailors.' He turned to another man nearby and shook his head to him. Daydan turned sharply not initially having noticed the other man who had a rather large shillelagh in his hand. He cleared his throat and lowered his left hand under the table to his boot, feeling his own dagger in his hand for a moment gave him a sense of security. If needed the dagger might well serve as a deterrent if things got nasty. Once reassured he returned to his eating and proceeded to finish off his meal while he watched the press gang circle the tavern looking for easy prey. The drunk who had fallen to the floor earlier was an easy target and he was soon lifted up and carried between the two men to some galley to sleep off his booze, but he would be long out at sea by the time he awoke.

After eating his fill and drinking down his Ale he made sure he was not too drunk to be able to make his own way home without looking like an easy target. While he was very capable of looking after himself, it was much easier to not get into such a situation in the first place. By the time darkness fell the streets were always full of opportunists. He kept to the more open areas along the river taking a different route, the buildings were smaller, much more tightly packed and of crude build quality. Some broken and deserted, others down to the foundations and looted for anything that was reusable. He soon found himself in a familiar area, a landing spot that had a relatively chalky bed. Often the river men here were covered in chalk, wading back and forth to their boats, a faint trail led from the small landing area towards the local streets and homes. He knew exactly where he was now, Cheyne walk, a satisfying grin formed on his face as his mind turned to rest. The thought of being in his own space where he could try to catch up with the events of the last few days and think about what he should do next. He had the chance to make a difference, to spread the word about his discoveries and theories, to at last be able to honour his father and his grandfather's dreams of uniting all of the peoples and all the classes in one common goal. Or he could keep his promise to Mary, to leave this land and start over somewhere else. To be free. For the first time, he felt a sense of peace and that finally everything would work out right, he turned himself towards the narrow streets and quickened his pace for home.

A short walk up the chalk stained road from the river, he felt a light sensation on his hand, he slowed down a little and turned to his side, as he did so, the feather on his top hat glistened with colour and he felt a small embrace. In the evening light he paused for a moment as his eyes slowly focused upon a familiar face, it was Mary, her spirt was very transparent and she was barely visible, but she was at his side holding his hand smiling to him. Normally they might be mistaken for a young couple walking the streets together, but he was as far as others could tell completely alone, but he could see Mary. Her smile was warming, she was dressed in a simple outfit that suited her simple carefree style. Her long flowing peasants dress off her shoulders and flowing down to her ankles, her legs were stockinged, and to tease him she would show some of her thigh lifting her dress a little. On her small feet she wore a simple pair of shoes. The front of her dress showed a tasteful amount of cleavage. He hair was free and cascaded down over her shoulders. She looked happy, and as she held onto him, he heard her voice in his mind, humming softly to herself.

'You must be patient, all will work out, you will see.' She stopped him and turned to face him, standing on her tip toes, they kissed in the darkness, the handsome mystic and his ethereal lover. She squeezed his hand and started to run ahead of him dancing and singing to herself. It was odd to him that no one else could see these apparitions but he could always see them very clearly. Sometimes he could see others that were not known to him, but his companions who seemed to be there when he most needed them made him feel like he was never alone. Mary danced up ahead tip toeing delicately through the street avoiding puddles and carefully picking her steps with the grace of a dancer. With every few steps she would turn around and smile to him just to double check he was following behind. How could anyone want to hurt this harmless joyful woman. He walked on trying to pick up his pace a little so he could catch up with his light-footed companion. He was more than a little relieved when the familiar streets near his home loomed into view. His lovely companion had vanished into the night, the thought of his large comfortable chair made him feel a little refreshed already, as the stresses of the day disappeared into memory.

Chapter Eleven

Time for change

Outside it was typically cold and damp, the strange mist from the Thames left an eerie grey fog hanging in the air, as the fog mixed with the smoke from the chimneys in view. Many of the dwellings here were little more than slums. He felt a slight chill in the air but thought little of it, being cold was a fact of life, it made the joy of being near an open fire in one's own home such a pleasant memory. There was no better feeling, than having your feet up on a hot stove in your parlour with a pot of hot water on the boil for some tea, and a hot bowl of stew in hand. He grinned happily to himself as he made his way into his home. After a good night's sleep, he would have a very eventful day ahead, one way or another. It was going to be an interesting day, a day of reckoning. A hearty meal was going to be very important, if things went wrong, he might not eat properly again for days. His simple stew was tasty, and he added a few more ingredients to the pot of leftovers from the night before, he was not a man who wasted anything, if something could be reused or reengineered to serve another purpose it seemed like the right thing to do. After reheating the stew and having his fill he put the rest in an empty jug and would take it out with him when he left. He knew of a few people nearby that would be grateful.

Daydan spent most of the night packing away some things into his saddlebags, and the old wooden travel trunk with large leather straps. He left his lab as bare as he could, most of the chemicals that he could sell he did, some he kept and the rest he burned. His smaller tools were packed into his trunk, and some of the larger heavier tools he left by the forge. Anything he could use that was light and easy to transport he packed into his chest. One change of clothes, a couple spare shirts and that was it. As he looked at his meagre possessions, he realised how little his life amounted to. One travel trunk and some saddlebags. Everything else, he would have to leave behind. After packing he stoked up his fire and made sure that his Jug of stew would bubble nicely while he slept. He made himself comfortable in his chair and pulled his heavy coat over himself to help keep him warm. His mind was spinning, and with the thought of an unpredictable day ahead he knew he had to try to get some sleep. After much time shifting and turning in his chair, frustrated he got up and put his coat over the back of his chair. He rolled up his shirt sleeves. It was no use, he had to occupy his mind somehow. He walked over to his small alchemical laboratory and started to mix a few chemicals together. Collecting a few items, he took some sacking twine and dipped it into some honey letting it soak. Next, he dipped the twine into some gunpowder, that he made himself from natural sulphur, ground charcoal and saltpetre. The string he then dipped into a bowl of wax to seal it. The gunpowder, he placed into small clay pots and pushed a length of the dipped twine inside, then he closed the opening with some candle wax. The wax acted as a tight waterproof airtight seal. It could be removed and replaced easily enough as the wax was relatively playable in normal conditions. He placed the sealed pots into his trunk, carefully wrapped them in some sacking to prevent the clay pots being broken if the trunk was mishandled. He kept two large blocks of his homemade soap. They were made using fine ash from all of the wood burning and carpentry. The Lye and other animal fats were easy to obtain, pig fat or better still beef fat could be obtained from the local farmers. Or he could obtain large quantities from his neighbours on the floor above his workshop. People had a very bad ethic, not really understanding what could be used and reused over and over again. Even in these hard times. Other ingredients he added to the soap were just to add a pleasant perfume, things like honey, and olive oil were easy to acquire and relatively cheap. Most of the soap he would sell, it was an efficient way to make money very cheaply. It was perhaps rather a time-consuming thing to do, but not exceedingly labour intensive. It was considered a luxury to wash with some perfumed soap, far nicer than using just water, or the plain soap that one could buy from the market.

An important item of his things he wanted to keep was a microscope which he enjoyed using to document things, images that were very difficult to see with the naked eye but under a microscope it interested him how nature had patterns in the way things grew, and how structures formed together. Along with his microscope he had a sea captains telescope, it was a very nice piece made from brass and rose wood, his trunk looked sadly rather empty, so he filled it out with some sawdust and old sacks just to stop the items within from flopping around and getting damaged. He looked around the place that he had called home and felt a little sad that this could all be over, even in the back of his mind he presumed that his ideas would not be welcomed, perhaps his father before him felt the same way too. As far as he knew his ancestors have been following the same path for centuries, only he it appeared was able to summon the souls of the dead from their corpses. His father never mentioned that he could perform such a thing, or his grandfather, but they understood that life energy was not just simply here and now, it was eternal, it could never be depleted, just changed into a new state. He thought about his lecture as the light of the morning began to peep through his street level window giving a little natural light to his basement. He gave his embers a final prod and putting the last of his wood on the fire, he stirred the contents of the jug and tasted the warm stew with a wooden spoon.

He grinned happily to himself, another useful item to add to his trunk, his small cooking pot. His life wasn't so pointless after all. He began to laugh to himself a little as he watched and stirred the stew as it began to heat up and start to boil and bubble. Maybe, he would be dining on something better than potatoes and cabbages tomorrow, or something worse. Rat, or maybe a raw egg. Until today, he never really thought of this place as home, but now he had to leave, it was the only place he ever knew, a place of comfort and safety, a place to work and study, a place to rest. A place to be at peace with himself. His large trunk he left by the door and replaced the large key in its hiding place, his saddlebags he put over his shoulder and put his hat upon his head. He picked up the jug of stew and taking his cane from the table he looked around the place that had served as his whole world for the last few years, letting out a sigh he closed his eyes regretfully as he shut and locked the door behind him. His pace was slower than normal, perhaps a little reluctant to leave his place of safety, concerned about revealing who and what he was and his ideas, it was his turn now, as his father had done before him and his grandfather and his grandfather before him. He remembered the stories his father told him about when he use to travel with his father, they were often stoned and beaten for their beliefs and strange ideas, one thing did not add up though, his father spoke of ancient times, hundreds of years ago, how was that possible, surely he must have confused his dates. He missed his father deeply and never knew his mother, but he remembered very clearly how fondly his father spoke of his mother and it always bought him happiness hearing the stories he would tell.

He knew the area of London he lived in quite well and manoeuvred his way through the tiny streets with ease, through the many markets where young ragamuffins would chase after travellers begging for money. He offered one such lad the jug that he filled with the last of his stew, he knew that other children would be nearby. If they were lucky, they would be able to avoid the harsh workhouse, but often they had little choice. They would become child labourers, unable to keep up with the work of the adults and forced to do the more dangerous tasks. He felt a little relief as he gave the jug to the boy. The dirty faced lad stared back at him and held the large jug in his small hands. The boy never spoke, he just stared and warmed his hands on the warm jug, he raised it quickly to his lips and drank slowly and cautiously from it at first, then reassuring himself that it was safe and good he drank from it heartily chomping on the fragments of potato and cabbage. When he lowered the jug from his lips, he wiped his face with the ragged sleeve of his oversized coat. Daydan smiled to him tipping his hat as the lad wiped away some dirt and remnants of stew from his mouth, the boy smiled back. He then dashed off into a corner behind some barrels, and to his surprise when Daydan watched the boy, three other small children emerged from a pile of innocent looking rags and broken barrels and wooden boxes. They took it in turn drinking from the jug and passing it on to their companions. It was a sad yet pleasing sight, he was happy that he did not tip the stew down the gutter in the street. These ragamuffins might last another few days with such a treat. The oldest of the children who could not have even seen his tenth birthday politely removed his ragged hat to him scrunching it up into his hands in thanks and bowed his head. He turned away from the children and shifted his saddlebags more comfortably on his shoulder, within moments, he felt a tiny hand grip a finger from his trailing hand. Daydan stopped and turned, then realised what it was. He dropped to one knee and smiled. A small girl, very young, held his finger tightly, she was dirty and scruffy but had the smile of an angel. He slowly took his finger from the little girl's hand and put his hand on her shoulder and then carefully stroked her matted dirty hair combing it gently away from her face. Her little eyes sparkled as he watched her. He knew what she wanted, but he could do nothing to help, he let out a sigh and shook his head slowly. She stared into his face almost pleading with him to take her away from these streets. How could he, he was a loner, his life did not lend itself to children or family, he had to always be ready to move. He stood up and walked away. For a few streets the little girl followed after him, and her gang of ragamuffin friends followed closely behind her. Eventually he lost them, his faster pace and their distractions of the many other opportunities for rich pickings from passers-by. Perhaps they were gone, but for some time he remembered that little girls face clearly implanted in his mind.

With some time to kill before he was due to speak, he headed for a tavern that he knew was very close to the university, it would make for a good spot where he could calm his nerves and prepare himself. The tavern was called The Kings Head, it attracted a very mixed group of patrons, it also served a good broth and ale. Aside from his nerves he was in relatively mixed spirits, the chance to sit amongst people laughing and having a good time would be a nice change from being alone, especially seeing that this time in particular his future was unknown, it seemed like a good idea to enjoy a little rest bite while he could. It was clear that things were starting to come full circle again, he knew that as soon as he made his talk, he would either be accepted as an enlightened individual and people would be able to see the need for change. If not, he would be feared and ridiculed for having such a radical and blasphemous idea, not only was it blasphemous, but to many it would be considered treasonous.

Whatever the outcome he would need to be ready, there would be little point trying to live a normal life here in this city after such a display. Telling people in positions of power that there was the necessity and potential for everyone to be equal, would most likely be considered as insurrection, and a cause for lawlessness. It was bad enough with the troubles all over the empire and the rumblings of the Jacobite's from the north, without sewing discord right on the Kings doorstep. It was a time for people to understand that the purpose of life is to evolve and to learn, to enjoy, not a struggle to acquire wealth and power. Although the two could be seen to have a very parallel path, without doubt there is a fine line between the two, the pursuit of wisdom and knowledge often brings with it the opportunity for positions of power or the accumulation of wealth. It is perhaps the fear of losing these things to another that so often causes conflict. Would lesser educated individuals be better able to understand the concept or is lecturing to the so-called intellectuals or the, "Enlightened," the best way forward. His father must have had the same ideas and struggled with the exact same dilemma he was going through. He told him of similar attempts that he himself tried in cities that he travelled to in order to try and pass on his wisdom. In each location he was shunned and narrowly escaped with his life. Jerusalem, Cairo, Morocco, Rome, Athens, Paris, and more, now here, in the great city of London, in the time of Enlightenment and the Awakening, were people enlightened, were they really awake. Power and wealth corrupted. Knowledge and understanding were the key to everything.

It would be easy to become reclusive and just hide away keeping his ideas to himself, using his knowledge and wealth for self-gain, and who would blame him. He had a vision of the future, a vision of a time without war, greed, hate, envy. He dreamed of a time where the only goal was the pursuit of knowledge and enlightenment, a time where life and consciousness were eternal. The idea was indeed radical, and extremely difficult for most to understand, but he believed that he understood the way forward and it felt good to be on that path. When he arrived at The Kings Head Tavern he made for the fireplace and began to warm up his hands glad to be in from the cold, rubbing his hands together on the head of the flames soon took the chill of the air away from his fingers. He looked around at the people in the crowded establishment, people laughing and singing, shouting and misbehaving in a rather unthreatening manner. It was nice to see such harmless fun, and it put a soft smile on his cheeks for a moment as he nodded to some of the patrons who tried to share a drunken joke with him. He found a seat rather close to the fire and got the attention of a serving girl for some ale, it could be his last drink of beer for some time. The thought sent a chill down his spine. One of his favourite past times was watching people going about their business, watching their behaviour, their attitude towards the people around him. The interaction between any two people was fascinating to watch, he would often fill in the gaps during a conversation trying to guess from his observations how one or another of his subjects would react, he found that it really didn't take all that long to be able to make very accurate predictions. By the time the serving girl returned with his mug of ale he quickly ascertained that one man was cheating on his wife, another was blackmailing a former friend, an officer in the guards had designs on promotion, and the serving girl thought he was worthy of some flirtation, most likely for extra tips. He grinned as she leaned over placing down a wooden bowl of broth in front of him, slowly sliding his mug of Ale across the table showing a large amount of her bosom. He tried hard not to laugh at her obvious ploy and deposited some coins into the most convenient location before grabbing the mug of Ale by the handle and raising it to her in a toast. Taking a long hard drink, he finally placed the mug down on the table rather unceremoniously and wiped his mouth with the sleeve of his coat. 'Thank you.' 'A pleasure me' lord, is there anything else you'd be wanting.'

He shook his head and simply smiled leaning back in his chair. 'This will do fine thank you.' The serving girl pulled up the hem of her dress a little showing her ankles and skipped off looking around for someone else who looked like they had a few extra coins to throw her way. *'She is not for you.'*

A female voice mumbled softly into his ear from behind. He turned his head slightly towards the direction of the voice in his head and as he did, so his eyes caught the tell tail blue light of a spirit, he tilted slightly leaning back a little further to be able to see to his side. *'She is not for you'*

It was the ethereal spirit he had taken such devoted care of earlier, whose affairs he felt he needed to put right, she was behind him. Her hands were on her hips. She looked to him with steely bright blue eyes and turned her head slightly as if expecting a response that she might not entirely agree with. It was Mary, and she appeared to be looking at him distastefully and was ready to respond. 'I know.' Daydan spoke clearly and softly.

Her eyes widened, that was not the response she was expecting at all, she looked away sheepishly and then back to her gentleman saviour with a tiny smile beginning to form on her lips. 'I like good manners, so if someone is polite to me, I will always be polite back, that is after all how a gentleman should behave, do you not agree.' He smiled to Mary winking playfully to her ethereal form that only he could see as far as he could tell. The very beautiful apparition of Mary if seen by anyone would have caused a stir, without any shadow of doubt, but thankfully they had no onlookers that he needed to explain to, so he continued drinking from his mug of ale. He looked to Mary and took another swig of the Ale and turned back to her, noticing that she had not yet taken her eyes off him since he spoke back to her. She folded her arms across her chest buoying up her small cleavage. *'Why do you not have a woman sir.'* She asked calmly and politely looking seductively towards him already having an idea of his answer. 'Because I am still in love with you, and I have not yet met another who is worthy.' He smiled to her and pulled up one leg, sitting sideways in the large wooden chair trying to make himself as comfortable as possible on the hard-wooden seat. Mary looked around and pointed with the open palm of her hand. *'My love, it is not hard to meet a wench in London, look around,'* She looked sheepishly to the floor and smiled looking up to him teasingly. *'You still have feelings for little Mary do you.'*

He preferred not to answer such a direct question again, he already confessed to her. It was not nice being put on the spot. He took another drink of ale trying to avoid answering and looking away focussing on the other revellers. Mary moved closer to him taking his hand and looked into his eyes lowering herself to his eye level. *'Tell me sir, will you not tell me sir.'*

He felt a little uneasy, a spirit can always remain if they have closure to attend to, his answer could take away any closure, it could also be the cause of Mary not moving on. He looked to her playing with the Ale mug as he watched her affectionately. Letting out a breath he felt himself slump slightly in his chair and looked up to the apparition of the lovely young woman trying to smile. *'You know I have feelings for you, I always will. You are my girl.'*

Mary was shocked, she was not expecting that response, in life he was older than her by several years, but he made her feel wonderful and so full of life. She stood up straight looking deeply into his eyes. He smiled and reached out his hand to her, Mary slowly wrapped her ghostly hand around his and stepped closer to him stroking his face with her cold ghostly touch. Again, he spoke carefully. 'I don't want anyone else; I just want you.' Mary waved her hand dismissively and pushed him back to sit down in his chair and sat on his lap touching his face. 'We cannot change the past, only learn from it.' Mary said quietly. He smiled to her. 'I know.' Before Mary could answer he put his finger over her lips, she never uttered another word on the subject, she pursed her lips and kissed his finger softly. He smiled to her and traced the line of her mouth with his finger. Mary took his hand and kissed the tip of his thumb and then sucked softly on the end taking it slightly into her mouth, she smiled gently to him looking deeply into his eyes, her lovely bright eyes sparkled with excitement. He watched her soft lips suckle the tip of his thumb until she gently pulled it away from her mouth. *'Mary, my dear sweet girl, you need to move on, you must make your peace and move on, please.'* She fidgeted on his lap getting comfortable and smiling back to him watching his face. *'Soon. I promise.'* Mary put her arms around his neck and lay her face on his chest holding him tightly, even he could feel the tenderness and comfort in her ethereal embrace. He sat still for some time watching her and the other patrons until some hours had passed, eventually her form faded, his drink had long been drunk, and the revellers had changed. With his companion gone, he remembered the task ahead.

I good while after Mary vanished, he finished off his ale and stood up looking around. He wanted to see if anyone had been watching him and his odd behaviour. Satisfied that he had not been watched by anyone unsavoury, he proceeded to the main entrance of the tavern and walked outside glad for a taste of the fresh air, rather than the hot sticky sweaty smells of the overcrowded tavern. He would have to consider his talk very carefully, and the likelihood of being arrested or having to flee for his life was a very real one indeed. He carefully put together an escape plan and was prepared to not be able to go back home afterwards. Outside the Tavern he had a message sent to the old grave-robber. Everything was set, and as he walked to the University his pace picked up a little. As a precaution, he arranged that his trunk would be moved to the docks so he could rendezvous with it latter. If things turned out for the worse, he would not have to venture to his home of the last few years and he could easily slip away. He knew that no matter what happened tonight, he was going to leave London and England for good. Mary was right, it was time he lived his own life, a new start in a far-off land. The walk to St Pauls Cathedral was a long one, but it gave him time to brush up on what he intended to say at the lecture. No one would believe him without evidence, that was for sure. It was also likely that any evidence he produced on the subject would also be scoffed at, and dismissed, even if it was staring them in the face. Some people just would not accept change, others feared it, many condemned it. He thought about his ancestors again, his father, what they must have gone through to try and bring about change, even then, in times of superstition, ignorance and witchcraft. He remembered his father talk about so many scholars from the past, freethinking men with new ideas, if it had not been for them many of the sciences of the day would never have been. Men who lived over a thousand years ago and more, even today, great minds were emerging all the time, this had to be the right time, it just had to be. As he walked, he was nervous about his presentation and his mind was spinning with possible questions. Part of him was relieved that it was such a long walk to the university, another part of him wished that the day was over and whatever outcome was to be, it had already played out. He walked smartly, head up and standing as tall as he could with his back straight. His cane skipped lightly along with each step, his saddle bags over his right shoulder and his riding boots making sure footing on the well-worn road. If his life in London was going to be over, he was going to go out like a gentleman. Just over halfway on his journey he walked past the Houses of Parliament, a large group of spectators formed, and he could hear cheering and shouting. He normally kept away from such gatherings, but the disruption was directly in his path, so he walked far enough away to be able to skirt around the disturbance, but close enough to get a good view. When he peered through the crowd a group of soldiers were stood to attention in their red coats, holding their muskets to their chests like they were ready to march into battle. The crowd were wowed by their drill and the drummer sounding commands to the soldiers. It all looked very smart and was quite a spectacle for the gathered crowd, the soldiers were probably back from some campaign somewhere around the world. He stood nearby and watched for a moment, the men demonstrated their marching and paraded up and down, but the real highlight was when they raised their weapons, the front row knelt down on one knee, the middle row stood up behind and the rear row poked their muskets over the shoulders of the men in front, then with a huge volley some thirty muskets fired off at almost the exact same time. The crowd applauded and congratulated each other undoubtedly for being part of such a magnificent country whose power and influence straddled the entire globe. A moment later he heard a familiar voice yelling at the soldiers, he looked around to see the men standing to attention. An officer on a large white horse was inspecting the troops, another officer stood by watching the cavalry officer, most likely of senior rank, inspecting his men. His horse moved slowly up the line sniffing and bucking slightly at the men, their heads barely up to the mounted officers saddle. Every now and then the mounted officer leaned down to a soldier and must have said something displeasing to the soldier because he saw their faces change, but they stood still, not flinching other than the steely look of defiance in their eyes. The cavalry officer pointed to one of the soldier's muskets and the soldier handed it to him, the musketeer pointed to the musket, and the cavalry officer cocked back the flint and pointed it over the heads of the soldiers. The clicking sound of the unloaded musket bounced off the buildings in a sharp cracking echo that eventually disappeared. The mounted officer threw the weapon back at the musketeer who fortunately managed to save the weapon from crashing to the floor. The cavalry officer kicked his horse on, much to the relief of the paraded soldiers and the infantry officer. 'Your friend, he may have a fine steed, but he holds a weapon poorly, and I would wager he wields a blade like a woman.' Angus watched as the officer rode slowly away. 'That man is no friend of mine.' The idea that this was the man who raped Mary and caused her death in a roundabout way made him numb with anger, but what could he do. It was Captain Atwood and Daydan could feel his blood boil within, he clenched his fist thinking about Mary. He turned away from the soldiers and parliament square and began to walk away towards St Pauls keeping the river close by. As he walked, he made his way under one of the bridges and suddenly felt aware that he was being watched, in the darkness of the shadows under the bridge he saw his ghostly companion, it was Angus the Highwayman. He had his arms folded across his chest, his two pistols tucked neatly into his belt and his short rather barbaric looking cutlas sword sheathed on his hip, he flicked the tresses of his wig away from his neck back over his shoulder and stared to him. *'Are you really going to do this.'* Angus spoke softly to him. He nodded to him not stopping, just simply slowing down a little. He looked towards the highwayman's face at first and then lowered his eyes. Daydan nodded. 'I *must, I must try.'* He thought about his decision and all the promises he made. Angus moved away from the stone of the bridge and adjusted his attire before following a few steps behind.

'Then my friend, sadly, we must part ways, I will go north and join my countrymen, we have an old score to settle with your king.'

Daydan stopped walking for a moment, looked to the ground and then turned to the highwayman and smiled. *'He is not my king. And, are you not part Frenchman.'* Daydan smiled to him slightly teasing his ethereal friend who returned the smile, but soon after, his face expressed some sadness. Angus put his hand on Daydan's shoulder and smiled.

'And proud to be, I am half Scottish, and I am also half French.' He grinned. *'And half Irish!'*

They both chuckled a little, Angus was always so full of life, a man's kind of man. He knew if they were to part ways it would be a sad day. He looked to Angus and nodded politely.

'I understand.' He looked at the man, even in his ghostly form he had a presence about him that was familiar, he could be at home in any group of men, or indeed most likely with the ladies. He wanted to know so much more about his life, his adventures, and to learn more from him about soldiering. Angus walked at his side leaning his arm on him adjusting his tricornered hat. *'Let us go and ruffle some feathers my friend, I am in the mood for a fight.'*

Chapter Twelve

No turning back

For the last leg of his walk along the Thames river to St Pauls, he was in conversation with Angus, his ghostly form was no longer visible, but he could hear his voice in his thoughts as clear as if he was standing right next to him and talking. The two friends talked back and forth for a while until he too eventually disappeared and was just the strange distant memory of a friend's voice in his head. He would hold his lecture at the College of Physicians, along with the company of Barber-Surgeons, the ferocity and squabbling between these two factions would not make his lecture easy. Physicians argued that barbering and pulling teeth was not practicing medicine, they were no more than beauticians and butchers. On the other hand, mortality rates for surgeries were very high, it was still a very new science. Breakthroughs in the field were being made all the time, all the better for people like himself, the grave diggers and undertakers trades were always in demand, especially in a large city like London. On the other hand, these physicians at the collage were unlike the physicians around the rest of the country, they didn't really practice medicine, they preferred to study medicines and anatomy in lecture rooms and live in wealthy homes attending to their wealthy clients. His task was not going to be an easy one, there were intellectuals around that might be able to understand his words. It was not so long ago that people believed the world was flat, although he was keen on the idea to try and enlighten people, he knew that it could potentially be hundreds of years before people had the wisdom to understand such radical ideas. In the future, discovery and understanding were inevitable, if he could sense the undeniable energies that penetrated all things, the vibrations that he felt in his own body and the things around him, surely others could feel this energy and power also, even if they could not understand it or where it came from, he had to try. As he walked enjoying the city views along the river, he felt oddly relaxed, like a man from a different time. A time when knowledge, adventure and understanding were paramount, belief in old outdated superstitions would be the stuff of memories. There were good people around, people who worked towards a greater good, but there were many who were greedy and driven to acquire power and wealth, these people he found dangerous and of great concern, but predictable.

The day started out rather bright and warm with nice sunshine, but as he walked, the clouds over head became darker. In the distance they were very dark grey and visibly heavy with rain, there was a torrential rain shower on its way or a huge storm brewing. Either way, he would most likely be making his escape tonight, in even more unpleasant conditions. He pulled up his heavy coat around himself and changed his walking pace from a leisurely stroll to a much faster stride. Looking over the roof tops ahead he could see the top of St Pauls and he smiled. The Royal College of Physicians was close by, his destination, the end of his life in London, or the beginning of something really amazing. He could almost feel his pace turn into a run as he felt a clear rush of excitement within him. It could work, this could be the time, in his mind he played over the lecture he so carefully planned. Nothing was written down, everything was put to memory on the advice of his father, if things went really wrong, then at-least there would be no written word for which he could be judged. He was finally relieved to leave the riverbank and to be able to stand upon a fully stoned street. Some areas of London were very nice and modern, but others were just slums. The great fire of London came at a good time, forcing construction in stone rather than the old decrepit wooden buildings, some were incredible feats of architecture, especially the more elaborate buildings. This gave way to museums, collages, libraries, the signs for an awakening were all around, but how awake was everyone. And that was not to say that there was still much room for improvement, the gap between the rich and poor was vast, slums still grew up rapidly in less habitable areas. There was always a growing population and there was always the promise of opportunity for workers.

Standing outside his final destination he looked up at the building, a simple design, perfect for lectures and presentations. There were a few people around but seeing the clouds over head most seemed to have been packing up their wares and heading for home early. All except the small groups of academics and other interested parties, making their way to the lecture hall, people from very different walks of life, but all very influential in their own way. He heard many foreign accents in the conversations. Suspicious glances eyed him cautiously, this is exactly what he was told to expect, maybe the knowledge he had was not for others to understand, maybe it was simply a curse. Another curse, he bowed his head to some strangers as they passed him by reciprocating with a polite nod of their own. He took an old sprig of lavender from his pocket that he used to scent his cloths and keep bugs away. He gave the sprig a long lingering sniff, the smell always reminded him of the countryside. Vast open space, rolling green hills filled with colour, sweet smelling flowers, ripe yellow corn fields and hot sunshine. The sound of birds and bees all around, and a cool summer breeze.

What if this time things were different, his mind refused to believe the possibility. He wanted to be accepted, to be free of this life of loneliness, to have friends, companions. Maybe it was his destiny to be always on the move, alone. When he thought of his ghostly companions it didn't make him feel so alone, but they were simply an echo of their past, they too wanted to move on. The song of the universe was calling them, and in the end, they would return, it was the way of all things, the way things would always be. With his mind steadfast, he knew he reached the right decision, that this was no way for a man to live, being driven from one place to another, time and time again. Living his life for his father, and his father before him. It was their dream to be accepted, not his. As for Daydan, he really did not care if he was accepted, as long as he could be himself. Maybe they were wrong. Maybe we are not meant to understand.

He sat on a low stone wall not far from the entrance of the lecture hall, around were horses tied to railings, carriages with their drivers, the last stragglers making their way home or to the lecture. Overhead the clouds were almost black and small splashes of rain wet the dry ground. At first it was slow, small raindrops randomly hitting the ground, then with every few seconds the rain increased, within minutes the rain was tumbling down splashing on the floor and forming puddles, torrents of water heading for the drainage channels. People covered their heads from the rain, as if the rain itself could cause harm. He never understood why people covered their heads from the rain. From clean water. He stood up and removed his short top hat and looked up into the falling rain letting it splash on his face. It felt so refreshing, cleansing. He breathed softly and closed his eyes, the rain made him feel clean and pure, with an unparalleled sense of wellbeing and calm. The worry of the lecture was behind him, he would perform the lecture as best he could, but this time, it would be the last. It would be the last time he was going to be chased from his home for his ideas.

If London could not recognise the potential future of man in his words, so be it. There was opportunity all over the empire, all over the globe. A man could make a good life elsewhere, through hard work and commitment. He stood in the street enjoying the rainfall and mentally checked his escape route in his mind. The idea of having his travel trunk moved to the docks, so that he would have the majority of his most precious possessions with him, was a nice thought. He slowly walked to the entrance of the building, there were no other lectures this evening, only his. The notices made quite an impact on the local thinkers and leaders, not only locally but also across the channel. There were still a few people gathered in the hallway discussing the outcome of the lecture that had yet to take place. Most were already dismissing the idea of his lecture, people already made up their minds before even hearing anything at all. A sad thought indeed, that intelligent men could not think for themselves, but had to rely on old teachings, even these men of science. His lecture title simply read. MAN, AND THE STARS. The title really said nothing, just enough to spark interest. To think people already had an opinion without hearing him speak was strange. He was no accomplished academic himself, but he studied, followed the rules of science, listened to the lectures and attended the presentations, just as many others did. He always kept an open mind. For him it was a constant struggle to acquire the funds for his education. In London education was paid for, it had little to do with talent and all to do with wealth, position and opportunity. His idea presented the opinion that everyone was equal, that everyone deserved the same start and the same quality of life. Already he heard the rumblings of the disconcerted. He heard one conversation in the hallway as he approached the lecture room where he was due to begin.

'If there is no class system, who shall do the work. I shall not I tell you; I shall not do it.'

'A silly notion, man is not equal, some are better, and some are not.'

They agreed with each other noisily and as Daydan approached, their murmurings reduced in tone and volume. He nodded politely to them raising a smile and walking on past. 'Gentlemen.' He grinned to them waiting for a response, but they just watched him walk by in silence. He checked his attire carefully before walking into the lecture room, he would remove his hat and jacket and keep them close to hand, especially his cane. The papers he had signed and copied were inside his saddle bags, safe and sound along with his most precious items. They were of little value in monetary terms, but to him they were important enough to want to keep them close by. A loud booming voice rumbled from behind him, as a large man forced his way through the gathered stragglers, still arguing and debating in the hallway. 'Ah, good, am I late.' The large fat Judge marched heartily towards him, his big rosy red cheeks and large red nose gave away his eagerness to be where he was. It seemed to him that the general opinion of his lecture was that it was utter rubbish, but some saw reason in his idea. Perhaps not acceptance, but certainly thinking beyond the teachings of religion, class and politics. He thought about much of what he would say and how it might affect or even anger those present. It would be nice to think that these intellectuals of society could open their minds to a possibility that as a species, they have the potential to achieve perfection. An immortal life among the stars, because we are just that, the very essence of the stars, each and every one of us. He looked towards the large out of breath man and nodded to him politely. 'No sir, you are not. You have time to calm yourself and find a seat, I will begin shortly.'

Daydan slowly unbuttoned his heavy coat and cleared his throat one last time as the fat man put a chubby hand on his shoulder.

'Good, this is a show I would not miss for the world. Good luck.' He began to laugh out loud, his laughter echoed down the corridors of the lecture theatre as he walked off out of sight. Daydan followed close behind heading for a large beautifully polished rose wood door, the sound of the assembled crowd on the other side of the door indicated that the lecture room was at full capacity, and the audience was becoming restless.

Chapter Thirteen

The lecture

From the elaborate doorway into the lecture room, he could see out into the mass of faces, there was a rather heavy layer of noisy chatter coming from the lecture room. This particular room was primarily used for lectures on medical matters, mostly anatomy, where bodies were cut up in front of about thirty to forty very eager medical students, most of whom wanted to be surgeons themselves. Sometimes live surgeries were performed, demonstrations of existing or new procedures. Often the procedures would end in a rather unpleasant death, in a time without any real pain relief, post-operative trauma was a killer. The desire for people to study medicine, anatomy and to become surgeons was very high. Other than attending these lectures the only other way to be able to study anatomy, was to either find a corpse to be able to study at your leisure, or to become a medical student in a theatre of war in some far-off forgotten land. The most common method used was to hire the services of a grave robber, however, if they were caught the penalty was death by hanging. Oddly, if the corpse was unclothed it was not considered a crime, but a corpse wearing little more than a sock, the crime was committed, and the noose was waiting.

The extremely opulent lecture hall was in an oval shape, at the centre was a table around waist high that a patient, or a cadaver would be placed upon and then dissected, on this occasion the table was completely empty. At the lower level was a wooden rail of a highly polished dark mahogany or rose wood, simply carved spindles adorned the rails, depending on the tear that the spectator was on, the higher the tear, the lower the detail in the woodwork. The lower handrail was most often leaned upon at the elbows, sitting on the bench but leaning fully forwards so that the onlooker could get an eye level view of the performance. Behind the lower handrail was a bench seat going from one tip of the oval to the other, behind that bench was a step, and another simple rail and then behind that another step and a bench seat. There were seven tiers of this pattern all rising in height so that the people watching from the top had as good a view as any of the others to the front. The style was also repeated on the other side of the room and looked like a miniature oval colosseum design. Daydan walked out of the shadowy doorway and strode deliberately into the very centre of the room and stood by the table. The room was suddenly silent, all that was heard soon after he entered was the tap of his boots upon the floor, aside from a couple of barely audible mumbles from the eagerly inquisitive spectators. He looked around at all the faces and almost smiled as he viewed the very powerful, influential and well-respected representatives of the city of London, England and beyond. He paused for a moment tapping his walking cane on his riding boot as he stood in the centre of the room. Turning slowly, he placed the cane upon the solid wooden table and removed his short top hat and unbuttoned his heavy coat.

He turned and looked up to the centre of one of the rows where he saw a man surrounded by several military officers and officials. The King himself, Daydan cleared his throat. He nodded politely and began to place his things upon the table and took the saddlebags from his shoulder and put them on the table, then he took off his heavy coat placing it next to his cane and short top hat. He carefully adjusted his waistcoat and looked up to the king. 'Your majesty, your honours, professors, doctors, my lords, ladies and gentlemen. I feel truly fortunate that so many of you have come to hear what I have to say. I want to try and show you that this is not something that is just in my imagination, a theory. This is part of our evolution, because I believe that in essence, in the future, we will exist as pure conscious, energy. Free to travel any distance we choose, immortal, like gods.' An eerie rumble of whispers drifted softly around the room. 'This is perfectly real I assure you, and the evidence happens right before our eyes, time and time again, only we are unaware of the potential that exists within each of us and all around us. If only we open our eyes to our true nature, to the potential of our very unique species, we would realise that we are such extraordinary beings, with such incredible potential.'

Murmurs rumbled around the room again, some nodded congratulating each other agreeing that indeed, they were extraordinary. He could also hear some of the negative comments coming from his attentive audience. Daydan wasted no time in moving things forward, the real difficulty in this lecture was to get people to stay focused until the very end. He paused for a moment as the noise of whispers between the seated spectators filled the air. He held his hands behind his back and walked the length of the centre table and back again. He turned slowly to face the more influential members of his audience and paused. King George the II himself, and a small group of his most trusted officers, officials, and the Bishop of London to name but a few. He stood in plain view of some of the most powerful and influential people of the British Empire. He took a long deep breath and breathed gently as the words seemed to roll off his tongue, as if he rehearsed them a thousand times before. 'It is time gentlemen, for us to put aside our petty weaknesses, pursuing power and wealth. In our distant future, these things are irrelevant, what matters is knowledge. Understanding our universe and our place in it.' He paused for a moment. 'In our future, time and distance are irrelevant, the entire universe is our playground, but we must cease with these basic negative emotions that distort our potential. Greed, jealousy, envy, the pursuit of status, wealth and power.' He looked around at his privileged audience to lock eyes with some of the most powerful and wealthy people in the land. He could sense that his speech was not going down well and was not being received as he had first hoped, much as he predicted. His fears and memories of past speeches flooded his memory, he paused. He knew he had to keep talking, if just one of these people could be open minded enough to just consider his words it would have been worth it. 'But sir.' A young man stood up, a foreigner with a very broken English accent, German or Austrian. Daydan nodded to the young man not expecting questions just yet, but the distraction would allow him time to think. The foreigner continued. 'If we are to evolve into entities without emotions or feelings, just pure thought and energy, what is the point of existence.' Daydan smiled, someone was listening, he walked closer to the young man and spoke in such a tone that others would have to be silent or not hear his response. 'Imagine consciousness, without greed, jealousy, envy, would that not be joyous.' The young man pondered for a moment and looked around at the dignitaries and men of learning much older than himself. 'But without compassion, joy, love.' The young man remained silent and spoke no more, he looked away slightly, deep in thought, he put his hands behind his back as Daydan had done, almost mimicking his stance. He looked to the young man thoughtfully, was this what the human race would eventually become, emotionless entities able to explore the stars at speeds incomprehensible even by our own imaginations. Living a life without love or joy, what was the point. He looked away from the young man and combed his fingers through his hair and walked up to the centre table clearing his throat. Almost in a whisper, as if speaking to himself. 'Consciousness without joy, happiness, love. Are these things not precious.' He pondered his own thoughts for a moment as his audience listened for more.

Daydan turned and walked the length of the floor again looking left and right trying to make eye contact with his audience. 'Energy is everywhere, it exists in all things, we just lack the understanding at this time, but we will learn, just as an infant learns to walk, even without guidance, we will learn. Close your eyes gentlemen, we can feel this energy all around us, within us. When we die, our energy, our soul leaves our body as pure conscious thought, it is fleeting and lasts little more than an instant as it proceeds on its journey to the source of the universe, of all life. All things possess energy, substance, natural unblemished things possess a purer form of energy, but it still exists, it is the natural order of things. I have realised that the best way to explain this is to show you. So,' Talking and whispering began to fill the room, and the room had a nice echo that amplified the whispers. He let out a long breath and prepared himself as he began to summon one of his dearest companions. He took his cane from the large wooden table in the middle of the lecture room and held it in his right hand. Slowly his hand and his silver ring began to glow with a pale blue light, the red dots on the blood stone glistened to a bright red, and gently increase in brightness. He slowly lifted up his cane and closed his eyes. When he lifted the cane higher to the light, tiny blue sparks of light began to dance above the cane until slowly more specs of light appeared, until they too began to coalesce and take form. The audience stared in astonishment at the strange unfathomable blue collection of tiny lights growing in number and forming into a human figure. A strange ghostly shape, slowly becoming more and more defined in clarity and detail. It was Mary. As her form grew more recognisable, she began to slowly walk around the table at the centre of the lecture room. The audience at first seemed terrified, but with Marys joyful and graceful movements and appearance, they simply stared on in bewilderment and shock. She smiled so beautifully, and he could see that her graceful movements in a way calmed the onlookers to eventual feelings of amazement and interest, rather than any terror.

He turned slowly looking up into the faces of his audience, his time was short, and he already knew almost half the listeners were already uneasy. 'How do we define life, it lives, it grows, it evolves, and in most cases, it can reproduce, but is that perfection, are we perfect.' He looked at Marys ethereal form and smiled. 'Mary is self-aware, she can hear us, communicate with us, and even in some cases touch us, yet she does not eat, sleep, drink or breathe, and in this state, she can never reproduce as we understand it.'

He swallowed uneasily as Mary lowered her eyes and made an involuntary caress of her stomach over her clothing.

'This energy lives, what I mean by lives is simply that she is conscious of her existence. She is between our world and the world of the dead. 'When she is ready and so chooses, she can return to the source, from where she will be reborn. She, or rather her soul's energy can return in a new life, waiting for the right spark, the right moment.' Mary looked sad, a sadness in her eyes he had never seen before, she began to dance for them. Slowly turning and moving cautiously looking at her captivated audience, she looked towards him and gently took his hand in hers. Her expression changed to a look of peace and calm as she kissed his hand softly and smiled looking up into his eyes. 'Emotions have energy too Daydan,' Her hand cradled his cheek and she smiled deeply to him as she watched his face. 'Emotions like love have the most beautiful energy of all, thank you for your love my lord, for I am not worthy you anymore. But maybe someday.' She stroked his face and traced her thumb across his lips and softly dipped the tip of her thumb into his mouth, the tenderness of her touch, even as a ghost was so pleasurable.

She removed her hand from his cheek and took a slow step backwards and bowed to him gracefully and put her arms across her chest like the dead Pharaohs did. Mary closed her eyes and tilted her head to one side and slowly, very slowly at first, her ghostly form began to break up as small specs of light of blue and white began to move upwards in a strange spiral of smoke, as if rising from a fire. The misty cloud weaved slowly, some of the light moved across the room into Daydan himself, and the rest moved upwards, making their way effortlessly through any barrier in their path. Mary's beautiful form slowly became less and less visible, he stared helplessly as he watched her leave, his heart sank, his only love disappearing up into the ceiling and inevitably into a cold dark raining cloudy night sky right before his eyes. Some of her light moved into him, and he remembered all of their good times together and the deep sense of love that they shared. He lowered his head and let his eyes peer disinterestedly to the floor, a tear began to run down his cheek. He shook his head, heartbroken at the loss of his sweat and gentle friend.

'Please don't go.' He repeated his plea once more, much more softly, much more desperately. 'Sweet Mary. Please don't go.'

Marys light was eventually completely gone, the room was utterly silent. His heart ached. He heaved a heavy breath and smiled weakly a little to himself, she had been such a good person in life. Her ghostly visage was almost pure white with a soft pale blue light, and now she was gone. Still deeply saddened to see his Mary leave him, he touched the blood stone ring on his right hand and caressed it gently. The ring on his finger began to glow brightly. At first, small pin pricks of light could just be seen dancing between his ring, his walking cane, and the beautiful peacock feather that was tucked neatly into one side of his top hat. Slowly the lights began to form, every moment more spots of light joined the mass of lights to slowly form new figures standing next to him. One of the audiences stood up at the back of the lecture room behind the king.

'Love, is for poets and fools, and that woman, was nothing more than whore, I bedded her myself at the theatre, this man is a fraud.'

He turned sharply and looked vengefully towards the voice, an officer of the cavalry standing behind the king pointed an accusing finger towards Daydan snarling with a twisted expression on his face. The assembled spectators watched the scene fixed rigid to their seats as two ghostly forms began to become more and more clear, the air in the room seemed to grow suddenly cold. One of the figures was the tall powerful slave Jin, and the other was the highwayman Angus Turin. The spectators starred at the two ghostly apparitions not sure how to react and then looked at the cavalry officer. If the speaker was a fraud, how was he able to provide such a magnificent performance, these new apparitions were a terrifying pair to behold, several spectators were clearly afraid while others looked sceptically at Daydan looking for any signs of foul play, or tricks.

He stood still and looked between his two companions in defiance. He held his cane tightly in his right hand ready to fend off an attack, he put on his hat and lay his coat across his left arm ready to make good his escape. The saddlebags he carefully packed and kept as best as possible out of sight under his coat that now weighed heavily on his left arm. It was a necessary precaution, things were beginning to turn out just as he suspected they might, whatever the outcome, good or bad, he was ready. It was very clear that even as their ethereal presences began to take shape, in these harmless forms, there was an air of violence and terror coming from his two ghostly companions. Whereas when Mary was dancing in full view, the atmosphere in the room was much more peaceful and calmer, even exquisite.

Some of the audience stood up intending to ask a question as was the etiquette in these presentations and lectures, another young man in his twenties challenged him in his Scottish English accent. yet before he could acknowledge the several genuinely interested observers, an object flew from the audience and struck him squarely on the temple. Daydan staggered and steadied himself holding onto a nearby handrail with his right hand still holding onto his cane.

'Fraud.' One spectator shouted, 'Heretic.' From a seat not so far away the yell of the King himself. 'Traitor.' Daydan had seen this before, many times and it was a scenario similar to those told by his father as a warning. People simply were not ready, the fear of losing their position, their wealth, they just did not understand, and they did not care. Even after all this time they were simply not ready, or they just had too much to lose by giving up their comfortable lives while others suffered. He ducked his head down and pulled a handkerchief from his pocket and put it against his temple to soak up a small pool of blood that had formed on his head. He used his coat and saddlebags to shield himself from any more missiles. Another spectator threw an ink pot and another his own walking cane.

His companions required no instruction or guidance. Before Jins form was complete, he roared and leapt over some of the handrails and began to hit out from side to side with his club violently. His eyes were open wide and his teeth snarling at any who dared venture close enough for a fearsome blow. Most of his blows were of course ineffective, flailing wildly left and right targeting anyone that tried to get near to their friend, but some blows hit home somehow. The target flaying backwards in fear from the crowd of bodies behind them. Angus pulled out his flintlock pistols and took careful aim at the two most powerful men in the room, one at the King and the next at the Bishop, when the pistols fired one could see the ghostly lead balls fly true and straight into the chests of the bishop and the other into the forehead of the King. They both staggered fearfully checking themselves in disbelief for wounds totally disorientated for a moment. Others stared at the king in horror and panic. With both pistols fired and with the calm and composure of a seasoned fighter Angus tucked them onto his belt and pulled out his very savage looking cutlass from the scabbard on his hip. He pointed it towards the military officers by the king who approached him slowly with their own elegantly crafted beautifully made curved sabres. Angus slashed at them skilfully, more to keep them at arm's length than to strike. His movements were skilful and clean, any trained observer would have seen instantly that the highwayman possessed great skill with his blade, even if it was a very barbaric looking weapon. He easily kept the majority of the crowd at bay with his display of fine swordsmanship. Daydan quickly made for the nearest door out of the lecture room.

With confusion all around the room, the less brave members of the audience made a dash for the other doors to escape, others tried to make a grab for him. The braver spectators hurled themselves towards the slave and the highwayman trying to protect the king. There was complete chaos and panic, and as planned a very small window of opportunity to make good his escape. An opportunity that Daydan did not lose a single second of thought upon. Once through the first door into the corridor adjoining the lecture rooms, he quickly pulled a wooden bench across the doors path after slamming the door quickly behind himself. The bench did little to slow his pursuers but as the unruly crowed forced their way blindly through the door not expecting the bench in front of them, the first few pursuers fell over the bench causing the rest to fall over them. Those few seconds assisted greatly in his escape allowing him to dash through the last few remaining doors barricading them quickly while still on the move with anything that came to hand. He slammed each door behind himself as hard as he could, his own form of defiance in a desperate situation trying to flee from a lynch mob.

He could hear screams and yells from deep within the building, whatever it was the slave and the highwayman was doing to keep them at bay, it was certainly causing a scene of utter chaos and mayhem. Daydan grinned to himself imagining the chaos and panic that his friends were dishing out. Perhaps in some small way they were able to get some payback for past wrong doings against them. Once outside again he headed for the street. A smile formed on his lips as he saw a familiar face tied a short distance away.

He wanted to keep his promise to the old woman and to Mary, but if the Atwood man ever faced off against him again, he felt that he would not be able to help himself, anger swelled up inside him as he thought about Mary. Everything she had been through, losing her like this, his emotions were running wild, a part of him wanted to turn and face his accusers and take as many down with him as he could, another part of him just wanted to flee, to make a fresh start and to leave this idea of trying to change people's way of thinking behind. Maybe there was another way, a better way to be the eternal hand, a better way to live his life.

His pace only slowed a fraction as he closed the distance between himself and the cavalry officer's animal, the horse recognised him and bucked his head several times in acknowledgement. Daydan smiled to the animal and took a quick look behind him as he ran head long towards the finely saddled animal.

The rain still tumbled down, and in the distance the rumble of thunder echoed through the dark night sky, the stars were hidden now behind thick black clouds and the rain left a cold bitter chill in the air. Thankfully it was the rain and stormy weather that seemed to deter most of the pursuers from their chase. The majority of his audience were not the sort of gentlemen to run or do anything quickly, it was mostly the younger or military men with the taste of blood or some kind of glory at capturing such a villain.

No matter who was chasing him, his mind was set on the promise he made to Mary, her touch still felt oddly warm on his lips. He could still feel her beautiful presence even though he saw her leave. Even when she said her goodbyes, it still felt like she was with him somehow, just like before, he breathed uneasily and tried to not think about her for now.

Chapter Fourteen

The grand escape

It was all over, yet again he tried to explain his understanding of the mysteries of life and death and the strange world in between, the vast untapped pool of energy that was everywhere. Yet again he was ridiculed and hated. His father's dream would have been so different, this age of enlightenment, this age of awakening. He pushed on hard running down the street to get as far away from the collage as possible as fast as he could, he could hear Jin and Angus's screams and yells in his mind as they fought his pursuers some distance behind him, hacking and slashing and gesturing menacingly to the few braver men that tried to chase after him. He could still hear the shouts of, traitor, heretic, blasphemer, fraud, freak, monster and fake. He growled angrily under his breath as he made it to the very end of the long street. The white horse ahead stood bucking its head, slightly shaking from the cold rain that ran down its powerful body. The night air was cold, the rain still tumbled down. The dark heavy clouds indicated a fierce storm was brewing. The night air was thick with heavy rain and static energy, rain was common here, yet this time the rain made the night feel even more hostile. He knew it was pointless going home, he pre-planned his escape well, having partly guessed that this would be the outcome, he knew that within hours of getting to his home there would be a lynch mob outside with rope and lanterns ready to chase him or burn him out. Luckily, he put his own plans to work earlier, high tide would be in the next few hours, and the small vessel he had chosen, could slip nice and easily up the Thames to a waiting ship that could take him away once again and out to the open sea. Part of him was happy and relieved to be leaving this life behind, the guilt he felt about not following in the footsteps of his father and grandfather had faded into the night. The only promise he vowed to keep was his promise to his beloved Mary. Now, he had to get from the collage and back to the Thames without being seen as fast as he could, outside in the dark streets away from the larger buildings the horse drawn carriages with their drivers were lined along the side of the road, most likely waiting for his more influential audience members. He ignored all but the fine animal ahead of him tied to a rail near a convenient stone water trough. He recognised the Atwood horse immediately, it was a fine animal that the Captain was unworthy of, even for that of a cavalry officer. It was very clear that this officer was not a gentleman after all. If ever the two would come face to face again, it would be a duel to the death, of that he was certain. Without another thought he marched over to the horse and stroked its long nose letting the animal sniff him and remember his odour. The horse was tied next to another horse, a mare, he mounted the largest of the two, the beautiful tall white stallion with an elegant military style saddle and bridle. With a slight tug on the reigns he took the reign of the other horse and kicked his own ride gently to move on. Instantly the fine animal began to trot slowly through the street, closely followed by the mare. Their shod hooves clacked rhythmically on the partly cobbled and muddied road. Behind him he could just hear the shouts of the small crowd he left behind, still the shrill of their accusations filled the night air, he ignored the screams and proceeded to kick the horse on more into a gallop, still holding the reign of the second horse. Several pistol shots echoed through the night, but they were reckless blind shoots shooting into the darkness at echoing unseen targets. The horses bucked a little but were soon eased by their able rider. He kicked his steed on again clicking the inside of his mouth to encourage and steadying his mount. The stallion seemed unconcerned by the shooting, or shouting in the distance, perhaps it was no stranger to unrest or the battlefield. He remembered the scars on the animal the first time they met, were they from battle, or were they the wounds of a mistreated animal. He leaned forwards slightly giving the animal a pat of reassurance and encouragement. 'C'mon boy.' The animal whinnied in appreciation and picked up its speed a little. The faster gallop felt good, the more distance he could put between the angry mob and himself the better, his life probably depended on it. Daydan smiled, now they would have to add horse thief to the list. The horses effortlessly galloped on towards the river, the streets were now mostly mud, but with the horses, he certainly had the fastest and more convenient mode of transport available. The walk to the collage had taken him several hours but his ride to make his escape back to the river would take him a fraction of the time. If he could stay ahead of the news, he should be able to make good his escape, to where exactly, he was still uncertain where that path would lead him. Far behind Jin and Turin's ghostly forms had already vanished, under such a barrage they would have little choice, but they would be able to return later, the energies of the physical world and the meta-physical world were always at odds with each other, drawing energy from each other in a strange mysterious symbiotic relationship. Someday perhaps, they would be one. All things would be clear and seen as pure perfect conscious energy, limitless and infinite.

'Giddy up boy.' He encouraged the fine animal forward once more and let go of the reign of the mare alongside, but rather than slip away and head for home she trotted on next to the stallion much to the amusement of the rider. They all made a fine sight in the rain and the dark misty night sky as they headed unhindered for the river.

He arranged to meet Charlie at the chalky wharf with a small boat and his trunk, that would take him out to a ship at the docks of the Thames. This was where the larger ocean-going sailing ships would be moored up and unload their cargoes. It would be a slow boat ride, but a safe one, the chances of anyone suspecting him of being on the river in a boat making his escape would be very unlikely. It would be reasonable to expect a mob to form outside his temporary home, but until they decided to break in and try to take him by force, it would be too late, and once inside they would realise that he had already moved his possessions out. By that time, hopefully he would be long gone. Eventually he came upon the small chalky muddy road that lead down to the wharf, a landing place for the smaller boats, some from up the river inland and some from the sea. These boats were much smaller trading vessels, the small docks rested on a soft bed of chalk, where they were less likely to be bogged in bad weather. This wharf had been used for many centuries. The locals often found antique finds from civilisations long since departed. Charlie, if his stories were true was from a long family line who lived and traded with the vessels that often moored there. 'Chalky,' as he preferred to be known, often joked about naming the wharf after himself if he ever had the money to buy it.

With the wharf finally in view he stepped down from the stallion and patted him down. The smell of the horse was rich in the air, not that he had run him hard, and there was no signs of distress or sweat on the beast, but it was a smell that he remembered from his youth in the Middle East, he couldn't remember much else. The smell of fine horses and how comfortable he felt around them never left him. He spoke softly to the stallion as he reassured the animal and then with a playful slap on the hind quarters, he sent the animal on its way. The two beasts jerked away easily and trotted off, wherever they were going they knew the way back, and seemed to be pleased with their little excursion and freedom. He tipped his hat to them respectfully, watching them canter off into the night, then he turned and walked across a chalky muddy road onto some well-placed planks of wood to try and avoid slipping into knee deep mud. The chalky base of the wharf had benefits, it was soft enough to allow drainage, and it made navigation very easy for the river masters being able to see the wharf very clearly from right across the river.

'You survived; can't say I'm surprised.' Charlie approached him holding out his hand for payment, Daydan grinned to the much older man and put his hand into his coat pocket and pulled out some coins and handed them to Charlie. 'As promised.' Tom, the younger man Charlie always had with him ran up to them, he tipped his simple cloth cap and looked the very part of a sailor, which was odd as he never ever went to sea. 'Your trunk is on the Sloop sir. I put it there mi self.' He coughed into his hand. 'Bloody evy it was too.'

Charlie slapped the back of the younger man's head playfully. 'Don't you be try'in it lad, the gentleman as already paid.' Charlie shook his head with a big smile on his face. 'Sorry boss, you take care, it has been a pleasure. Ooh, while I remember, the sloop will take ya to Blackwall docks, that's where you can get a Galleon to take you to the India's or the America's, but raver you dan me, savage places them are, not like ere. Ere we're civilised. And the pick ins is bet er.' He smiled.

Daydan looked up to the dark cloudy sky and was aware of the thick rain clouds over head, a light rain was still falling everywhere. In the distance he could hear the slow tumble of thunder, but from the blackness of the sky he knew a big storm was brewing. It would be an interesting journey wherever he chose to flee to next, but at least he would be safe, safer than here. Maybe this time he would do things different, the idea that one would work so hard to blend into society and then destroy it by becoming an enemy of the state seemed very pointless indeed. Why had his father and ancestors put so much time and effort into try to convince a people to change their ways, that was just as much a part of their nature as was the colour of their eyes. He put his hand in his coat pocket and pulled out a silver coin and handed it to Tom, he gave him a smile and returned his hand to his cane. The old man stared at Tom with a look of surprise on his face. 'Young Tom Beaufort, you give that ere, shame on you.' Charlie tried to snatch the coin from the young man's hand, but Tom was far too quick. Daydan had to laugh softly to himself, he tipped his top hat to the two men and started walking along a low wharf to the small sloop awaiting him moored at the end. He hunched his shoulders a little to protect himself from the rain and when he almost reached the Sloop, he felt a presence nearby. He turned and saw the ghostly form of Angus begin to glow and become clearer. As he watched the highwayman's spirit form, he seemed to be uncharacteristically relaxed, he stopped in his tracks and turned to him and bowed his head respectfully. The Highwayman held the hilt of his cutlass and watched him carefully, he shook his head and looked up at the night sky as the rain fell in a strange kind of slow motion to the floor. 'I'm done too.' The highwayman's tone was calm and thoughtful. He approached slowly, Angus had a vengeful temper and had been a very useful ally, but it was obvious that he was not an adventurer, at least not like this, not anymore, his days of stalking the highways for easy targets and rich pickings were long gone, and even when asked why he hadn't made peace with himself, he could never answer. To lose yet another friend, companion, this would not ease his conscience one bit, Angus spoke finely. A clear-thinking mind, and of the three companions Angus in a way seemed like a brother. It was sad to see them leave, but he knew it was the right time for them to move on. first Mary, and now the highwayman. Truth was, a spirit is a soul in limbo, waiting, lost, trying to make peace, on their way to the source to be reborn, death was not the end. It was just a part of a never-ending cycle of renewal. He held out his hand to the Highwayman spirit, and in the dim light of the wet rainy night the two came together, two entities from alternate worlds coming together one last time.

'It has been fun my friend, thank you. I wish you well on your journey.' The words from Angus felt solid in Daydan's mind, he would miss him for sure, he looked to the highwayman and smiled warmly looking at their unlikely other worldly handshake. 'You too my friend.' As their hands pulled apart, he watched Angus turn away, he began to walk slowly down the wooden wharf and with each step his energy slowly began to dissolve away vanishing in the rain upwards and along the ground like small wisps of smoke. He watched him patiently until his friends faded form had completely vanished. When his friend completely disappeared from sight, he felt a piece of him had disappeared too, a side of him that when things got tough, and the odds were stacked, Angus would always be there to turn the tide.

Feeling saddened by the loss of yet another friend he stepped up to the small sloop, the boats master held out a hand to him to assist him onboard and pointed to a seat at the stern. Looking more closely to where he was directed, he recognised a part of his trunk under an old tattered sail used to cover the cargo. 'You'd best sit there with your gear. We'll be go'in, now you're ere." Daydan simply nodded to the river master, he settled himself down comfortably for the journey to the docks. The small craft sailed slowly along the river, at some points he could see commotions on the key side, but he was invisible to them, the escape was well planned, and the main search was now disappearing into the night. He folded his arms across his chest shielding himself from the rain as best he could, he looked over many times to the mainland and felt relieved he would be moving off to another land to start over. All he had was a few precious possessions and what money he could muster along with some silver and gold to trade. He began to envy the people in their nice warm homes, safe and secure, huddled up around their fireplaces with their loved ones telling stories and laughing. Able to think about the future, raise a family, have roots. Wasn't that what life was about, enjoying the simple things. Looking up to the river master as he sailed his boat effortlessly down the cold looking muddy waters of the Thames, the rain splashed down in the boat and onto the Thames making visibility difficult, the boat master gestured to his passenger with a flick upwards of his chin. 'Where would you like to go to, the India's, the America's.' Daydan wasn't sure what to say. He looked to the river man and breathed an uncertain sigh. 'Which would you choose.' His fate was now in the hands of the river master, no matter. The river master shrugged his shoulders, he looked to him for a moment and then turned his attention back to steering his little boat. 'Dunno, I only ever lived on this river, never wanted to go anywhere else.'

Daydan shuddered, the idea of spending one's entire life without adventure, without challenge, it felt uncomfortable, cold, very unfamiliar. Looking at the river master he seemed happy, even in the cold rain of this night, he seemed content. Maybe it was himself that was wrong, he always felt impelled to be more, to do more, to see more and to learn more. He blinked his eyes and watched the river master as he skilfully sailed his little sloop smiling to himself. When he saw his passenger watching he began to whistle to himself. With the rain and cold the whistling lifted their mood as the craft slipped through the rough water. Daydan closed his eyes and pulled the sail over him, he felt sleep begin to creep up and take him, he was tired and exhausted, the gentle rocking of the small craft made it easy for his mind to slip away. A smile formed on his lips as he felt all sense of time and feeling drift away. The delightful relief of sleep finally got the better of him.

Asleep, his mind took him to a far off place, bright sunshine warmed his face, he was sitting on the porch of a modest house with a large chair swinging from some chains, a lovely woman with dark red hair leaned over a new born baby at her breast, feeding the infant tenderly, singing an old song in a strange language he never heard before. He sat close by her with his arm around her watching her breast feed the baby. Her voice was beautiful and soft, almost a whisper, so comforting. Her singing was gentle and full of tenderness. Away from the porch two young children played in the hot sunshine sitting in a dirty puddle throwing sloppy hand fulls of mud at each other, laughing and giggling looking back to him and waving. He watched the scene in his mind, the gentle woman, the children, the modest home, even the weather. His mind focused on this fiery haired woman trying to see her face, but her head was down focused on breast feeding her child as any mother would. He leaned back in the swinging porch chair and let his arm run along the back to the mysterious woman's hair, then he stroked her bare shoulder gently with his fingers and could feel her soft warm skin. With his lightest touch he was willing her to look up to his face, slowly she began to lift her head turning her head to his. Who was she, what woman could turn him from his solitary life to a family man so easily, in his dream he was clearly happy and content. From the look of his home and his young family, they seemed to be doing well, he looked out into the distance beyond where the children were playing and all he could see were fields and fields of small trees, neatly planted, in long orderly straight lines like a huge formation of soldiers. He wanted so much for the woman to look up at him in his dream, her body looked alluring and healthy, slim and beautiful. Her hair was a dark red like rosewood, and her skin a beautiful pale white like marble. If only he could see her face, she teased him as she fed the young child from her breast looking down, her eyes peering through the fringe of her red hair at him. His fingers teasingly caressed her arm gently. It felt so real, so vivid. He let out a sigh and closed his eyes tightly in his dream with a grin of content satisfaction on his face, he relaxed fully ready to give himself up to his dream.

Chapter Fifteen

Out to sea

A sudden shove awoke him from a cold yet restful slumber, his dream was still in his thoughts half expecting to awaken next to his mysterious fiery headed companion, he peered out from beneath his heavy coat and a large section of sail cloth, then he looked up to the river master who had given him a considerate yet forceful prod to awaken his slumbering passenger. 'Your ship, it's just there yonder.' He pointed to a beautiful sailing ship with tall masts. A few of the sails were unfurled and loose, flapping in the wind, ineffective but looking very ready for action if needed. The fine-looking tall ship he noticed, had a line of guns on the upper deck, not what he was expecting of a merchantman bound for the new world. The little craft he was on eased itself towards the larger ship, some line was thrown over the side, the River master took the line and then tied a heavy rope to it that was quickly fed in place of the line. The heavier rope was then tied around his trunk. Then he heard the grinding of wood as a winch hoisted his trunk up high into the air. A second rope was lowered down with a loop tied into the end, He looked oddly to the river master who gestured with his foot, realising what to do next, he put his booted foot into the noose and held the rope getting ready to be hoisted upwards. 'Why this ship.' He said to the boatman. The boatman pointed to a flag at the rear of the ship that they were next to, the flag was a simple one, the Union Jack, and another flag, one he had never seen before, it had a St George's cross in the top left corner by the pole, and then horizontal stripes of red and white. He turned to the boatman. 'I don't understand.' The boatman almost ignored him as he went about readying his small sailboat to pull away as soon as his passenger was gone. The boatman turned the rudder so as to make a speedy get away as soon as he could raise his sail again. 'Sir, this is the Jane, a Royal Navy ship of his majesty the King, you are listed as the ships Barber Surgeon, rather fitting so I understand.' He grinned to him. 'Trust me. If you wish to disappear, this is the ship on which you should flee.' He grinned a little. 'Besides, I have my instructions.' He gave his passenger a final pat on the shoulder and then whistled up to the crew above onboard the ship. Suddenly, he was hoist high into the air and up level with the lower rigging, then a swing arm squeaked, and he was turned and lowered onto the deck. The Captain in a Royal Navy Uniform and tall grand wig greeted him and then turned to his crew. 'Gentlemen, let us to sea, with all haste.'

There was a flurry of activity on the deck of the ship as the officers and crew ran around unfurling sail, hauling in the anchor and lashing down the last of the supplies onto the deck, or lowering it into the cargo hold. The ship looked oddly loaded, piles of supplies were covered in sail on the deck, the ship itself was not a war ship, though it had a battery of sixteen guns, eight on each side of the main deck. They were very cleverly hidden behind blast shutters. It was a very fine ship; the craftsmanship was very smart and luxurious yet simple. This was a ship built for stealth, speed and cargo space.

Suddenly, shots were fired from the riverbank, a man stood on the docks shouting at some soldiers to open fire, the soldiers directed by a young officer ordered his men to hold their fire. Daydan could just make out the silhouette of one officer grab a musket and prompted a soldier to load it. The soldier refused and the young officer took the musket from the infantry man and loaded the musket for the other officer but stood his men down. It was Atwood, somehow, he had tracked him to the docks, and he was shooting at the Royal Navy ship, much to the bewilderment of the marines and officer nearby. The tall sailing ship was readying for sea and the men were busy running around unfurling the last of the sail for the open sea. Daydan's trunk was swinging precariously from the yard arm as more important duties were undertaken. The line for the trunk was lashed to a wooden belaying pin on the rigging mast. The sight of his trunk swinging wildly overhead was rather worrying, but no one else seemed to care, they had more important things on their mind. He turned to see Atwood pointing and looking at him through a Captains telescope on the far bank, and then grab the musket from the marine officer's hand. As he watched, he saw the smoke rise from the musket and then a moment later a whooshing sound as the musket shot hit his trunk with a thud, then with a sudden crack of noise, his trunk exploded, a loud thundering bang. Black and grey smoke mixed with cloudy wisps of white smoke was all around them. Everyone ducked down for a moment at the loud noise. There was a shout from above as one of the men fell from the rigging crashing through the ropes to break his fall, he finally landed on the fore deck with a crash, he paused for a moment and then yelled out in pain as he tried to stand upright but his arm and shoulder were badly disjointed. The sailor knelt on the floor holding himself up with his left hand trying to get up, his right arm useless and dangling oddly. Soon after in the chaos and the cloud of smoke everyone continued back on with their duties rushing around to get seaward again. The smoke from the harmless explosion billowed up into the air, some of the heavy debris from the truck fell overboard into the water making several plopping sounds, more landed on the deck. A piece of sacking cloth floated harmlessly through the air and then slowly down in pieces either into the Thames or onto the deck. The officer on the land clenched his fist yelling at the soldiers and the other officer, they ignored him standing to attention refusing outright to fire upon the Royal Navy ship, especially one flying the colours of the company.

He saw the injured crewman and realised quickly that as the ships surgeon it was his job to help him, he wasted no time and stooped down to the sailor who was disoriented and in considerable pain, he helped him to his feet. The sailor was a thin athletic looking, with light brown skin, wearing nothing more than a light canvas shirt, trousers and bare feet. He carefully observed the man's injury gently feeling over the disfigurement. He gave him a reassuring smile and nodded to the man who looked terrified and confused towards the stranger and his smart looking undertakers attire.

'It is dislocated, we need to fix it.' Daydan looked around and pointed to the man's canvas shirt. 'I'll need your shirt, quickly man.' He carefully helped the sailor out of his shirt, most of the men were going about their duties but a couple of his crew mates watched with interest, wondering if he was going to lose his arm as most navy butchers would presume to do. When the seaman's shirt was removed Daydan twisted the shirt in his hands turning it into a thick rope. Flicking it around and around several times to make a sling and wrapped it around the man's chest, then he told the two onlookers to hold their crew mate down, they used a handrail and stood on the far side holding their crewmate. Daydan took the man's hand firmly in his own hands, he took the dagger from the sailor's waist and put the crudely made wooden handle in the sailor's mouth motioning for him to bit down on it. Slowly and gently but with steady force he pulled and twisted the arm towards himself, there was steady resistance and then a moment when the ball joint nudged itself back into the socket of the sailor's shoulder.

There was a sudden look of relief on the face of the sailor, the four men stood in silence for a moment and the man's shirt was handed back to him as his dagger fell from his mouth and onto the floor next to them. A broad smile showing a row of large white teeth emerged across the man's face, he slowly rotated and manoeuvred his arm grinning happily and nodding to the ship's new surgeon. Daydan stooped down and picked up his knife handing it back to him. 'Go steady with the arm, there could be damage to muscle and tendons, we will not know right away. Just go steady.' The sailor nodded, it was unlikely that he would be able to, 'go steady,' he was a sailor at sea after all. He moved over to one side and made for the rigging climbing up a rope ladder and up to the top of the first sail and then began climbing the ropes higher up into the sails of the ship, all he could do was watch the man's agility as he moved skilfully through the rigging. There was hardly any indication at all that he, only moments before dislocated his shoulder.

The crew were all busy as they made ready for the open sea, one sailor lowered his blackened trunk to the deck, one third of the trunk had been blown away in the explosion, much of the contents had been blackened or fallen into the sea. Luckily the blast only appeared to have marked most of the contents and not damaged them, a few homemade candles and blocks of soap slid and rolled along the deck of the ship, a pair of long under garments hung over a rail near the edge of the ships rigging and was quickly tossed overboard. Hardly useful now with the ass scorched out. The plopping sounds from the Thames must have been his microscope and telescope, two of his most prized possessions making their way to the bottom of the old river, maybe a few of his carpentry tools too.

The docks were by now way off in the distance, well out of range of any muskets, Daydan frowned at his unfortunate turn of bad luck, just as things seemed to be going so well. He looked around at the hard-working disciplined crew. Already he seemed to have made a reputation for himself as the two sailors who assisted him with the shoulder dislocation pointed him out to some of their crew mates. He ignored the suspicious attention from the crew and looked for the ship's captain. Something wasn't right, he just felt it, but no matter how much he investigated the scene upon the ship, he just couldn't get that feeling out of his head, he remained silent and watched carefully. As he observed the crew, a young man approached, a lieutenant from his uniform, when his head turned to greet him, he saw a face that looked familiar. 'Ah-ha, we are in good hands men, the ships surgeon has a good heart. And hopefully a fast saw arm.' The young lieutenant laughed. Daydan looked more closely to the lieutenant and tilted his head slightly. He pointed his index finger but said nothing. It was the young man with the blue eyes from the stocks a few days earlier, he grinned and smiled nodding his head. 'Good to see you again, this time in much happier circumstances sir.' He held out his hand in greeting. 'Likewise.' Holding his hand and clasping his left hand over his right hand. 'Welcome aboard sir.' His voice lowered and a small smile broke out. 'I am lieutenant Rothschild, and this ship is the Jane.' He paused and his smile grew broader, 'for now.'

The young lieutenant smiled and stepped away putting his hands behind his back and looked out over the lower deck watching the sailors hard at work as they skilfully put out to sea during the bad weather. 'Come along lads, lets be to sea and to some adventure.'

'*AYE AYE, sir.*' A crewman bellowed. 'C'mon boys.' The ship was a hive of activity, one of the sailors started to sing and some of the others joined in, just as a loud crack of thunder hit the air and a flash of lightning streaked across the night sky. The ship began to move faster and faster cutting a neat line through the Thames. The ships new barber and surgeon familiarised himself with the deck of the ship, he watched the crew working in the rain as the storm seemed to hit them relentlessly, but they didn't seem to care about the rain. Before long the tall ship eased its way down the Thames towards the open sea. Within hours it was heading out past Southend and around through the English Channel to the vast Atlantic Ocean. Even though the skies were opening up and the rain and thunder was crashing around the crew, they were in really high spirits, it was like they were going home and just couldn't wait to get there. On an ocean-going ship, he certainly felt rather out of his depth. He never saw sailors so fearless and excited to be going to sea.

The ship rolled violently up and down, yet it seemed to skip effortlessly across the water. Once the ship was well underway and heading through the channel two sailors hauled what was left of his trunk up to the upper deck for him, one of them pointed to a door leading into the main part of the rear, where the captains and officers' quarters was located. 'This way sir. You may as well rest, this storm ain't letting up till a while.' The ship tossed and bucked in the rough sea, but the Jane was a fine ship, built for ocean going voyages, it cut easily through the storm. The Royal Navy Flag fluttered overhead and at the rear, the large sails filled with a strong powerful wind and he felt a huge sense of relief that he was leaving England. It felt like he was being released from a prison sentence, and no matter what, he was never going back there again.

He tried to salvage what he could from his battered trunk. Trying to think positively he pondered his new situation. When one of the officers showed him to his small cabin next door to the captain's quarters. For such a ship of the Royal Navy, there were usually more crew, not to mention more officers, to ensure that the men were kept in line. There were also no marines onboard. Something wasn't right, which made him even more uneasy. Cargo wise it was a very well stocked ship, but the crew, putting to sea undermanned was surely dangerous. He listened at the captain's door overhearing voices as two officers talked on the other side. 'So, after Dartmouth, what then.' He heard the young lieutenant respond. 'Then my dear man, we are lost at sea.' Realising that he was actually eves dropping, he moved to where his trunk lay, checking the contents of what few things were still there. He put his short top hat down and took off his heavy coat and placed his cane upon the small cabin bed and sat down next to it. He placed the saddle bags next to him and stared at what few possessions he had left. His heart pounded as he thought about the papers he was given; he checked his saddlebags for the certificates that were still tied very securely into some pig skin. They were rolled up and tied with a long leather strip. He tried to figure out in his head what was going on, was this a trap, had his enemies finally caught up with him and completely outsmarted him. He scratched his head and resigned himself to the idea, that whatever his fate was to be, he would at least be well rested. Daydan let out a long yawn and lay back on the cabin bed and pulled a blanket over himself and used his heavy coat over the top like a blanket for some extra warmth. The smart ship tossed up and down and from side to side, he tried to sleep amidst the violent movements of the ship and the noise of the creaking vessel, the thunder, and the men singing overhead. He wasn't used to the seas motion and a couple of times got up for a sip of water, that for the time being seemed to ease his impending sea sickness. The ship creaked endlessly, at times it felt like it would smash apart, but it didn't, it seemed to handle the storm with relative ease, as did the sailors.

He must have slept for some time. When he awoke, it was dark, and his slumber was shattered as he was thrown out of bed and onto the floor from a side hitting wave. The ship easily handled the manoeuvre and righted itself very quickly as it rocked to and fro. He put on his heavy coat and left his hat and cane on the bed, pulling his coat tightly around himself, he went up on to the main deck to see what was happening. Once on the upper deck he could see land, but it was no longer Devon or Cornwall, they were far behind them. He walked up to the young lieutenant standing next to the Captain and pointed to the land in the distance. 'The coast of Ireland.' The Captain nodded to him as the ship tossed and turned in the heavy rain and rough seas. The fog on the sea was intense yet the ship and its crew masterfully cut a line through just south of the southern coast of Ireland, and out towards the open Atlantic. The rain lashed the crew and the ship, but they still seemed to be indifferent about the conditions, indeed they still seemed excited and in very high spirits. 'Overboard lads, you know what to do, let us be quick about it.' Some of the sailors unlashed some canvas sail from some piles of cargo on the deck, they began tossing it overboard, damaged planks of wood, sail, rotten food, bits of rope and broken barrels, even the carved name plaque of the ship. HMS JANE, and a large Royal Navy Flag. Now, all behind the ship was a trail of debris, rubbish floating on the rough sea in the middle of a storm. By the morning it would all likely end up somewhere on the southern shores of Ireland, should the storm allow. 'Gentlemen. Hoist the honourable colours.' A whoop of cheers erupted from the crew. 'Hoo-rah.' He watched as the Royal Navy Colours were cut from the ship and dropped into the sea along with all of the other debris, then the colours of the Honourable East India Company were unfurled and raised. Enthusiastic cheers rang out from the crew as they congratulated each other. Their suspicious passenger scratched his head. Daydan still watched carefully trying to put everything together as he saw the Captain and his lieutenants shake hands and laugh. Daydan went to his cabin and stared at his smashed trunk and left some of the personal items within, the few pieces of clothing, a couple of his favourite books, research notes. Nothing of any use or value that would be of benefit to his travels to the new world. Anything that was not of use he left in the broken trunk and carried it all up onto the upper deck. Once on deck he tossed his broken trunk over the side with his unwanted items going over the side along with the other debris. Some of the crew watched him smiling to themselves. The storm raged on and the ship bobbed violently heading for even rougher seas, yet the crew sang on. Even with the ferocity of the storm the fine ship seemed to dance over the waves as if it was mocking the storm. The captain approached Daydan with his lieutenants holding the hilt of his sword and tossing his captains hat and wig overboard. His lieutenants laughed and looked to their confused ships surgeon. 'So. You are the mystery Thirteenth shareholder sir, are you not.' The young lieutenant Rothschild announced as he stroked his chin. Daydan nodded still very confused. 'I guess so.' The Captain put his hand on his new ships Surgeons shoulder. 'Worry not, the Jane is lost at sea this night, all part of the plan, insurance don't you know. This is the Mary May. Merchantman of the Honourable East India Company. 'It is my ship. A captured vessel from the Spanish. On paper.' He smiled and tapped his large nose. 'All will come clear my friend, all will come clear.'

Now he was even more confused, not as too what just happened, but more as to what was to happen. It was as if the whole voyage had been planned, if it had been planned, what was the purpose, he was no longer just a working passenger as the ship's surgeon. Now he was a key member in an elaborate fraud, a fraud so elaborate it was perfect. He disappeared so completely, any and all records of him leaving London had ceased with the sinking of the Jane and the loss of all hands. He walked up to the foredeck of the ship and watched it crash into the sea, up and down, no matter how hard the storm hit the vessel she sailed onwards. It was indeed a beautiful ship, crewed by hardened sailors who knew their posts well. As he stood hunched into his heavy coat watching the sea crash on the bow and the ship toss and buck its way ahead. The lightning and storm raged on, the thunder roared, and the lightning cracked and flashed through the night sky as the rain lashed the ship relentlessly. Easily onwards the beautiful fast ship sailed on through the crashing waves and wild relentless sea. England was far behind now, still the storm raged all around them, yet for the first time in many years he felt a sense of peace. The future was unknown, chaotic, but it would never be the same as before, there would be no more lectures, no more trying to change the pace of evolution. If man was going to struggle and continue to crawl its way out of that primal soup, as they did millions of years ago when life first began, then let mankind move at its own slow crawl. No matter what, he would ensure that his children would be more wisely schooled, his ideas and beliefs he would keep to himself, he was utterly determined never to have to flee from any place like that ever again.

Chapter Sixteen

Nothing is as it seems

He stood alone and stared upwards as a hand gripped his shoulder and turned him slightly. 'The Captain requests your audience sir.' He turned to the young lieutenant and nodded politely. Looking up to the stars briefly, Daydan followed the young lieutenant. Nothing was said as he walked behind the young man, he carried himself as always like a gentleman should, tall and upright. Even now, the uncertainty gnawed at his imagination, when faced with impending danger, and this moment felt dangerous yet not final, he prepared himself for whatever was to come. When they arrived at the door to the officer's quarters the young lieutenant opened it for him ensuring that Daydan went through first and he followed. He then pointed the way through to the captain's quarters, straight ahead. He had no idea what to expect, everything seemed to be pre-planned and it made him feel very uneasy, but he tried his very best not to let his trepidation's show. He stood up smartly with his hand touching his pocket where he kept his razor, knowing that he had his dagger tucked in the top of his boot, if he was going to have to fight for his life, he would go down well.

The old Captain was sat at his table and when the two men entered, he stood up to greet him. Two other officers were sat around the table with a third man whom he had not seen before. Daydan nodded to each man politely and approached the large table scattered with charts, maps, tables and scrolls. From the maps he could see and recognise the coastline of the Eastern America's, the Caribbean and the Gulf of Mexico. There were also several leather-bound purses that he expected to contain coins. The Captain drew out a dagger and threw it on to the table where it rattled and vibrated sticking directly into one of the maps near the coast of the America's. He looked to Daydan and frowned. 'We have a proposition for you my friend.' The captain spoke in a forceful tone. Daydan was not really in a position to discuss business, so the abrupt attitude of the Captain seemed rather brash and aggressive, he was unarmed to a degree and outnumbered as well as surrounded. He looked around trying to think of an escape plan. He slowly clenched his hands into fists, feeling the energy around him pulse and enter his body. The only logical escape was to take a run and try to dive through the very small window behind the captain. But that would land him miles from anywhere in stormy seas. The Captain stroked his chin thoughtfully, he then leaned forward onto the table looking deeply into his surgeons' eyes. 'Somehow, you have stumbled into a very unique position my friend, either by chance or by plan,' He paused looking deeply into Daydan's eyes trying to study him. 'Either way, you are here, and therefore we must proceed lawfully it would seem.' Daydan had little faith in the law, he had even less faith in businessmen, he sniffed the air slightly in defiance. The captain looked around to the other gentleman assembled and then back to his newly appointed ships surgeon. 'We would like to buy your share of the company, now, here. Would you agree, you can go to the America's as a rich man sir, a very rich man indeed. Start a new life. And want for nothing.' He looked towards the captain and folded his arms across his chest, then looked around to the other assembled officers. 'And the alternative.' The captain removed his hat and wig and scratched his bald head, giving each of the men assembled a look. He turned to Daydan once more and pointed a forefinger to him. 'Hardship, doubt, challenge, hard work, excitement, adventure, mystery.'

For some reason he found considerable comfort in those words, hardship he could handle, in fact he quite enjoyed a challenge, had his entire life not been one of the same. Wealth, luxury, none of these things played a great role in his life thus far, none of them held any appeal. He spent his entire life running, learning, studying, researching, hours in dusty long forgotten corners of libraries, trying to find the secrets of life and death, of creation itself. Secrets that he believed revealed themselves under the strangest of circumstances. He looked up to the captain holding him in his eyes without blinking. 'Sounds exciting, what are you offering.' The captain smiled and rubbed his head, behind him the young officers released their holds on hidden daggers under their tunics and stood more easily. Was he being tested. He looked to the young Rothschild and scanned his face. He looked coldly back to him and then smiled. 'Sit gentlemen, sit, let us drink and talk.' The captain mumbled softly. As the captain sat down, he pulled a smart crystal decanter from a fancy mahogany cabinet and placed a number of glasses on the table for each of his guests, then he slowly poured equal measures of rum into each glass. Daydan could smell the sweet rich scent of the rum from the other side of the table and smiled. He pulled out one of the chairs and sat down looking to each of the other men assembled. The Captain raised his glass and made a toast. 'Honour gentlemen, and the company.' The other men raised their glasses and repeated the toast, Daydan too raised his glass in salute and backed the glass of rum in one gulp, he turned to the Captain and reached down to his boots with both hands pulling up his ornate ivory handled stiletto dagger, he placed it on the table in front of him and laughed. 'I think perhaps it is time we all come clean.' He said looking to the Captain. 'There is a plan afoot correct, and I am an unwitting party, a party that is interested in this venture of yours. Very interested indeed.' The captain laughed, he was clearly a man not to be underestimated, but somehow, he had been thrust into this strange world of mystery, and he clearly had skills that would come in very useful. The old captain began to stroke his lips with his forefinger.

'Perhaps you are aware of your history my friend, and maybe you are not. Through out time great powerful kingdoms have risen and fallen, Empires, Dynasties, this is not by chance sir, this is by design, with each rise and fall of a civilisation, power and wealth is simply relocated, always on the move, always invisible. Always in control.' Daydan huffed a small tone of agreement through his nose and continued to listen. The captain poured some more rum into each glass only this time he filled the glasses to the very top and overflowing using a second decanter to complete the refills.

He thought hard about what the captain had implied, in his travels as a young boy, his father told him of great civilisations that had been destroyed and the knowledge they possessed, some great sciences lost forever. Man was being shaped already without knowing it, shaped into a kind of slavery, an ignorance, knowledge was being kept secret, discoveries left to the libraries and colleges of those fortunate enough to have access. It all started to make sense, his own struggle to enlighten and awaken was at odds with the Company, surely, they knew this, or did they. Did they see him as a threat, or did they simply see him as a private enterprise that just got lucky, or did they see him as an ally, someone with a knowledge that could be manipulated to their own ends. He was beginning to think over everything that had happened in London recently, had it all been chance, had those tormented souls he had set free been all part of a greater plan. Was he simply a pawn in a huge game or was he truly a master. It felt that on this magnificent yet small vessel in an immense storm that could at any time sink this ship with all hands in a heartbeat, he felt suddenly very small and insignificant. He looked to the captain who took a sip of his rum and leaned back in his chair as if he didn't have a single care in the world. Who were these men, why the elaborate cover up. 'It is time to build a new empire gentleman, you are its architects and champions, the America's, new, unspoiled, full of opportunities, in two hundred years that place, as raw and savage as it is now will be the most powerful empire on earth. And you will all be rich beyond your wildest dreams.' He was not one to be excited or blackmailed by wealth or power. The desire for wealth meant nothing to him, but the idea of adventure, knowledge, learning more about life, that was something he found difficult to resist. The opportunity to learn more held a fascination that he could never turn down, it was indeed a most cruel weakness.

The gentlemen around the table laughed, not only the older man but the young lieutenants too, one of them swallowed the entire contents of his glass and slapped it down on the table hard. 'In two hundred years we will all be long dead, what is the point.' The other assembled gentlemen laughed and agreed with the younger man and looked to the captain for reassurance. The Captain stood up sharply and leaned across the table. 'That maybe so gentlemen, but Rome was not built in a day, and your ancestors, your children and your children's children can carry on your work, and he.' The Captain pointed an accusing finger to Daydan with an extended arm that could only be directed to one person. 'He will be there to see it.' For a moment there was utter silence, then a little titter of laughter, then a little more laughter. The Captains expression never changed, he stood by his statement, he seemed so adamant and sure of his accusation that the other men's laughter turned to stares of disbelief. Daydan slowly stood up and raised his glass, he carefully took a small sip of the rum from the edge of the glass and held it up giving a warm friendly smile to the men around him, he sipped again from the glass of rum. Looking over the top of the glass, he grinned.

'I will certainly do my best. Of that gentleman, you can be sure.' As the newcomer in the room, he felt like he was rather naïve about the company and what was happening exactly. The Captain however seemed to have a very good idea of what was going on, he explained to him about the trade routes far off in the east, the orient, the silk trade and opium trade. Tea and exotic animal skins from India, precious stones, gold and ivory from Africa. Trade was key, it generated wealth, and wealth generated opportunity. For the wise businessman opportunity brought with it, other rewards. Daydan's views of wealth and class were at odds with the company. He sat and listened to the captain for hours that night, they all did, and as they exchanged stories of adventure and the captain told of the thirteen shareholders, the thirteen stripes on the company flag. The thirteen shareholders who owned the largest portions of the company, all thirteen had shares in excess of one percent, he remembered his small share on the documents, odd that it was so prized. But quite humble that the company made such a big thing of his share. He questioned the captain one time asking jokingly. 'If each stripe on the company flag represents one of the major stake holders, which stripe belongs to me.' The captain coughed roughly and slapped him upon his back laughing. 'Why, the bottom stripe of course.' He thought no more about the lowly position he held, but it gave him a sense of purpose, a new idea for a future in a new world, a new beginning. As the night continued, the rum slowly got drank, and the tones of their voices got louder, his smile grew broader.

The sound of laughter escalated to the early hours that night as the men drank and talked of the future, their plans and their ideas for fortune, to build a new world, to learn from the mistakes of the past and make this one better than any that had come before. The tall ship dipped up and down over the waves as it sailed on its long journey ending finally in the America's, the lamp light of the captain's cabin stayed on all night and well into the next morning and long after the sunrise. By the time the men retired to their bunks, the storm of the day before and the rough seas had calmed considerably, the wind was good and favourable for their short stop in the canaries. Just enough time for some more cargo and fresh supplies before they were to travel to the America's.

Chapter Seventeen
Ship of ghosts

The last couple of days after leaving the southern coast of Ireland the ship sailed out to sea on a west south westerly course, the sea was rough, but after the stormy night, the following day the storm had thankfully faded. Not that the crew's spirits seemed to change at all. They worked hard through the night changing crews for rest sleep and food. The next day with strong winds and rolling seas they worked tirelessly tending to the ship. Daydan had never seen so many men committed to their work before, their skill as sailors was a joy to watch, up and down rigging, tending to the ropes, repairing any equipment that needed tending too. The next day he spent rather allot of time in his cabin looking over the few possessions he managed to save from his travel trunk. The few clothes and some of his carpentry tools, everything else was either damaged or destroyed or lost in the Thames when his chest exploded, luckily the damage to his things that he was able to salvage was minimal. A fortunate error on his part with incorrectly mixing his ingredients for making the gunpowder, or perhaps his ingredients were not of a good enough quality. On the small cabin bed, he lay out a cleanish shirt, some undergarments, a mallet, chisel, a hammer head, a hand saw, a draw knife, a plane and an old wet stone for sharpening knives and blades. Not much at all, in his saddlebags he had his change of clothes, shirt, pants. His certificates of ownership were still securely tied in their pigskin leather bundle and tied with a long piece of leather. Inside the centre of the bundle was a small sharp knife. The saddle bags also contained some flints for lighting fires if needed. A pair of stones that he carried for as long as he could remember. Not much of a collection for one wanting to start a new life in some far-off land. The sum of his entire worldly possessions. Most of what was damaged in the explosion, some old useless scrolls of his fathers and badly damaged clothing was tossed overboard with his broken trunk, when they steered away from Ireland. What possessions he managed to recover he repacked into his saddle bags and old sack he managed to scavenge from the ship's stores. The ship still dipped and bobbed in the sea, but much more gently now. The creaking of the ship at first especially in the storm made him feel uneasy, like it would break and crack in two at any moment, but in time the strange noises were rather therapeutic, and the ship had a strange eerie rhythm to it. He pushed open his cabin door to the small corridor where the four rooms led off from each corner of the corridor, all for the officers of the ship. He heard the Captains voice mumbling softly and proceeded to his door and knocked politely not wanting to forget some gentlemanly etiquette even if they were on board a sailing ship under the flag of the company. Oddly, only days before having changed its signage from a Royal Navy ship to a privateer's merchant ship under the crown. 'Yes.' Daydan pushed on the Captains door, it partly opened but caught the floor, the door was obviously in need of maintenance, so he leaned a shoulder against it giving it a forceful nudge, the small door gave against his weight and opened easily. When he entered the Captain's cabin his eyes were drawn to the captain and the young lieutenant looking at the charts that were sprawled out across his desk. 'Quite an adventure my boy, mapping the America's, do you have funding.' The young lieutenant turned and acknowledged their visitor and turned back to the captain's charts. 'I do sir, the navy has an interest in the maps, and so does the company.' He smiled to the captain and began to roll up one of the charts. 'I shall have a good career, adventuring and exploring.' He stepped away allowing the Captain to see their guest. 'My apologies gentlemen.' Daydan spoke clearly as he entered looking like a man who just overheard a conversation that he was not privy to. The young lieutenant Rothschild walked around him, and opened the door moving easily past him. Smiling, looking directly into Daydan's eyes. The young man exited the Captain's cabin and closed the squeaking door behind himself giving it a forceful yank as it clipped the floor. He remained facing the exit as the old Captain stood up and arched his back stretching himself and then laughed a little under his breath. 'Everyman has vices, a weakness, some of us have many.' The old Captain laughed. He heard him pull out a chair hearing it squeak along the floor. What exactly did the captain mean by that, Daydan frowned slightly, he must have missed something. 'Come and sit. I would like very much to know more about our newest asset, our mysterious thirteenth shareholder.' The old captain cleared his throat and rested his elbows on his desk watching his newest crew member carefully. Daydan turned slowly having given the man more than enough time to be ready for a guest. He moved toward the Captain and sat across from him, sitting in a chair not as grand as the captains, but a nice chair all the same. The old man stood for a moment and pointed to some charts on his table and looked over them carefully and then back to his guest The captain was clearly a very fine sailor and navigator, from the calculations on his map and the knowledge he showed as he spoke. He felt the ship was in very good hands indeed. There was a sextant on the desk, an instrument that he read about in journals, but this was the first time he ever saw one, he looked toward the captain rather intrigued. 'Sir, I did wish to ask if I could explore your ship, maybe make use of myself, help with repairs, learn some of the skills of the crew, I could perhaps cook. It will after all be a long journey to the America's correct.' The captain sat at his table and took a chunk of rather stale bread and picked up a knife cutting a piece of cheese from a block on his table and took a bite. 'Life at sea is not for everyone my friend, it is hard, food is scarce and rationed, as is the water. We wash with sea water if at all, it is not ideal, fresh water is far to valuable to waste. As for cooking, little food is cooked. Fires onboard are unlucky and require fuel.' The captain paused for a moment while eating and then spoke again unashamed of his ungentlemanly eating habits. 'Of course, you are free to roam as you wish. Assist if you can, the crew will oblige you. And be grateful, just don't be a nuisance.' He nodded and smiled to the captain a little relieved that he would not be stuck in his cabin for the entire journey. 'I should like to first thank you by fixing your door.' He smiled to the captain and pointed to his cabin door. The old man laughed and tore the remaining chunk of stale bread in half and offered the other half to his guest. 'I have grown rather use to that doors stubborn character, I shall miss it, but if you wish. It is our flaws that give us character, and this beautiful young lady has much character believe me.' He shook his head to the offer of the stale bread and stood up to observe the captain's charts. The captain watched him with interest and moved closer pointing out their intended route to the America's. Using a drafting compass to indicate their estimated travel across the map. He rolled it skilfully with his wrist along their intended course, pointing with his other hand. . 'We are here, south westerly of Ireland, we will travel for the rest of the day out to sea, and then south, south east, just out of view of the Portuguese coast. Then we make a heading for Canneries, our aim is to make land before we get spotted by another vessel while out at sea, if we can do that, our logbooks will be perfect, and our disappearances as the Jane will be complete. We will pick up fresh supplies in the canaries and maybe buy and sell a few tonnes of cargo. Whatever the situation, from then we are a merchant ship flying the colours of the company.' He nodded to the captain and watched and listened intently as he continued. The captain smiled slightly seeing that his guest was captivated by his explanation and enjoyed showing off his navigational skills.

'Then we cut across west north west and hope to spot land in the Virgin Islands. From there we will offload some more cargo, resupply and maybe trade some more cargo. From the Islands, we have an easy journey on to the America's, it is this crossing where the monsters be.' The captain laughed slapping down his outstretched hand onto the vast Atlantic Ocean. Daydan frowned slightly. 'Monsters.' The captain laughed showing a mouth full of bread and cheese and a row of not so healthy teeth. 'An old seaman's joke boy. Here there be monsters.' The captain's eyes then turned to a look of an unemotional blank stare. 'The sea has no master, but she is a cruel mistress.' The old man sat down and ate his mouth full of stale bread and cheese swallowing it down this time before speaking again. 'You have been a seaman long sir.' He asked trying to break the uneasy silence. The captain took a cloth and wiped his mouth like a gentleman after a meal and began to twirl a large silver ring on his hand, set with a polished but uncut ruby. 'Over fifty years at sea, I have seen many things, horrible things, and done horrible things too. After my education I was sent to navy school in Portsmouth and served on my first ship as an officer before my 16th year. I had my first ship at 22years, quite a feat. I was in the royal fleet most of my life and made admiral.' He smiled. 'Can you believe that of an old decrepit fool like me.' Daydan shook his head. 'I had no idea you were an admiral sir.' The old man leaned back and let out a long sigh. 'Not anymore, I still have much influence in the navy, but now, my interests are in the company, so I do what must be done, and I enjoy it, these old sea legs are not good on land, I do not desire to live my life any other way than how I live it now. When I die my bones belong to the sea, and my soul to the wind and the rain.' He huffed gently and looked patiently towards his newest crew member. 'So, tell me, how did you acquire your fortune.' Clearing his throat uneasily. 'You know, we have been waiting a very long time to meet you, a very very long time.' He chuckled softly to himself. Daydan watched the old admiral carefully, he felt like he was being a little deceitful, not wanting to give away too much about how he acquired his share. Whether it was fortunate or not, already the old woman's prediction of them being a curse seemed to be starting to come true. Things certainly felt like things were proceeding without his knowledge, understanding, or control. 'I was given them.' He cleared his throat noisily. 'As compensation.' The old man raised an eyebrow frowning slightly. 'Compensation. indeed, when might I ask.' He looked to the old man studying his face, there were questions behind his eyes obviously, but so it seemed were answers. The old captain knew something. He folded his arms across his chest and looked the old admiral squarely in the eyes. 'Recently, within the week actually.' The old admiral stroked his stubbled chin and grinned. 'From whom did you acquire them.' Daydan remained silent, he let out a long breath and started to prod at his boot thinking of a possible subject to try and change the conversation to. 'A woman.' The admiral sat back and made himself comfortable interlacing his fingers and started tapping his lips with his forefingers very slowly. 'The duchess.' Daydan stared at him for a long time before speaking. The silence was broken finally with a single hand rubbing the old man's eyes slowly. 'Mary. Mary Atwood, the Duchess.' Daydan shifted uneasily on his chair, how could that be, she lived in a nice house, but it was a house, not a huge manor on a vast estate. 'Atwood sir, yes.' The old man grinned. 'She is a very smart woman, and a very shrewd businesswoman of incredible ability, her family name she can trace back to before the crucifixion, how many families can boast that my friend.' Daydan shook his head, his mind was spinning with questions, what the hell was going on, why did he always feel that he was no longer in control of his life anymore. 'Her name is not Atwood, that is the name of her husband, her name is,' The old man frowned. 'I cannot even pronounce her name, did you read your certificates thoroughly sir.' He nodded back to the old man. 'Yes, very.' The old man turned to him with a thoughtful look in his eyes. 'A mystery, I suggest you read through them very carefully my friend, she is no fool.' Daydan stood up and nodded to the old admiral as he made for the door, before he could open the door the old man spoke softly almost in a whisper. 'Argyll. Her true name is Argyll.' He stopped in the doorway but did not turn to face the old man, he paused for some time thinking of questions to ask, but something inside of him stopped him from saying another word. He opened the door and pulled it towards himself as he stepped out into the small corridor adjoining the other cabins and then closed the Captains door behind himself. He quietly and thoughtfully went back into his own cabin, closing the door to his cabin behind himself he went over to his saddlebags and pulled out the papers wrapped in pigskin and untied the leather cord that bound the documents safely together. He sat on his cabin bed and lay out the papers in front of himself and began to read every single word, over and over again. As he remembered, nothing was amiss, everything was as it should be, the contract, the transfer, the signatures. He looked at the date next to the signatures, he suddenly grabbed the other documents, the dates were wrong, he poured over them scratching his head. The date of the transfer was some forty-five years ago, forty-five years to the day, he sat on the cabin bed and stared at the pages. A date he had never celebrated ever in his life, the day he was born. He looked over the documents again and again and the same conclusion came to his mind. It could not be a coincidence; the odds were to great. He sat back on his bed and lay himself down. Closing his eyes his thoughts wondered wildly over the discovery he just made, the old sea captain knew something, but what was clear to Daydan, the old man could not possibly know. The captain obviously knew allot more than he was letting on. He closed his eyes and slowly began to drift off into a restless head spinning sleep. The ships bell clanged over head as the ship rolled upon the sea, he could hear the ships sails flapping in the wind sometimes out of the small open window in his cabin. The eerie rhythmic creak of the ship. He breathed softly and opened his eyes; his cabin was dark. He watched the stars through his small window bobbing up and down with the ship's movements, he closed his eyes and lay back on his pillow. Then he saw the lights, the tiny specs of light he so fondly associated with his friends. He smiled and waited for a moment, but rather than it being the form of the slave, a form he had not been expecting slowly appeared before him as he lay on his bed. Marys form became clearer and he could see her smile, she straddled him and began to untie the upper part of her dress. Her smile was so pure, her eyes so clear and blue, even in this dim light. His hand stroked her cheek as she sat upon him, she took his hand in hers moving it to her lips and letting it touch her mouth. 'Mary.' He said softly to her as his fingers caressed her mouth tenderly. She looked into his eyes and lowered her face to his slowly, with their lips almost touching she looked deeply into his eyes. 'There is no shame in our love my lord, none at all, fear not, all will come clear. You are far more than their company, far more than a name, I will come to you, I promise.' Mary leaned fully upon him in a passionate kiss. She felt so good, her lips, the weight of her body on his, the gentle hum she made as she kissed him. He blinked and closed his eyes more tightly and then opened them. He sat up suddenly, she was gone, just like that. Did he just dream what just happened. Was that his imagination, did Mary come back to him. He stared around the room looking for something, a sign, her light, after a moment he lay back on his cabin bed again and looked up out of the small window to the few stars he could see. He felt lost somehow, confused. He lay back and put his hands behind his head and closed his eyes desperate for sleep to calm his mind and give him some rest from his chaotic irrational thoughts.

Chapter Eighteen

The Canaries

The next morning, he woke on his own, no one interrupted his slumber. When he opened his eyes, the daylight poured in through the only window in his cabin, he stood up still dressed in his clothes from the day before, pants, shirt and his boots. He stretched himself out and looked at his carpentry tools still laid out on his bed next to his saddlebags. His boot knife was still tucked into the top of his boot to one side, very visible without his long heavy coat on. Daydan judged that such a show would not be out of place on this ship somehow. Letting out a final yawn he made his way up onto the main deck and stood at a rail looking out to the open sea, he breathed in deeply and smiled as the cold wind pushed on his chest and lungs, but it felt so good, the clean salty air and the wind in his hair, he closed his eyes and let the sea spray and wind caress his face.

'Do not let her seduce you my boy.' The captain's voice rang out across the ship from the stern quarter deck, the best part of the ship to view his entire vessel from. He didn't look at the captain immediately, for a short time, he just enjoyed the wind and weather on his face as if he was all alone. After a few moments of peaceful bliss, he looked up to the captain and smiled. 'We all have our vices sir.' He laughed at the captain who nodded and laughed back. He beckoned for him to join him on the quarter deck and pointed to a spot at his side. He nodded and walked past some of the hard at work crew members and up a small but nicely carved vertical flight of steps. Once up he stood near the Captain who was close to the wheel man steering the ship. He watched the old captain as he pointed out some of his crew members and explained a little about each man's role. The old captain was very proud of his crew, and even more proud of his ship. The crew all looked happy at their work even with an Irishman shouting orders almost continuously. The crew obviously really did not need to be told anything, ropes were coiled, sail either catching the wind or lashed, the deck was clean and free from clutter. As he looked more closely at the crew, he noticed that many were foreigners, more than half, all nationalities and all creeds, it was interesting watching them work together with little more than a look or nod. The old captain kept looking upwards to the slim dark-skinned man at the highest point on the ship, the crows' nest. This spot was not a large nest like on the warships, this was small, just enough room for one man, and that was a squeeze. The brown-skinned Sailor pointed to the horizon and signalled to the captain who then gave orders to his wheelman adjusting their course and turning the ship out to sea slightly. The captain turned to his guest and smiled.

'He was a slave I think, on a ship we.' He paused. 'Acquired.' Without waiting for the captain to finish he noticed that there were a few of his crew that were dark skinned, there was even an Asian crewman, Chinese from the top knot upon his head that trailed down behind him carefully platted and groomed. An Arab, a Turk and Portuguese, it was quite a spectacle, quite a collection of nationalities and languages. He turned to the captain and smiled putting his hands on his hips as he watched the men hard at work.

'They look like they could handle anything the sea could throw at them.' The captain nodded. 'And then some.' The captain nodded politely. 'Each man is easily able to do the work of at least two men. Without exception.' That day on the deck of the ship was one of discovery, as the men worked, he assisted where he could. Learning from the crew how they wanted the ropes coiled or tied ready for re-use, lashing down cargo, the sail and the supplies on the deck, nothing was left to chance. Later that day he repaired the captain's door plaining a small portion from the bottom edge. Much to the appreciation of the captain and his officers. He learned that the Chinese man was the sail maker, prior to that a tailor, how he came to the ship was unclear and he did not ask to many questions about anyone but knowing something about each of the crew was rather reassuring. The Chinese man spent most of his time making or repairing sail and items of clothing for the crew, he could do some quite extraordinary things with some material, needle and thread and a sharp knife. He soon settled into life onboard ship and wherever he worked to help out he watched the crew carefully, by the end of their journey he hoped to be a passable sailor. In the evenings, if the weather was calm enough some of the crew would gather on deck and sing songs and play music. Some had instruments that he had never seen before. A Scottish sailor played a fiddle, another a flute, one Spaniard played a Vihuela, some would bang along on a barrel or piece of wood or tap iron rods together. The nights were long and sometimes they would exchange stories and adventures from far off lands. With a crew of such diverse origins and so many different cultures and languages, it was interesting to see how well everyone cooperated with each other and respected each other, for the most part. Minor scuffles broke out sometimes, often a misunderstanding of some kind, but they were quickly tamed by the Irish master shipman, who seemed to do little in the way of work other than yell at the crew. He observed the crew's manner closely, the Chinese man bowed to people constantly and had a fixed smile upon his face. The Arab would pray several times a day sometimes looking to the captain for an indication of an eastward direction and then drop to his knees. On occasion the Turk would join the Arab for prayers, but more often than not the Arab preyed alone.

One evening, after a scuffle had broken out due to an exchange of words the Irishman called two of the crew over to settle a dispute. Both men were told to avoid each other earlier that day. Sure enough, when the men sat to relax a little and the night watch took over, the two men stood in the centre of the deck and glared at each other. A tall thin white Englishman and a very dark skinned large muscular Moroccan faced off to each other. A bell was rung, and the two men raised their bare fists to fight out their differences. Looking at the two men the fight was pointless, the Moroccan was much larger, stronger and younger than the Englishman, at least twice his size. The smaller of the two was considerably faster however, and with each powerful swing from the North African the white man dodged him easily and moved around quickly ducking and avoiding his blows, he kicked the African in the shins many times and jabbed at his face landing a few lucky punches. Every once in a while, a powerful swing from the African glanced across the Englishman with a huge sigh of relief from the rest of the crew. If just one of the Africans blows connected the fight would surely be over, slowly, the Englishman was tiring and the Africans punches got closer and closer and much more powerful, his anger growing as the fight continued. The fight went on for a few minutes until finally the African landed a punch that sent the tall Englishman, skidding across the floor after initially being lifted into the air by the force of the blow. The African stormed over to where the Englishman lay trying to recover from the blow while holding his nose, drops of blood dripped rapidly onto the floor. The African reached down and picked the man up with one hand forcing him against the main mast of the ship. 'I am no slave Englishman.' He squeezed the white man's throat tightly. The thin man was off the ground choking trying his best to apologise. The captain fired his pistol up into the air. 'Enough.' 'Gentlemen, enough.' The African continued to squeeze the thin man's throat. The Irish shipmaster struck the African across the arms with a rigging pin and glared to him shaking his head. The man loosened his grip slightly just enough for the Englishman to splutter out an apology, 'Sorrry. Joke.' The Irishman pointed the rigging pin to the African and shook his head to him again very plainly, the large African let go his grip on the chocking Englishman and watched him fall to the floor wheezing for breath.

The African sneered through gritted teeth. 'Only a coward becomes a slave.' For a moment there was a complete silence on the ship, then, three other dark skinned sailors walked towards the African and glared to him, they showed the scars on their wrists from the manacles they had been chained to, the thin African who always seemed to be aloft dropped from high up onto the floor, landing in a crouching stance at first to break the fall, but slowly stood holding a knife in his hand, he too showed the scars of slavery on his wrists and lifted his shirt from his back to show scars from a whip, beatings and branding irons. Then the china man stood in front of the African and pulled aside his shirts tall neckline to show a large scar and mutilation around his neck from an iron collar. The five sailors stood before him defiant and clearly angry at the accusation that any slave was a coward. The Captain was still on the main aft deck watching the proceedings, he called out simply. 'Mr Cooper, if you please.' A white man Daydan only saw a few times repairing the barrels and cargo containers limped forwards, he wore one boot on his right foot, his left foot was wrapped in rags, he put his foot up on a step and untied the rags to show a foot that had been cut off at the toes. He looked at the African and lifted his eye patch showing a brand that had destroyed and cauterised his eye, then he put the patch back over the hideous wound on his face and then raised his left hand. His little finger had been cut clean off. The African turned away disgusted at the sight, he swallowed and looked to the captain. Then he nodded to the captain respectfully in silence and looked away. The captain cleared his throat and spoke again in a soft compassionate tone. 'He is not finished my friend.' The African looked at the mutilated Englishman again, looking him up and down, Mr Cooper stared back at him and dropped a tear from his one good eye, then he opened his mouth wide and let out a sound that no one had ever heard before, a sad sound like a man in agony and pain. His tongue had been cut horribly from his mouth.

The African staggered back and bowed his head turning away shamefully and put a powerful hand on Coopers shoulder. The two men eventually exchanged a look of admiration for each other that touched the hearts of everyone watching. The African turned and picked up the battered and beaten thin Englishman and brushed him off carefully. Everyone looked on between each other, it was a moment that left a mark on everyone's mind. A shared admiration for their crew mates, a comradeship that few would ever share again. Slowly the crew returned to their singing and gambling and their stories, the thin Englishman tended to his blooded nose, and the African sat next to the Cooper and the two men smiled to each other in silence shrugging their shoulders.

When Daydan looked up to the Captain he was not looking at his men, he had his hands behind his back smoking his clay pipe, looking out to sea towards the horizon, and the point where the sea touches the starlit sky. There was such a beautiful majesty about the night sky, especially at sea, it made one feel utterly insignificant, yet at the same time part of something wondrous, beyond imagination. The days were full of work and when the wind was up the crew worked hard to get every bit of speed they could from the ship, when the winds were calm, they would pass the time maintaining the ship, or themselves, but mostly he looked forwards to the evenings. The languages he could hear, the men singing, the music they played, he could understand why the crew enjoyed their lives on the open sea so much. Some of the men would gamble with dice or cups. Arguments ware settled swiftly with a bare fist fight under the orders and watchful eyes of the captain. It made some light entertainment for the crew and gave a chance for some of the more boisterous men to blow off some steam. The routine was simple, work hard, make sure the crew were far too exhausted for any mischief. Most would retire happy to their hammocks ready for sleep after a shot or two of rum, some food and a song. The Captain himself while clearly respected by the crew would sit apart, smoking his simple clay pipe and just watching out to sea, his tall flamboyant wig clearly set him apart from the other men, his clothes were no longer the dark blue or black of the Royal Navy but flamboyant colourful jackets and breeches. He was approachable and always acknowledged his crew politely when they looked to him. After a little more than two weeks, they sailed calm and rough seas, yet the ship handled even the hardest storms with little difficulty, one late morning the watchman from the lookout high above the deck yelled out.

'Captain captain, Land'o land'o.' A cheer rippled through out the ship, the captain nodded up to the crewman and looked to the direction he was pointing, the captain slightly adjusted the ships course with the wheelman. Land on the horizon was a comforting sight and the crew put in extra effort in getting as much speed out of the ship they could. Port meant some rest, a chance to receive pay and get drunk, perhaps even to find a not too fussy female companion, most of the men were anything but handsome. Although the captain was pleased for the sight of land, he often looked over the back of the ship, reliving memories, perhaps also regret. They would sometimes talk and share stories, but the old captain although a respected figurehead of his crew had something that clearly weighed heavily on his mind. Before they were seen by any other ship or the coast, the captain ordered their colours be changed as they sailed towards the coastlines of the Canary Islands. The new colours were Spanish, England was still at war with Spain and had been for some time, even though hostile engagements at this time were few and far between, pirating and privateers were encouraged by their respective governments. The captain was no slouch when it came to gain an upper hand no matter how cunning or deceptive, he had to be. The Canaries was under Spanish rule, so it made perfect sense to blend in with the local traffic rather than appearing to be an obvious outsider. After a few hours the ship dropped anchor off the coast of Tenerife and the port of Santa Cruz. Long before the war with the Spanish, these islands were popular with pirates. Many of the inhabitants transported from all over the seafaring world, but with a strong Spanish occupation and the majority of inhabitants being of Spanish Origin most attempts to overthrow rule were quashed quickly, by the very able local militia who seemed to not really care who thought was in control, the local militia ruled themselves. A Spanish military presence and navy was always present, so this rag tail ship and crew would need to act their part well. The captain wrote a note, and had it passed up to the lookout with a small purse of coins, from the very top of the ship the bare footed lightly clothed dark-skinned sailor dove fearlessly into the sea making a tall but precise high dive into the waves below. Moments later he arose some distance away from where he entered the sea, swimming towards the land. The captain along with some crew manned the rowboat that was put over the side and began to row towards land. The island had a deep-water port, suitable for the ship, yet the captain moved the ship away from the port but in full view of the vessels nearby. Daydan was unsure why this was, some kind of navy etiquette, caution on the part of the captain. He watched for a moment as the ships rowing boat moved closer and closer to the port, the dark-skinned sailor reached the docks long before the rowboat, and they watched him run along the jetty to a man who pointed further down the docks. He handed the man the tightly folded note and the purse of coins and pointed to the captain. It was not possible to hear the conversation, but the captain and the jetty master spoke and laughed together. The small number of crew stayed in the rowboat and the bare footed sailor stayed close behind the captain. Some time passed with lots of shoulder patting and laughter, the captain then pointed to the ship and the rowboat began its journey back, without the captain and his barefooted bodyguard who remained on the jetty. When the little rowboat was back onboard the ship, the crew skilfully sailed the ship slowly to the jetty under less than half sail. One of the men approached the quarter master with orders and the crew set to work. A sailor who returned walked past Daydan and smiled. 'The deal is done, twenty barrels of gunpowder, five barrels of nails and a dozen bails of wool. And one crate of muskets.' The quarter master stood close by checking his inventory and pointed to some of the crew to begin moving the cargo up onto the deck. Most of the cargo was hoisted with a wooden block and tackle onto the deck and then swung to a point where it could be easily hoisted over the side and onto the jetty.

'Looks like someone is upgrading their fortifications.' The quarter master set about marking some of the barrels and bails. The items were marked in his own way for quality and he mixed the cargos ensuring that some of the poorer quality merchandise was added in and some of the best quality merchandise was clearly marked for the captain to open up to show the purchaser if needed. He smiled at how well everyone knew their roles, the crew, the officers, everyone was efficient and skilled, he could see why the entire ship operated as it did, through mutual respect and hard work. If people could do this on a small ship, why not everywhere. This was his dream in action, this was what he was trying to achieve on land, he folded his arms across his chest standing in his shirt and began to laugh out loud, as his laughter grew the crew smiled and looked to each other and began to sing sea shanties as they worked.

The ship was tied up and the crew started to offload the traded cargo, a gangplank was lashed to the ship leading onto the jetty for easier access. It didn't take long to unload the cargo from the ship and when the cargo hold was resealed the crew waited patiently for orders. The captain looked over his ship and then to his crew gathered on the deck, he motioned to the quarter master and pointed to the ship's capstan. A cheer filled the air knowing what was to come. 'Twelve hours shore leave gentlemen, we sail with the morning tide.' He nodded to the quarter master. 'Give them their pay. They've earned it.' Another enthusiastic cheer rang out. 'Hoorah.' The crew roared a cheer to the captain and pushed their way to the Capstan, eventually forming a line, the quartermaster handed each man some coins. Two shillings per man, without exception. Each of the crew when paid made for their closest friends and moved ashore in their small groups to enjoy their brief but well-deserved shore leave. The large half naked African watched the Cooper sitting alone working on some empty crates and barrels putting some pitch and sacking cloth into the cracks, the African shoved the White man and gave him a smile indicating toward land with his head. Cooper looked away shaking his head, the African prodded him again. Cooper threw down his knife that fell into the bottom of the wooden barrel he was working on, and gave a small smile back to the larger man and nodded. Slowly, the two men walked and limped side by side, the large African put a reassuring hand onto the white man's shoulder as they both looked toward each other slowly making their way down the jetty to the busy cantina. The remaining crew set about their work, it was their watch, and later their turn would come. He watched the luckier members of the crew head to the cantina and listened to the silence on the ship, the waves gently lapping the side of the ship, the ropes slapping the mast, sail rippling gently in the wind, it was a comforting sight, and the sounds were southing even to someone as inexperienced a seaman as he was. The gentle rhythmic sounds even he was starting to feel a sense of comfort in them. He looked around the ship, a small crew remained onboard, there were a few small chores to do, but mainly they just relaxed, kept watch, took it in turn to rest. Late in the night the Captains lamp was dimmed, and the sailors were still, a lookout kept an eye on the gangplank watching for returning sailors or possible intruders. The best spot on the ship was aft, a platform over the officers' quarters that slopped slightly to the main deck down one of two flights of almost vertical steps. He stood in the rear area alone, his mind wondered to London and his small workshop, the people, the open green parks and the cramped streets with their slums and the huge opulent homes of the rich and powerful. He was a little surprised that he did not feel homesick in anyway, but then, in his short life this far, he moved locations so many times, even gypsies moved around less than he did, and certainly not as far. Leaning slightly onto a hand rail running across the back of the ship he felt a presence close by, he turned slightly and realised that it was Jin, his form slowly materialising before his eyes in the starlight, the giveaway tiny lights of energy were swirling together more and more intensely until his visible ethereal form stood at his side. His friend looked up at the stars and then back to him, his visage did not show that he was speaking, but Daydan could still hear his voice in his mind as if he were, he turned a little to face him. 'My people are close.' Daydan nodded lifting his right hand from the wooden rail and pointed into the distance Eastward. 'Yes, they are close.' He smiled softly to the large powerful man as he brandished his ebony tribal club in his hand. 'I feel them, I hear them, calling me home.' He put his hand upon the ghostly shoulder of the slave and smiled to him holding back his sadness. 'Then you should go, go home to your people and make them strong again.' The African stood up tall and puffed out his chest and smiled to him, with a polite nod he put the club into the waistline of his trousers and began to turn, then he stopped still. He took the ebony club from his waist and knelt down on one knee presenting the club in his hands to his friend. His balled head looked down to Daydan's feet, yet he heard his final words clearly in his thoughts. 'Remember me.' Daydan smiled back but didn't take the offered club in his hand. 'How could I ever forget the greatest war chief that ever lived.' The tall man stood up and smiled, he tucked his club gratefully back into his cloth trousers and turned slowly. As he began to walk off the ship, he appeared to be walking on the very air its self, with each step his light and aura began to slowly disperse across the sea in the direction of his homeland, until he was just a ripple of light moving across the gentle waves like sea foam, floating on the sea towards the great African continent to the east. All he could do was watch, he felt a loneliness that he never felt before, closing his eyes he breathed in deeply feeling the loss of his friend and the sadness heavily on his chest, wiping his face he looked up and watched the sea kiss the heavens far off in the distance, the night looked so perfect, as a bright silvery moon reflected its ribbon of light across the distant horizon towards the ship. After gazing up at the stars for some time he was required to take watch on deck, it was an easy watch, they were after all docked. The ship was quiet awaiting the return of the crew and for any last-minute cargo the Captain could acquire before setting off to the America's. He chuckled lightly to himself greatly lifting his mood as he watched the men stagger in from the cantina a lot worse for wear, drunk and disorientated. Some had been into fights, most likely with other crews but no serious injuries. He stitched a few cuts with some sail cord and a thick needle borrowed from the Chinaman. The crew seemed to accept him as the ship's surgeon, or whatever else he could do. Most of the men just collapsed on deck finding anywhere to lay and sleep off their well-earned hangovers. Before the sun rise the next morning, he returned to his cabin and brought with him up onto the deck his walking cane and his top hat, that he always wore when conducting business. He took his cane and skilfully removed the sword from the ebony wooden shaft and moved to the hand rail looking out to sea, he held it with two hands one on each end and brought the flat of the blade down hard on his knee once and then twice, the strong blade would not break so he just took the blade and tossed it with the cane shaft over the side of the ship into the waters below. The items made a pair of plopping sounds as they fell into the sea, and a moment later the thin African lookout dived into the sea looking for the silver handled sword cane that sank quickly to the bottom.

Daydan looked up at the starlit sky with the full moon high above lighting up the sea nearby with a vivid silvery hue. He looked to the moon sadly and held his top hat tightly by the brim and stared up into the stars above.

'It was all a lie father, our destiny, our calling, all a lie. I will not live my life as you did, always on the run, always alone, I want a place to call home, to settle down, have a family. I want peace.' He pulled back his arm and tossed his hat as hard as he could high into the air, he watched it for a moment and then turned away so he could think more clearly. Looking away from the sea he walked towards his cabin or for just anywhere comfortable to rest his head for a few hours. Just then a warm strong freak gust of wind whipped around the ship, the sails fluttered and the Spanish flag bellowed in the breeze, something hit him on the back of the head and when he turned, his top hat bounced onto the ground at his feet, his eyes were drawn to the colourful peacock feather that decorated the hat with its length of black silk trailing down behind. He blinked taking another look at the hat that he just threw out to sea. He closed his eyes tightly trying to block out the hat and sword from his mind, then he lifted his hand, it seemed to burn in slow motion from some kind of blue flame, it glowed intensely causing him to blink again, and when he did he could see all of the ship, but through a kind of filter, all around was blue, and from different objects the small inky blue specs of light drifted between objects. Living objects gave off so much more intense blue light. It was as if he could see things in an unknown spectrum, he closed his hand quickly, nervously. With a defeated smile he stooped down and picked up the hat and put it on his head grinning slightly. 'Okay okay, but I'm going to be doing things my way now father.' He thought about the strange blue light that he remembered so vividly. Although he was tired and exhausted, he couldn't stop thinking about his old ethereal friends and how much he missed them.

Chapter Nineteen

Buts & barrels

The crew were stirring early onboard the Mary May, many of them staggered onboard after the night in the cantina and crashed out exhausted but content with their drinking and the chance to let off some steam. A little rivalry with some of the other ships was expected, but this crew was diverse and adaptable, the size of the ship they crewed was large for the amount of crew on board, which meant they had to work much harder, but the reward and the equal share of plunder should they be able, was well worth the hardship. The sloop-of-war had a huge cargo hold and a well-stocked gun deck, the ship was always at around half strength but that never stopped this crew. The ship had a wide but shallow birth making it good for getting right up close to land or sailing inland up the shallower waterways if needs be. The Mary had eight six-pound cannon on each side of the ship, they were mostly just armed with shot and chain, only really used up close to clear the decks of enemy crew or to tear through the sails so the target ship could not escape. Most of the time they were hidden under canvas or behind carefully disguised blast shutters. With a ship of this size, if the ship were to come under attack, the Captain would have to think very carefully and tactically how to deploy the ship in such a way that the enemy remained on one side of the ship. They simply did not have the crew to have enemy on both sides of the ship at the same time, that would be suicide, and that was not an ideal situation. This captains' tactics were always speed and cunning, or just run to fight another day. With a crew of no more than forty-five men on the Mary, that should have one hundred men, and with a cargo weight of around thirty-five to forty tones. Unlike many of the Royal Navy ships that were ruled with an iron hand and a good flogging for any breach of rules or discipline, the captain-maintained order through respect, and a good pay-out. Trade and piracy had their advantages, but it was a double-edged sword, with a fate that could change in a single moment.

Daydan awoke early the next morning on the cargo deck, seagulls flying and squawking overhead, he was covered in sail cloth to keep himself from the weather, as was most of the cargo. The crew were either hidden under canvas or below the main deck secure in the cargo hold. Stretching and letting out a big yawn with many of the awakening crew he looked up to see a warming sight. That moment in the morning when daylight begins to creep through the curtain of night and the changes of light on the distant horizon sending a ribbon of sunshine over the surface of the sea to their ship, heralding the beginning of a new day. Being moored at a jetty they simply lay back on the canvas, enjoying the rare relaxing start to the day and embracing the welcome heat of the morning sun, chatting about their exploits and exchanging stories of the night before. The captain emerged from his cabin putting on his large elaborate wig over his bald head, he retired in private to the far side of the ship, finally turning to a crewman he watched them on deck enjoying the sun. 'Where is the quarter master, he is not in his cabin.' A crewman looked back to the captain blankly and shrugged his shoulders. The Irishman appeared from under some sail cloth and drained the last of his drink from an earthenware tankard he acquired from the cantina. He slowly lay down the tankard next to himself and looked up to the captain who was still trying to put his wig on straight. 'He went ashore earlier, something about passengers and cargo, he said you knew, Serrago, something.' The Irishman scratched his head. He slowly stood up scratching himself more publicly and let out a yawn. The Captain tired of his wig and just held it in his hand down at his side. 'Serrano.' The Irishman passed wind noisily and stood up as tall as he could stretching out his arms and scratching his ass, he looked up to the old captain. 'No. I'm sure he said Serrago or serragoes.'

Some of the crew stood up as they heard shouting on the dockside, commands and marching soldiers, the old captain turned to the sound and adjusted his shirt watching the jetty. An officer and a dozen soldiers marched up the jetty to where the Mary was tied up and started yelling commands to his soldiers to halt, stand to attention and look smart. The crew of the Mary were little impressed and began to tease the soldiers mimicking their regimental attitude. The captain coughed clearing his throat, a clear sign not to antagonise the locals. The officer marched up to the gang plank and was about to step onto the ship when the Turk and the large African stood in his way with their arms folded across their chests. The Spanish officer looked at them clearly angry that they dared bar his path, the captain very slowly descended the very steep stairs from the upper deck and slowly made his way towards the Spanish officer making perfectly sure the Spaniard knew who was in authority on his ship. 'Señor Serrano esta viniendo Samos su escolta.' The Spanish officer snapped his heels together, clenching his buttock cheeks tightly. The crew began to laugh again. One or two of the men mimicking the Spanish officer's showmanship. The captain pulled a slight face to the officer and nodded his head. 'Si.'

The Spanish officer clicked his fingers to his soldiers, who turned and ran on board scuttling off into a corner in their small group, watching the very diverse rough looking crew, most unarmed but about a half with little more than a knife or blade of some kind on their hip. Even though vastly outnumbered, the sailors could do little against fully armed and fully trained soldiers with their muskets ready and their swords or bayonets attached. The soldiers stood in their tight formation group with their muskets standing upright. There was an odd kind of standoff as the groups of men sized each other up, the soldiers looked well-disciplined and well trained. The sailors looked like they knew how to fight dirty if they had too, the men shifted slowly around the deck and up into the rigging making sure that no two targets were in the same direction. The old captain approached Daydan and the other two officers, Mr Rothschild and Mr Kennedy. Both men looked oddly to the Captain as the four men moved closer so they could talk without being overheard. 'Someone important is getting a military escort to the Caribbean, passengers of ours.' The captain glanced over to the Spanish officer. 'We'll charge this passenger more if we have to take soldiers with us.' Lieutenant Rothschild leaned closer to the Captain. 'They could be trouble.' The captain nodded. 'We need to stay smart till we get out of port, we should be okay with the Spanish flag flying from our mast, but for how long, I could not say. Talk to the men, I don't want any problems.' The young lieutenant nodded. 'I'll see to it Captain.'

Daydan watched closely and listened to the captains words carefully, it was very clear to him over the last couple of weeks that the company walked a very fine line between what was legal and what was illegal, and it appeared that for this company, the end justified the means, even if it meant piracy, fraud and even treason. The company had a power all of its own and had contacts everywhere. Piracy on the high seas was commonplace, especially places like the Caribbean which was so difficult to protect or police a nation's interests, so far from its shores. Even with settlements and garrisons nearby, these places still needed to be manned and supplied. Piracy was it seemed perfectly legal when done under the colours of your own nation, Europe was at war, and war was always very good for business. The turn of events on the ship looked like an odd situation to him, and he was interested to see how the cunning old navy officer would handle it. Most of the men began to go about their duties, some went below deck to carry on with their rest. On the main deck a few of the sailors moved some of the cargo below and began making ready to set out to sea. They all looked to be totally focused on the soldiers, ready to react and retaliate in an instant. Daydan saw two of the sailors secretly load a swivel gun on the upper deck close to where the captain would stand, one shot from that cannon would cut a tightly packed group of soldiers into ribbons. They shielded the cannon from the soldiers and Spanish officer so as to not draw any unwanted attention. A short while later a carriage pulled by four horses moved up the docks and stopped by the jetty. An old man and a younger man stepped out and adjusted themselves looking towards the ship, then a young woman stepped slowly out of the carriage wearing a very elaborate dress and a large white wig, she looked awkward as she walked up the crude jetty with the two men ahead of her, the men were arguing about something as the woman watched her footing very carefully on the irregular planks of the jetty. Her oversized dress with large wide hips, the fashion of the day looked uncomfortable, and very impractical, anywhere else other than a fancy house or palace ballroom. She seemed to be extremely shy, avoiding eye contact, looking down at the floor walking behind the men like an abandoned puppy. The ships Quarter master arrived shortly afterwards on a horse drawn cart carrying large oak cask barrels. The Captain relaxed slightly when he saw the quartermaster and motioned to some of the men to assist with the unload and transfer. The barrels were going to be a late last-minute cargo for the ship, as well as the unexpected passengers, no doubt, whatever the cargo, the quartermaster would have bargained hard for a very profitable deal. Daydan put his hat on a rigging pin, rolled up his sleeves and made his way onto the jetty to assist with the unloading and transfer of new cargo to the ship. He started to walk towards the jetty when the thin African look out swung down on a rope from the rigging, he tapped him on the shoulder with his walking cane, the very same walking cane that he tossed into the sea earlier, the African smiled to him and put the cane into a hole next to his top hat, then he nodded politely to him and flexed his arm in front of him, rotating it and performing a slight strong man pose, so Daydan could see he was recovering well. Daydan smiled and gave the man a nod in recognition of his kind gesture. He looked out towards the jetty and saw the men manhandle the large oak barrels and decided to make himself useful and help.

The quartermaster got down from the cart carrying a small chest under his right arm and made his way up the jetty towards the ship, as some of the crew past him, he ordered them to transfer the barrels to the ship. The large barrels were heavy and had to be carefully rolled rather than carried, and once at the gangplank they were hoisted and moved across to the deck and then slowly lowered into the cargo hold. The quarter master handed the old captain the small chest. 'Five thousand in gold, to transport this lot to the America's, the Caribbean. Cuba.' The captain coughed encouraging them to keep their English quiet, he looked to the quartermaster and peered into the small chest, it looked like treasure, typical of the sort stolen and looted, a mixture of jewellery, gold, coins, gems, pearls, it all looked genuine enough, being on a ship and handing over fakes would not only stupid but insulting too. The captain would have a better look and inspect the payment later in his cabin. He looked up to the quartermaster and indicated to the barrels with his head, Daydan watched the man also wondering what was inside the barrels. The quarter master shook his head. 'Dirt and twigs.' The captain frowned a little wanting a more detailed answer. 'They filled the barrels with dirt from the mountainside and put these twigs or roots in them, I'm telling you it's just dirt and twigs, or roots. Something like that.'

The captain motioned to one of the men to show him a barrel, he called Cooper over to open one up, the disfigured man scanned the barrels and hit the lid of one barrel with his elbow, the lid tilted enough to allow the captain to see inside. The captain put the small treasure chest under his arm and pushed his hand inside the barrel and pulled out some dirt. He put his hand in again and pulled out what looked like small tree roots, a small root system and a trunk about two inches thick, it seemed that the barrels were indeed all full of these, that and some rather damp dirt. The captain looked to the quarter master for a moment. 'How long will these last without water.' The quartermaster shrugged his shoulders. 'They should be okay, as long as the dirt is damp and not sodden, they won't rot, and as long as it does not dry out completely, if they are in the hold and kept in the dark they should remain quite dormant, at least until we make it to the America's.' Daydan spoke quite fast and then realised he interrupted the two gentlemen. He lowered his eyes a little as an attempt to apologise for his rudeness, but the captain and quartermaster seemed to appreciate his knowledge and input. On the gangplank the two flamboyantly dressed men stepped onto the ship shouting at each other, they were overly dramatic in their exchanges and gestures causing quite a scene. When the last of the barrels was onboard and moved below with the others, the quartermaster greeted the two foreign gentlemen politely and waited for the young woman. She tried desperately to walk as lady like as she could but found the uneven jetty difficult to walk upon, especially when she could not see her feet or the ground beneath her, owing to the very large size of her dress.

Daydan watched her closely and then noticed the mascot on the front of their ship. It was a carved wooden mascot in the form of a half-naked woman, a mermaid. She had deep red hair, as red as blood, and it came down her chest to cover her beasts, but from the carving and painting it was very clear that she was naked. His eyes were drawn to the ships mascot and when he looked more closely it looked like the mascot smiled and winked back to him in a strange ghostly blue haze. In the daylight he thought he saw a shimmer of blue light and a ghostly female figure float slowly across from the ships mascot and fly gently right into the shy young woman on the jetty. She seemed to take no notice whatsoever, neither did anyone else, but he saw it. He shook his head and looked at his ring wondering if he was imagining things and his mind was playing tricks on him, sure enough his silver ring glowed with that soft pale blue light. The bloodstones natural darkness and the small red spots glowed with a vibrant unnatural intensity as if one of his companions was nearby, but he could not see anyone. He continued to watch the awkward looking young woman carefully as she looked up on occasion to see him watching her. Once all the passengers were onboard, the captain ordered the ship to make sail for the sea and the gangplank was pulled in and the mooring ropes unbound returned, and recoiled neatly back upon the deck, ready for the next port.

The older male passenger screamed at the younger man looking down his nose at him. 'Sembri un fagiano.' The captain turned to his officers. 'He said he looks like a fancy bird.' One of the crewmen interrupted the captain whispering softly. 'Peacock.' The insulted younger man looked to the old man and yelled back. 'Sembri un Contadino.' The young woman was rather unimpressed that none of the two men she was travelling with were assisting her, they were just arguing while she was trying to walk in such an unnecessary amount of attire. Her large skirts, huge wig and dress size were totally inappropriate for this journey, especially on a sloop of war like this. As far as the captain was concerned, they were paying passengers and they paid their fee in gold. The ship slowly moved away from the jetty and turned toward the open sea as the sails began to fill with wind again, they move slowly out to sea away from the docks. Their departure was relatively easy and fast, and it did not take long before the crew had all of the sails unfurled and filled with wind pushing the ship to the open Atlantic Ocean and a huge journey ahead. Sailing almost due west to the America's, every man without exception was happy to see the port slowly falling away behind them. The two passengers were still arguing and shouting to each other. The woman looked decidedly unhappy, uncomfortable and distressed, she hid her face from the gazes of the men very deliberately, like she was shy. She was just about to join her companions when she slipped on some of the ropes and would have fallen had Mr Cooper not grabbed her quickly and broken her fall. When she saw his hand with his missing finger, she screamed causing him to stagger back, suddenly stumbling on his mutilated foot, that made his eye patch slip up, showing his burned-out eye. She screamed again covering her mouth suddenly at the sight.

Immediately the soldiers and officer stood at the ready pointing their muskets, the woman gasped pulling back from the maimed crewman as he tried to cover up his eye, but before anyone could do anything else the younger male passenger struck the disfigured seaman across the face with his hand and pulled a knife. Daydan stood quickly and forced himself between the sailor and the Italian gentleman and pushed him toward the rail of the ship near to the rigging. The older passenger pulled out a pistol and aimed it. The captain immediately lifted his boot and kicked the older passenger off his ship with the flat of his boot against his rear. The young woman screamed again causing her wig to flop from her head, as she looked overboard seeing her father splash into the sea below trying to swim. 'Aaghhh, mio padre non sa nuotare.' With the sound of the splash the younger passenger immediately dived overboard very clumsily after his father, trying desperately to swim down and find him. The older man had not resurfaced. The captain looked worried. 'Oh, she said he can't swim.' The captain looked aloft to his lookout and whistled with his fingers in his mouth pointing to the man overboard. Removing his shirt, the crewman dived off the very top mast into the sea splashing cleanly into the water looking for the older passenger. At the same time two musket shots were heard, Daydan dashed forwards blocking the path of the soldiers so they could not open fire on the crew without shooting through him. 'No no no no.' Behind him one of the crewmen screamed out being hit by a musket ball in the shoulder, the other shot just flew straight through another sailor's baggy shirt but did not wound him. The captain looked overboard and watched, Daydan stared at the soldiers remembering his dagger in his boot, but one move to retrieve his weapon would surely cause the other soldiers to open fire. This time the muskets were pointed directly to him. The woman screamed out staring wide eyed as her brother splashed around in the sea still trying to find her father. 'Get a boat over the side quickly boys.' Mr Rothschild pointed to a small group of men. The small group of sailors untied the rowing boat and began to lower it over the side, Daydan was trying to calm the soldiers and stop them from shooting, still keeping himself between them and the crew. Finally a cheer rang out from the crew as the African lookout seaman emerged dragging up the old man from the depths, he spluttered and coughed frantically and was pushed up onto the rowing boat that was lowered down to the sea moments before, the younger of the two passengers joined his father on the small rowing boat. The old man coughed and called up to his daughter. 'Sofia.' The captain cleared his throat into his hand and looked at the small chest and then to the two men in the boat. He could see the soldiers facing off with his crew, and his ships surgeon standing right in between them. He whistled to the young Italian man in the small rowboat and dropped the money chest over the side for the young man to catch. The Captain turned to the soldiers and pointed to the small boat over the side. The port was still very much in view and not all that far away, but it was out of the range of any cannons at the nearby fort. The Spanish officer saw the stalemate as clearly as the captain did, his orders were to protect the nobles. He was obviously someone of importance, and the man was now overboard in a small rowing boat with his boisterous son. The two men were still arguing as the sailor swam back to the ship and climbed up a rope to his crew mates, who rightly patted him on the back congratulating him for his heroic service.

The soldiers began climbing down the rope ladder to the small rowing boat, the Spanish officer seemed to have a new target of interest, the chest of jewels that the younger man in the boat held under his arm, as he continued to argue with his father. When the last of the soldiers was in the small boat the father yelled up to his daughter while still swearing obscenities to his son. 'Sofia sofia.' She looked over the side of the boat and angrily pulled the covering from her head where her wig once sat. Her covered head hiding her real hair. 'No papa, rimango con le mike vita.' She screamed hysterically looking around at the sailors, some of the men tried to calm her but she lashed out. Daydan approached her slowly and tried to calm her putting his hand on her shoulder. The hysterical young woman immediately struck him with her right hand hard across the face. His eyes widened and he pulled her towards himself and sat down on some cargo, puttimg her over his knee, he began slapping her backside, but there was so much material and hoops to her dress that it was hard to find her at all under all of that. He pulled enough of her garments aside to reveal the fleshy mound of her small round backside; her undergarments covered her upper legs but was tied in such a way that her small round buttocks were open to the elements under her skirts. He tried not to think about what she would look like if he turned her over, as he slapped her fleshy little ass cheeks. She screamed kicking back and forth with her feet wildly, then she slowly stopped. He stopped smacking her backside. Slowly he pulled her dress back down to cover her and then stood her up standing up himself and then turning her to face him. All of the men watched still grinning from the show of the woman's bare flesh. Sofia stood in front of him and slapped him very hard around the face once more, but this time when she hit him, she did not pull her hand away from his cheek, she caressed his face gently but in such a way that no one else could see. Their eyes locked upon each other with a deep intensity. She slid her thumb slowly across his lips a couple of times, back and forth and gently pushed the tip of her thumb into his slightly open mouth, Daydan instinctively closed his eyes and kissed her thumb and softly sucked the tip. He suddenly realised they were not alone and what he was doing. He pulled away and bit his lip softly. Her taste was divine. Sofia watched him closely for moment, then she watched the other sailors as she pulled the bandages from her head and slowly let down her long dark hair. It fell down her back like a beautiful river of silk, her long dark hair looked completely out of place in her fancy white ball gown. She tried to clean off the the thick white makeup from her face that was the fashionable thing to wear, denoting a family's wealth and status. She tore at her overly complicated elaborate dress. She wiped the makeup from her face to reveal a dark red birthmark down the right side on her neck. It caused most of the men to turn away from her. A superstition, the curse of the devil himself. It was the size of his first three fingers, from her right earlobe down her neck almost to her collarbone. Daydan thought the scar looked a little like a horse's head, he smiled finding it quite cute. It wasn't unsightly to him, it suited her. To him she was very beautiful, he smiled slightly to her, the young woman turned away physically hiding the mark shamefully with her hand, sweeping her long dark hair down her shoulder and across her collar bone to hide the mark from view. She had a small amount of red lip colour on her mouth that made it look like she was pouting when of course she was not. Probably some other fancy fashion style derived from Paris, London or Rome, she clearly was not one accustomed to the elaborate trends of high living and ball gowns. They made her look clumsy and insecure.

Daydan turned away from the mysterious Spanish woman for a moment and moved quickly over to the injured sailor who took the musket ball to his shoulder that ripped through his shirt. Blood pooled on the shirt making it wet and sticky. He pulled at the shirt a little taking a closer look at the wound and then took his stiletto bladed dagger from the top of his boot and called the captain. 'I need some hot water,' he thought for a moment, hot water was very unlikely, 'Rum sir.' The captain nodded to the quartermaster who returned soon after with a small keg of rum, Daydan took a long healthy swig, grinned and wiped his mouth. The captains supply was a very nice rum indeed. He then poured some over his knife much to the horror of the crew who saw the rum dripping onto the deck by their feet. Washing the blade quickly but thoroughly he then poured some over the sailors wound who had by this time tore off the shirt still screaming with the pain. He used the pointed tip of the blade to dig out the musket ball, after the first failed attempt he had the sailor drink a few glugs of rum, then he tried again to find the musket ball digging a little deeper, after more blood and screaming from the injured sailor the musket ball gently plopped out at the tip of his blade and dropped onto the floor with a deep thud, rolling harmlessly across the deck. Daydan then searched a little deeper in the wound to try and find any other debris. He finally pulled out a small swab of materiel from the wound that matched the hole in his shirt, he poured the last of the rum over the wound and grabbed a pistol from the young lieutenant. He asked for some gun powder and poured some from a powder horn into the wound, then he cocked the pistols flint and fired it next to the gunpowder on the sailor's shoulder. There was a sudden flash as the powder ignited and cauterised the bleeding wound that stopped the blood loss instantly. The sailor yelled out in pain and grabbed angrily at the ship's surgeon trying to defy the pain. Daydan then poured the last drops of the rum over the wound to cool it down a little and to sterilise the wound. Then he swallowed the rest himself feeling rather nervous about the crewman and if he would survive his injury. Although he knew anatomy very well, he was not very use to working on the living or saving lives.

The seaman watching on stared at the surgeon as he worked quickly to save their comrade, even though the seaman was still obviously stressed and in considerable pain from the ordeal. Daydan slowly began to tear up his clean shirt carefully covering the wound with the fabric to protect the injury as best he could. He turned to the captain who was on the upper deck watching the drama below. 'He'll need to rest up, at-least for today, I'll change the bandages in the morning. He should be fine then.' He patted the seaman lightly on the other shoulder and smiled as he rose to his feet and wiped beads of sweat from his forehead with his arm. The captain nodded and the crewman's friends assisted him down to the cargo deck to find a hammock to rest up in. The young woman, now looking very different walked up to the captain and began talking to him about the barrels and her reason for travel, the captain questioned her several times speaking in her own language. The captain watched her carefully as she spoke. A woman on a ship at sea was bad luck, every seaman knew that. The captain started to step down from the upper deck and walked down towards the crew on the lower deck, the woman pointed to Daydan. 'Si.' The old man grinned widely. She walked up to the handsome ships surgeon and looked him deep in the eyes. 'Ho bisogno.' She paused for a moment watching his mouth intently as she moved closer to him. 'Sono la contessa Sofia Serrano, Sarah mio marito proteggi il mio onore.'

He looked into the woman's dark eyes that seemed to penetrate his very soul, the captain laughed to him. 'She said she is a lady, and you will marry her, so these dogs don't try to have their way with her.' Daydan stood up looking back at the woman. 'But.' She looked a mess in her overcrowded dress, she had the most beautiful long healthy shinny dark hair that when unfurled and straight almost reached the small of her back. The quartermaster pointed to a barrel on the deck. 'I think her luggage was also stored in barrels, along with her brother and fathers. I'll have them brought to your cabin.' Daydan recoiled a little. 'But what, wait.' He looked into the face of the young woman and then to the wide-eyed crew. He turned to the quartermaster and nodded. 'Okay okay.'

From above the lookout called to the captain and pointed to the small rowing boat on the water, the old Italian gentleman was standing up in the boat holding the small chest of treasures in his hands pointing it to the officer, the officer's gun flashed and the next second the old man dropped the trunk into the hands of the officer and fell into the sea over the side of the rowing boat, Sofia's brother stood up and stared at his father's body floating on the sea and then disappearing below the waves, one of the soldiers stabbed the young Italian in the back twice repeatedly with his bayonet and pushed him into the sea with his foot, with such a wound the young man soon disappeared under the waves, Sofia screamed hysterically seeing the murder of her brother and father so cruelly right in front of her eyes. She screamed words to the small boat that were little more than a shrill. Daydan grabbed her and pulled her close turning her head away from the small boat, the captain pointed to the scatter gun on his bridge as the young Spanish officer stood up in the rowing boat holding his right hand up waving a two finger gesture to the Englishman, a clear insult. The charge in the scatter gun was already set, the captain placed an extra charge inside the cannon and then pushed in another hand full of shot and chain. The powder monkey rammed it home, he turned the scatter gun to the target some four-hundred feet away. The officer smugly held the small treasure chest securely under his left arm. With an aim from the captain that seemed rather vague and matter of fact, the powder boy lit the fuse. The cannon flashed almost immediately sending its contents onwards. The captain and all nearby coughed from the smoke, when they turned they did so just in time to see a hot piece of chain and shot pepper the men on the small boat and watch the red hot chain fly true through the air and hit the officers right arm taking it clean off and cauterising it at the wrist. The officers hand plopped into the sea. Sophia had turned just in time to see the revenge shot being startled by the noise. She jumped uncontrollably and put her arms around Daydan holding him tightly. She began to sob into his shoulder unsure of her fate.

The soldiers on the small boat opened fire on the ship, the crew ducked and avoided the shots easily, it seemed like a puny response, a lone row boat with musket men onboard firing upon a sloop-of-war, at first the sailors jeered at the pathetic show, but a yell from one of the men turned their attention elsewhere. Mr Cooper staggered back clutching his throat and he fell to the deck sprawling across the cargo. His new African friend held him trying to help him to sit comfortably, but blood pulsed through his fingers from an artery in his neck. The hardened sailor looked at Daydan as he knelt down to assist him, the seaman shook his head trying to talk. But with no tongue it was not an easy task to make himself understood. He held the hand of the African and looked up into his face smiling and removed his own hand from his throat, again blood gushed from his neck in steady rhythmic squirts. Daydan immediately covered the wound with his hand but Cooper grabbed his hand and pulled it away, slowly his eyes closed but his face still smiled warmly. The African screamed out loud and deep. 'Nooo.'

He cradled his friend in his large arms. Daydan held the dead seaman's hand in his, he saw the ring on his finger glow gently as the man's spirit slowly eased itself away from its body, a sight completely oblivious to everyone else, but Daydan himself. The spirit smiled to him and looked happy, he looked fondly to his old crew mates and the new friendship he so recently just made with the large African. He nodded to the only person who could see him and began to slowly walk, floating effortlessly off the ship. He was not the broken regretful seaman he remembered seeing limping slowly around the ship, but a fine healthy young man with piercing blue eyes and a happy smile. His spirit walked easily through the deck rail and over the side diving headlong into the sea. His broken body looked content and happy on the deck of the Mary, relieved, Daydan put the dead sailors' arms across his chest in the traditional way and closed his one eye looking to the African who had him supported from behind. 'He is at peace.' He smiled softly to the man. 'This is what he wanted.'

The rest of the day had gone along with the normal routine of a ship at sea, Coopers body was washed and wrapped in sail, stitched by the Chinese man and assisted by the large African sailor. There was a strange quiet atmosphere on the ship that evening, as the captain made for the most favourable winds and asked about the wounded crewman. The weather was good and relatively mild as they pushed out to sea. The lookout at the very top of the ship watched out for other ships, but as soon as the Mary was far enough out to sea the Spanish flag was lowered and replaced with the Union Jack, and the St Georges cross on the Company Flag. The rest of the day was uneventful other than the countess figuring out for herself that this was not a Spanish ship at all but clearly an English vessel.

Eventually he helped the men move the countess's barrel to the officer's cabins and he assisted the young woman with her luggage moving it from the officer's corridor into his own cabin. The crew had better ideas for what to do with the two Italian passengers' luggage as it was traded and tossed from one crewman to another. Anything useful was shared, anything useless was tossed over the side. The young woman darted around the ship yelling at the crew trying to recover items of clothing for herself. Once inside his cabin she poured some water from a jug into a bowl and began to wash as she undressed herself. Daydan turned away shyly trying to respect her privacy, she laughed to herself at his manner and took her time tending to herself. She eventually stripped down to her underwear and finished washing all of the white makeup from her face and arms, then cleaned and wiped over her body with a cloth. She was careful not to show to-much flesh but delighted in teasing him, looking over her shoulder to catch him watching her. She was always careful to hide her neck and red birthmark under her long luxurious dark silky hair. She finally put on a long plain white dress, like a one-piece nightdress, with short puffy sleeves and an open front that would show the small mounds of her breasts. There was a thread of white silk that was tied to pull the two sides of the upper part of the dress together to cover her breasts, she tied the top of her nightdress in such a way that when up close there was little need of imagination. When she was done, she removed her undergarments and threw them into a small pile on the floor. She appeared to have separated her clothes into two plies, one pile to keep, and another to discard. She jumped into his cabin bed hiding herself under the simple cotton sheets and rough thick woollen blankets

She patted the bed to her front as she pushed back against the wall of the cabin bed as much as she could, trying to leave him enough room to sleep with her. She covered herself with the blanket and looked frightened. He sat on the bed and took off his boots but remained dressed, then he eased back towards her and lay upon his bed with Sofia behind him. She put her arm around him and held him gently, he listened for her words, but none came. Slowly her breathing softened and he felt her go limp behind him. He closed his eyes and smelled the young woman's distinctive scent close behind him. Her presence was pleasurable, and as much as he wanted to turn and have his way with her, something held him back, his feelings for Mary perhaps, he closed his eyes and rested comfortably with the young woman behind. Above, there was a small service for mister cooper, his body was dropped overboard with the sound of a splash being the only sound that stood out that night. Daydan closed his eyes. He lay quietly in his bed with Sofia behind him thinking about the events of the day, he tried to think clearly about the road ahead and the decisions he had to make for the future. But for now, rest called for him and he gladly began to think of the future. The young woman behind him held him as she slept, it felt nice, natural, and he felt for the first time ever in his life that he was where he belonged, his breathing eased, and his thoughts became vague as he slowly fell to sleep.

Chapter Twenty

Sofia

Waking up with someone so close was a very new feeling for him, he remembered the events leading up to this very unfamiliar situation. His impression of the hysterical Spanish/Italian aristocrat was initially unimpressive. Under all of her makeup and wigs, all the yards of material made her look like a child's doll, lifeless and unemotional. Every moment in her company she seemed to grow on him, some of her traits he found rather attractive. She also made him feel a little out of his depth, the only other woman he ever shared a bed with before this was Mary. This was hardly the same, this time they were thrown together out of necessity. She was obviously frightened of her treatment aboard a ship as the only woman, who was not a paying passenger. Daydan was a man who did not want to be a party to what would happen if he did not agree to this arrangement. The fact still remained, she was a very pretty woman when all of her makeup, wig and finery was removed. She was smart and seemingly well educated, and she behaved for the most part just as he would expect an independent woman to behave. Sofia was close behind him with her arm around him, she seemed very comfortable and unafraid. Like it was natural to her. His mind and imagination were in chaos with images and scenarios that he pushed from his thoughts. He carefully moved her arm from her slight embrace and rolled off the cabin bed, standing up on the wooden floor in his bare feet. Outside he could hear the creaking of the ship as it sailed west towards the America's. The captain said that the journey could take months, depending on the weather, but he assured them that mostly at this time of the year it would be just a little more than six weeks, maybe seven. So far, the captain's calculations and navigational expertise were very impressive, no one ever doubted his leadership or navigational skills.

The woman in his bed rolled over slightly stretching out her slim body across his bed enjoying the extra space, her eyes remained closed and a soft smile danced upon her beautiful thin lips. Her dark almost raven black hair had a beautiful sheen to it in the lamp light of the cabin, much better than the tall white highly impractical wigs that so many women and men found so fashionable these days. They were meant to be a sign of wealth and prosperity as the wigs were very expensive, the more elaborate the wig, the more influential and wealthier the owner. Daydan himself never cared for a wig, he always kept his hair neat, pulled back into a small tail and tied, from a distance his hair looked like a common short dark wig with a simple length of silk to keep his hair back. Sometimes, when he was working physically hard away from others, he left it free hanging. He would sometimes let it grow and then cut it short, but it was always neat and tidy. He never did get use to the idea of a wig, so he wore a hat, which was so much more practical.

This morning he took a small piece of black silk and tied it about his neck, then he found his stocking socks and put his boots on. He looked not unlike the other officers and senior crew, boots pants and a plain white shirt. The officers would sometimes wear their jackets, but the captain was not strict about any uniform, neither was the company. Provided the men did their work well they were left pretty much alone, other than the yells of the ever-present Irish master ship-man's voice. When he left his cabin and ventured out into the daylight, he first had to shield his eyes from the sunshine. The day was clear with a nice cool breeze coming off the sea, the ship bobbed and dipped as it ripped through the sea under full sail. It was a beautiful sight to behold, and the salty smell of the sea made breathing a pleasure. The men worked hard all the time; they had a very efficient routine for a ship that was very undermanned. He nodded politely to the crew as they went about their work. This morning, oddly, many turned their noses up at him or shoved past him aggressively. Not at all what he was expecting after his performance the day before. Their rude brash behaviour troubled him, perhaps the loss of Cooper affected them more than he realised, the mutilated slave was a very well-respected member of the crew. He sighed to himself, Cooper was happy when he passed, Daydan would not let their feelings change what Cooper wanted for himself, the look on his face, it was his time. He was taking a quiet piss over the side of the ship when a sailor shoved past him almost pushing him overboard into the sea, he grabbed a rigging rope just in time. 'Hey.' The sailor ignored him and didn't even acknowledge the crude inappropriate and potentially dangerous nudge. The Captain as always missed very little on his ship, even with his elaborate wigs and colourful jackets and self-absorbed appearance, he watched his ship and his crew like a hawk.

As the only member of the crew who would seem to acknowledge him this day, he slowly climbed up to the captains' aft deck, where he watched his ship and gave commands from time to time to his helmsman. He stood next to the old sea captain, just as he did so many times before, learning what he could from the old man of the sea. They would talk about all sorts of things, the company, business, his adventures on the sea, navigation, they were moments Daydan looked forward to. The captain had an uncomplicated life full of adventure, he envied the old man in many ways. He also knew he kept some daemons very deep down within his soul. Those were the moments the captain would for no apparent reason suddenly go quiet. He respected the old mans need for peace and silence and would just stand quietly and wait until the old admiral broke the silence with some smart remark about something or another. The Captain seemed to have something on his mind, he would glance to him for a moment and then look back at the crew or up to the sails and his look out. They exchanged glances for some time, and he was unsure exactly what was going on. Something was amiss, and it was beginning to get uncomfortable. The lookout above climbing in the rigging was going about his work with relative ease, untroubled by his injury a couple of weeks before. The sailor with the bullet wound was healing nicely too. He listened to Daydan's instructions to replace the bandages with a clean dressing daily until the wound sealed itself fully. As he went about his chores tending to the men, he could not understand the bad reactions he was getting from the crew and now the captain too.

'Did you bed her.' The captain said suddenly not even looking towards him. Daydan turned to face him abruptly. 'NO, No I did not.' The captain contorted his face and removed his large wig to scratch his balding head and then replaced his wig. 'A woman on a ship is bad luck.' The captain turned to him and put his hands on his hips facing him square on. 'Do you know why.' He shook his head to the captain. 'A woman is distracting for the crew, for obvious reasons, especially one who tries to lord over them. Sailors only have one mistress, the sea herself. The only welcome woman aboard a ship, is either a naked woman, or the ships figure head. Seeing as this woman onboard is a passenger.' The captain frowned. 'We are just to sea with a long, long way to go. And already there is unease onboard my ship.' The captain held his hands behind his back. 'It would be better to throw her overboard, before she divides my crew.' He looked to the captain and put his fingers through his hair and watched the crew as they worked. 'No sir, you will not do that. I gave her my word.' The captain was right, there was an uneasy tension onboard, so much more different than when they left England for the canaries. 'She is different, special, I do not know why, but I will protect her.' He looked to the Captain sternly, the old man glanced to him and then focused back up on the crew.

He realised how important superstition was for the crew, the unwritten rules, he gave the captain a polite look and nodded to him in confirmation of what he just told him. For the rest of the morning he avoided the crew as best he could, he helped with a few chores, tidying ropes, tying down canvas over some of the cargo, watching the crew for injuries or ailments. Later in that morning Sofia ascended to the upper deck, she was wearing a white shirt, one of his, and a pair of his pants, she looked completely different from the day before. Her hair was tied back hanging down her right shoulder covering her neck over her small breast. Her hair was long, almost down to the waist of her pants. She had small feet and wore no shoes, just like many of the men that made no sound on the deck as she walked. The men watched her closely as she strutted around the deck looking sideways towards the crewmen, when she saw the captain she climbed up to where he was standing careful not to fall off the steep stairs.

She put her hands on her hips standing tall, her very feminine figure left nothing to the imagination. Her small but firm breasts nudged tightly through the shirt. Her very feminine shape, silhouette and small rear were accentuated by the cut of Daydan's riding pants. She looked comfortable, very different from the woman who first stood upon the deck of the ship covered from head to toe in finery and makeup. She uttered some words to the captain who pointed down to him as he saw her turn to face him. At first, she frowned catching his eyes and his reaction. Slowly she took the stairs down to where he was tying up some of the cargo, she stood behind him with her feet apart and her hands on her hips. After a few moments of being ignored she gave him a hard kick with her foot, when he turned to her, she put her fingers to her mouth indicating food. Rolling his eyes, he slowly stood up and brushed off his hands, moving closer to her to take her to find some food. One of the sailors grunted and shoved his way past him. When he turned to look at the man some of the other sailors shook their heads in disgust. Sofia noticed the odd behaviour of the men and then turned to the gentleman who treated her with so much respect and kindness. They walked over to a barrel by the door to the officer's cabins together and he removed the lid tilting it slightly. Inside the barrel was fresh drinking water and a wooden ladle on a length of twine. Ripe green apples floated in the cool water. He scooped up some water for her to drink and then dipped his hand in to remove a large ripe apple. It was clean and cold and very juicy and refreshing. She slowly bit into the apple cautiously at first. A loud but satisfying crunch came from her mouth as she bit into the fruit. After the first bite she began to eat the fruit with an urgent lust to quench her hunger. They proceeded down into the cool dark bowls of the ship where the more fragile, valuable cargo was stored. Gunpowder, silks and tea, also a few barrels of fine opium powder. He took out his sharp stiletto boot knife and cut some meat from a ham that was freely hanging from a rafter. There were a few of these hams, very heavily salted to prevent insects and other growth. The hams would be consumed long before the end of their journey but initially it was a very good source of protein for the men, and a little taste of home. Later in the journey their meals would not be so glamorous. Gruel was most common onboard ship because it was easy to store oats, corn was easy to store too. The labour involved to turn it into flour was impractical, flour would be used and often salted but cooking was difficult, so most foods were eaten cold, even water was rarely boiled. If they were fortunate, maybe a few lucky catches would add fish to the menu but in general the men survived on very little but made up for it whenever they landed at a port or was able to go ashore for some much-needed supplies and fresh water.

Sofia's barrels were below deck, storing her precious vines. The vines themselves had been cut back to a minimum but the roots where possible were preserved to give them the best possible chance when replanting. She checked the barrels to ensure that the dirt within was damp and not dry. The earth could dry out on its own and the roots would be fine, for a short time. It was her families wish to set up a vineyard or farm in Cuba. Just as they had done in central Italy with great success. The romance of the new world had lured many adventurers. No doubt her plans may have changed now. Daydan turned to her in the darkness of the cargo hold and gripped her arm gently as he fed her a piece of ham from the edge of his blade. His touch was firm but gentle on her arm. She took the sliver of meat in her mouth and turned to him looking into his eyes while carefully ensuring that the ham went inside her mouth, as she spoke, she covered her mouth wanting to look every bit like a woman from a good family. 'My husband.' His hand brushed against her cheek lightly replacing some strands of hair that had fallen over her face, she leaned gently into his hand and smiled. Her dark ebony black eyes sparkled in the dim light of the cargo hold. His thumb again caressed her soft lips tenderly as she closed her eyes and kissed it delicately. She took his hand in hers and held it to her mouth with her hands and kissed the palm of his hand. As the ship creaked and rolled on the sea the two strangers shared a quiet romantic moment together. She looked up into his eyes and held his hand to her mouth in her hands. For the first time, Daydan watched a tear fall from her eyes and run slowly down her cheek. He smiled weakly to her using the back of his hand to wipe away her tear. He let out a soft sniff and took her hand leading her back up to the main deck. She lost everything, her family, her security, her safety, Daydan was her only hope, a complete stranger to her, thrown together out of necessity, but somehow, she felt a sense of belonging as she gripped his hand as they ascended back on to the upper deck together.

The men were busy working, some glanced disappointed to their surgeon for not having his way with her in the cargo hold, but the woman did look tearful and sad. It was understandable in the circumstances. Losing her home, seeing her brother and father murdered in front of her eyes. Most of the day was quiet and easy going, the weather was good and the wind favourable. Daydan and Sofia sat on some bails of wool that were covered by a sheet of canvas to protect them from the worst of the weather, they spoke to each other in their broken words, sometimes calling upon the captain or some of the crew to translate. Most of their conversation was to recognise items, behaviour or moods. Still the crew was unimpressed with their surgeon, but he seemed to care little about their reaction. He was enjoying Sofia's company and she appeared to enjoy his just as much. They would often laugh at each other's attempts to understand each other's languages. Sofia learned incredibly fast watching him closely. She spoke Italian and Spanish beautifully, she also spoke Portuguese, and now some English and some French. Her native languages of Spanish, Italian and Portuguese being very alike. She spoke a few words of other languages that he never heard of before. She observed the crew and the way they treated him and asked if he was a criminal. He laughed reassuring her that he was no more a criminal than was the rest of the crew. She had a great admiration for the old admiral who paraded himself around like a court gentleman, while on this fine ship sailing out into the middle of the Atlantic Ocean. Perhaps he reminded her of her father, Daydan smiled at the thought, that surely would amuse the old captain. That evening the men rested as they always did, on the main deck, sharing stories, singing songs, gambling and playing games. Again, some played their instruments, others would just sing songs that reminded them of home. Daydan and Sofia watched intently as the crew laughed and joked with each other, sharing a smile and a look that showed that even under such odd circumstances, the two of them shared something unique. When one of the musicians started to play a familiar tune, Sofia stood up suddenly in front of her chosen man, she began to dance, untied her hair letting it cascade down he back and over her shoulders. She was always carefully to hide the red birthmark on her neck. As she moved, her long hair slowly followed her movements like a dark ribbon of light. Her bare feet moved effortlessly over the wooden deck of the ship, her arms were like the wings of a giant bird, graceful and silent. Her finger movements looked so delicate and precise. As the musicians played faster and faster with more passion, Sofia kept in time with the music, her movements were longer, her jumps higher and her steps more complicated and elaborate, yet all the time graceful and seductive. She danced like a flamenco dancer, her fingers clicked beautifully and her arms and hands mimicking the melody of the music in the air. The musician struggled to go any faster, and soon with a final twang, one of the strings on the instrument snapped, Sofia fell exhausted to Daydan's feet, her small chest and abdomen heaved heavily under the exhaustive dance. Her beautiful mouth was wide open sucking in air as fast as she could, gasping for breath. He stood up sharply with Sofia at his feet and applauded her and the musician as loudly as he could. 'Bravo, bravo.' He looked down to Sofia at his feet and then turned around to the other sailors, they looked away refusing to feel anything other than disappointment to him. 'That was beautiful.' He nodded to the musician and leaned down to Sofia scooping her up in his arms as she breathed heavily, still gasping for air. She put her arms around his neck and held him tightly burying her flushed face into his chest. Over head the stars shone like diamonds in the night sky, the moon glistened over the sea with a mystical silver glow all around it. He cradled her in his arms and headed for their cabin carrying her gently as if they were on their wedding night and was carrying her over the threshold to their matrimonial bed for the very first time. He kicked open the door to the officer's cabins and pushed his own cabin door open clicking it closed behind himself with his heel. He sat Sofia on the small bed and stared into her face as she looked back to him, she was still breathing heavily as he watched her. Her chest lifting and falling frantically, but the heavy breathing was no longer from her exhaustive dance, something else was getting her pulse racing, something different, something new. She watched him so closely, studying his eyes, she slowly and shyly began to untie the neck of his white shirt, slowly opening the collar down to the centre of his ribs, her hand shook as she pushed her hand gently inside his shirt to stroke his strong powerful chest. He put his hand on the soft supple skin of her shoulder, then he moved forwards and took the two collars of her shirt in his hands and ripped open the shirt in one easy movement. She jumped; her small firm breasts pointed eagerly towards him fully exposing them to the candlelight. He moved slowly closer stroking her soft olive skin. He lowered his head and softly kissed her swollen nipples that hardened between his lips as he nibbled her gently. Her moan was soft and grateful. She was trembling, from fear or excitement, either way she never resisted for a moment. The hunger they now had for each other could not wait another moment. Gripping her small waist, he picked her up in his hands pulling her closer to his eye level to meet his lips. He kissed her passionately, deeply, and for a moment she resisted still trying to catch her breath, afraid. But his grip was strong and powerful, yet not rough. Her mouth felt the softness of his lips and she put her arms around his neck leaning in to fully enjoy the deliciousness of his passionate heart stopping kiss. Their mouths were hungry for each other as their kisses became more and more passionate. In the quiet stillness of the night, as the ship sailed towards the centre of the Atlantic to the Caribbean, a young woman's moans of pleasure and release could be heard through the night. Not just once that night, but several times, her moans were like the song of the wind in the sails of the ship, rhythmic, beautiful, her releases of pure pleasure were the sound of the sirens luring unwary seaman to their deaths. Not a single sailor slept that night, their thoughts were taken over by the memories of less lonely nights. They gazed upwards wide eyed from their slumbers listening to the soft grateful moans of the only woman on the ship.

When he awoke the following day, they were both naked, the stale musk of the night before was in the air in the small cramped cabin, and her scent was all over him. He awoke first and stood from the small bed putting a blanket over her lithe naked body to warm her.

He smiled as he looked at the beautiful woman he had just bedded and pulled on the torn shirt she had worn the day before and quickly put his pants on. He let out a yawn and went up through the corridor and out onto the deck, the sunlight was once again bright, and a clear sky overhead meant good weather. At first, he had to shield his eyes coming from the darkness of the cabins, but once on the deck the heat of the sun was a welcome feeling. He breathed in the salty air and felt his body relax. His eyes gently scanned all around almost still in a trance from his night of passion. Everything had a strange blue white haze, he could see shapes of energy in the wind and in the currents of the sea, in the sails above his head. He looked around slowly and saw the sailors going about their work, but they too had a strange glow, he lifted his hands up in front of his eyes and as he did so he could see them glowing gently, drawing energy from around him. He watched and smiled weaving intricate shapes in the air watching the energy, follow the motion of his hands like the flames of a fire on a torch. He looked around fascinated by the patterns of energy everywhere around him, everything looked so vivid, so clear, so perfect. A heavy object suddenly hit him hard in the centre of his back and he blinked, when he opened his eyes again the strange perspective that he saw previously was gone, his vision was back to normal and he looked unimpressively back to his flesh coloured hands. He looked up and turned himself towards his attacker. He instinctively raised his fists to defend himself, but it was unnecessary. 'Good, she wailed like a young lover should.' The tall muscular dark-skinned man nodded to him and laughed out loud in a deep rumbling tone. Daydan nodded back to the man politely making his way over to the water barrel and dipped his hands in to scoop out some water to wash his face, all the time looking more closely at his hand. Did he just imagine what he saw only moments before. He looked up and cleared his mind acknowledging the much larger man, a very strong powerful crewman. From all over the ship the crew were whooping and hollering, cheering him, he felt oddly embarrassed. He didn't feel it was a victory or worthy of cheers, or that she had been conquered in any way. She was nice, she was very smart and full of self-confidence most of the time. But also, shy, that was attractive, and likely she was a good businesswoman too from their conversations. She appeared to know her trade well, she would make a very good business partner and a very loving and desirable wife. He knew she was very aware of her birthmark. The obvious mark on her neck that she made every effort to keep covered. He personally didn't think it was at all important, just a discolouration of the skin, not unsightly or off putting, it was a part of her. To him, she was exquisite, like a work of art, in a way, the way she turned her head constantly made her look rather sultry looking. She was healthy and strong and, in his eyes, very beautiful, her very Mediterranean colour and features he found so appealing. As the sailors congratulated him and pat him on the back he thought more about Sofia. She was a very special woman, but had it not been for all of those mysterious incredible circumstances, they would never have met.

He sat for a while on the pile of cargo on the deck and thought about the events of the last few weeks. If he could go back to that night, walking up to the graveyard on the edge of the Thames, that dark stormy night to rescue a lost soul. Could he ever have imagined that his adventures would bring him here. He looked at the silver ring on his hand and smiled as he gently twirled it thoughtfully around his finger as if in some way it gave him comfort. He pointed the blood stone of the ring facing him in the open palm of his hand, the red spots of the stone were bright, like tiny rubies, but they were not glowing as they would when his ethereal friends were nearby. This was a more natural colour, still bright and vibrant, but gentle and unimposing like a piece of fine jewellery. A part of him missed Mary, her impromptu late-night visits as he slept, her carefree character, her smile and the curve of her lips. Sofia had so many of the same characteristics, she was smart, beautiful in her own very natural way, and sometimes self-confident. Both women shared a vulnerability that he found very attractive. Like they were experiencing every moment for the very first time, their eyes sparkled like the stars.

The weeks ahead were much easier, the ships routine was mostly steady, the Captain steering the ship for the best wind, carefully tracking and recording their progress on his charts and in the logbook. Each night the two lovers would make love, quietly. Some nights Sofia would be silent as they made love, slowly and carefully, gentle. But later, over their tot of rum or one of her carefully stashed bottles of red wine, they would sit up and talk and laugh and put on a show for the crew so at-least they would think that the ships surgeon was behaving as a man with a pretty young woman should do. During the day they would walk the ship together assisting the captain or helping the crew. Talking to each other and slowly picking up more words from each other's languages. It did not take long before their conversation grew more interesting. Sofia had a very clear plan of what she wanted in her future and of what she expected of a husband. A few days into their voyage the captain performed a simple wedding ceremony on the ship for them and recorded the event in his logbook. Before her journey, Sofia had been a virgin, she had little contact with men at the insistence of her father who intended her to marry into the aristocracy. Sofia shared quite frankly with him that until she boarded the Mary, she was a lost soul, unhappy, lonely, afraid, all she knew was her family vineyards in the mountains. She knew very well how to set up a farm having been uprooted many times. They were neither Italian or Spanish and were easy targets for either. Finally, the Spanish uprooted them from their conquered lands in Italy and ordered them to resettle in the new lands across the oceans. It was important for Spain that the new world be settled and populated with their own citizens. She explained to him about a new untamed land called New Mexico that her father told her about. Their first port of call being Cuba and then to find out news of this new world and its opportunities.

They were rarely out of each other's sight and would spend hours talking and laughing together. The crew got use to having a woman onboard, especially one like Sofia. She was polite and pretty, never flirtatious and always ready to help. The Chinaman took a shine to her early on and she helped him repairing sail and making garments. It passed the time, and she took to the new skill with ease. The Chinaman was a solitary crewman, he kept himself to himself, but every morning before sunrise he would be up on deck doing his strange slow dance. They would watch him as they waited for the sunrise and the splash of new colour in the sky. Some mornings Daydan would try to copy the moves of the old china man as he moved slowly and gracefully, Sofia would tease him, and they would all laugh together. It was not until one morning, he fell into his trance and could see the energy around him, forming and being attracted to the strange intricate graceful movements. As he copied the Chinaman, he could see the intensity of the energy in his hands and with a final symbolic thrust and stride toward the china man he sent a wave of energy towards the china man who fell backwards a few feet across the deck. Daydan dashed towards the china man laying on the floor who was laughing. Sofia helped him stand up rather shocked at what she just saw her husband do. The china man bowed repeatedly clasping his hands together and laughed. 'Ch'i.' They both dusted off the china man and a mutual fondness of respect grew between them.

He soon realised that the long plait from his head clearly showed him as a Manchu. Days after they would still sometimes practice together, but never again would he release that energy toward the china man ever again. Weeks rolled by, as they went about their routine on the ship he would often smile to his lovely young wife. She repeatedly told him of her dreams for a new life, a family. It was such a coincidence that they had the same dreams and desires.

Chapter Twenty-One

Land ahoy

After many weeks at sea, the endless routine, the slow but steady reminder that their supplies were dwindling, and the food stores were beginning to get thin. The crew and Captain were looking to the horizon for land fall. One morning he was awoken by banging and crashing coming from the captain's cabin, he ran next door to see what the noise was and saw the captain reaching under his cabin bed pulling out old maps and charts.

The old man was on his knees with his head under his bed pulling out dusty old pages and throwing them behind him. Finally, he stopped and slowly pulled back out from under the desk and stood up awkwardly, he was old, well past his years as a seaman. He dusted off an old chart and lay it out upon his table and weighted down the corners with some random objects, he turned for a moment to his uninvited guest and huffed under his breath. 'This woman, your wife, you are serious about this.' He entered the captain's cabin fully, closing the small door behind himself and sat on the edge of the captain's bed. He nodded rolling up his shirt sleeves and trying to make his torn shirt look a little more presentable. 'She is a good woman, she has virtue, and I find her very attractive. She is smart, funny, and I believe she would be a loyal and loving wife, what more could a man ask.' The captain coughed a little. 'She is a woman, a woman who is afraid and desperate, do not underestimate that.' The captain beckoned him over with his finger and pointed to his map. 'This is our route through the Virgin Islands, we should see land any day now, then we avoid contact but remain close between the islands until we reach Jamaica. The last time I sailed here Jamaica was part of the crown. I have business there so we will land and take on supplies. I will let the men ashore and resupply for a few days in port.' He looked to his ship's surgeon and then back to his map. 'These will be hard times in the Americas, very hard times, but for the right people, unimaginable opportunity wealth and fortune.' He watched the captain and followed his finger upon the map he had laid out. The captain was very accurate about his route, deliberately avoiding the larger islands and making his way for Jamaica. 'I have heard stories of an island called California, to the west, where the warriors wear gold armour. An island where there are no men, only tall beautiful dark-skinned women.' The old man smiled. Daydan nodded politely to him. 'I just want to live in peace captain.' He said softly as he smiled to him. 'Maybe raise a family, get some land, farm. Some horses.' The captain coughed and balled his fist. He shook his head. 'Then you should turn around and go back to London, there will be no peace here, not for a long time. Think carefully my good man.' He looked at the map showing the island of California on the west coast. All along the coastline to the south of the America's were forts and colonies. Much of the west coast of the America's were still uncharted, or only partly charted. The captain was right, this would not be easy. The captain moved back to sit in his chair and began to put some tobacco into his clay pipe and lit it from his oil lamp. The smoke bellowed from his mouth. The captain's old black teeth nibbled the end of the pipe as he watched his guest.

'Good maps are scarce here, there is still much to be explored and correctly mapped, Mr Rothschild, he is a fine young gentleman, he would make a useful addition to your expedition, I would seriously think about it.' He nodded to the Captain politely, the idea of more travel, overland. What was this strange land he spoke of, this land of dark-skinned warriors clad in gold. This was a vast land, wild and unconquered. For someone like him, with his skills, it could be a great place to build a new home and a new life. He thought about Sofia, and about the young lieutenant, perhaps a new adventure lay ahead. The captain leaned forwards putting his elbows on his knees. 'I see she is very taken with you, and she will give you many children. But she will not have an easy life, not one that she is used to back home in her palace.' He gave a smile shaking his head and watched the captain as he smoked his pipe. 'She did not live in a palace sir, she is an illegitimate granddaughter of one of the duchies of Tuscany, they fled, trusting the Spanish who uprooted them to be good to their word for resettlement in the mountains. Years later, they were uprooted again, she has lost her home before, their vineyards, their livelihood, and now her family. I am all she has.' He paused for a moment thinking quietly to himself. 'And she is all I have.' He smiled a little to the captain. The old sea captain pulled hard on his pipe and blew out long columns of smoke. He pointed the tip of his clay pipe to his map. 'I wish I was a younger man; I would venture with you.' The old captain smiled, he stood up and straightened his stiff back as he pointed to the map so he could see. 'From Jamaica, we will put to port at the Garrison of New Orleans, then I would suggest you travel by land as far to the west as you can,' He laughed a little and smoked some more of his pipe. 'I envy you.' Daydan smiled to the old man. The captain stood up straight and slapped him upon his back. 'It is not too late.' Daydan said smiling. The old seaman shook his head, he sat down in his chair rather tired and eased himself into a comfortable position. 'When the time comes, I will go down with this ship, the sea has been my only mistress. We are old friends.' He said those words with deep compassion and honesty, like he had already made up his mind. The old man searched through some more maps scrolls and leather-bound books, he took a small book from under the pile bound in leather and opened it up. Looking through some of the entries he stopped at a page and tapped the notes with his forefinger. 'There is a man you should meet' I have not seen him in years.' The captain read a few pages from his notebook. 'He used to help the Spanish missionaries settle these parts, Mexico is growing in strength, the Spanish, French, Portuguese and Britain, are all stretched to thinly. Economically it is suicide, history repeats itself time and time again. This is where smart people cash in on opportunity, that is why piracy in the Mexican Gulf is so lucrative.' The old sea captain grinned. He went to his bed close to where Daydan was sat and reached under his simple mattress and pulled out some black cloth, he shook it out hard letting it unfurl. The large cloth was a flag, deepest black, nothing else was upon the flag, just a large plain black flag. He looked at the captain and creased his eyebrows thinking to himself. The captain said nothing, he folded the black flag neatly into a triangle and put it upon his cabin bed and turned slowly. 'Come, today is a fine day, we should be on deck.' He followed the captain up onto the deck, but on his way out he took a last look at the flag on the captain bed, this old sailor was as cunning as they came. He watched the old man with admiration. The old black flag was a warning, death, the mark of a plague ship, it became adopted by the pirates to put fear into their enemies, and as time went on the pirates put their own identifying marks upon their flags. The captain was trying to tell him something, something important, something he missed. On deck the men were busy, the weather was good with a nice wind, the ship tilted slightly to one side making full use of the strong wind for speed. The crew went about their work with a little extra effort and eagerness knowing that land was close. Suddenly a familiar voice from aloft called out. 'Capitan, Capitan, look.' The seaman pointed to the horizon from high up in the rigging. The captain scanned the sea with his telescope and looked up to his lookout, the lookout pointed again. 'Ship.' The old man swivelled to the direction his lookout was pointing and stared through his telescope. 'It's coming right for us, a French man-o-war.' Above in the rigging the Union Jack flew proudly, and at the rear of the ship the company flag, but obviously with the union flag flying this was a viable target. The sloop was much faster and much more manoeuvrable but had much smaller and far fewer guns. The French ship cut a line almost straight at them. The captain had the sloop zig and zag across the water just as an amateur captain would do to try and lose their attackers. Slowly, as time went on the war ship gained ground and the sloop was coming in close to firing range, some of the crewmen on the ship were handed muskets and swords for the boarding party just as a precaution if things went wrong. The war ship was trying to cut them off forcing them in towards the islands, the captain watched the man of war from the rear of the ship and kept giving the wheelman orders and adjustments. The old sea captain watched as the man o war was almost lined up with the sloop. The captain ordered the wheelman to turn sharply 90 degrees, just as they turned a volley of shot pelted the water hundreds of feet in front of them. The canon fire startled Sofia, and she emerged from the lower decks in a white dress and bare feet. Having heard the commotion on the main deck she moved to the side of her husband holding his arm tightly, he pointed to the ship and put his arm around her helping to keep her warm as the ship skipped through the sea. The crew worked hard and were ready for the change of tac whenever the captain would call out. The ship would suddenly jink on the captain's orders, again and the French cannons would fire shots wildly into the sea. The captain continued to watch the French man-o-war behind them through his telescope staying one step ahead of the French captain all the time. The young lieutenant pointed and encouraged the men. 'Those scurvy dogs were waiting for us.' He looked to the captain and then back to the French ship. Just as he did the sloop jerked again to one side, the French ship tried to retaliate but as it chased the sloop each turn pointed the guns more towards the sea. They needed more time to bring the ship back level again so as to not lose their shots into the waves. With each turn the French ship fired off a volley of cannons, there was a short silence each time and then relief from the crewmen. The captain knew the shots would miss before the French even fired. After several turns and volleys, the captain yelled at his crew. 'Man, the starboard guns, ready to fire on my order.' Some of the men began loading the 6lbs cannons on the starboard side and made ready to fire lifting the small blast shutters. The French ship fired again and the sloop skipped along unscathed, then the captain changed his tactic, the next time the French ship fired and missed he had the ship turn about running back across the French guns that just fired and turned to the rear of the man-o-war, as the Mary sailed at speed past the rear of the French ship the captain called out. 'Fire.' All eight-cannon fired simultaneously right at the rear of the French ship, cannon balls and shot smashed into the enemy ship ripping through the captain and officers' quarters. Most of the shots penetrating deep through the bowels of the ship. Glass shattered all over the back of the enemy ship, large pieces of decorated wood tumbled into the sea. The 6lb cannonballs smashed open huge gaping holes. The crew of the Mary let out a huge roar of victory. The captain clasped his hands with delight behind his back, he was not finished yet. 'Wheelman, hard a port, steer directly away from them.' Again, the ship jinked and returned back onto a line with the enemy ships cannons still being reloaded, the light fast sloop, tilted under the weight of the wind in its sails as it cut a speedy line though the open waves. The sloop got further and further away very fast opening the gap between the two ships, it seemed the French man-o-war had given up the fight, keeping an eye on the enemy ship the captain had the Mary steer back towards the Caribbean and land. Sofia gave her husband a hug and smiled to the old captain. The old man stood proudly on the deck of his ship and watched his crew smugly as they made for land, his beloved old sloop survived again without as much as a scratch. The captain stood at the beautifully sculpted handrails and stroked the intricate design on the rails and breathed in deeply. 'Wheelman, steer west north west, lookout, watch the horizon.' The crew paused for a moment, if the captain said land was close, you could bet your life he was right. They jumped to their duties with a keen excitement and another victory under their belts. Sure, they had not gained any plunder, but escaping from a man-o-war whose only internet was to capture them, in prison them and maybe steel or sink their ship. They were very lucky indeed, a less experienced or skilful captain would have panicked and given up or lost everything. Relieved that the fighting was over, Sofia stood back from her husband slightly twirling slowly showing off her new dress. 'You like the new dress my husband.' He nodded to her. 'Very much, you look very beautiful, like a fine country lady.' She looked at her dress and pulled the puffy shoulders down to her arms showing the entirety of her upper body from her chest up, it was nice that he called her beautiful. No one ever called her beautiful before, all other men ever saw was the red birthmark on her neck, they mocked her. And she would turn away in shame. Daydan never looked to her like that, he always smiled. Sofia's dress was pretty and comfortable, the dress was made of fine cotton, front was patterned with white silk strands to pull it snuggly together. It scooped in nicely at the waist and then long and flowing to her ankles. He smiled watching her show off her dress dancing a little in front of him. She looked over to the Chinese man who must have helped her fashion the new dress, she smiled thankfully to him seeing that her husband approved. The Chinese man just continued with his work and bowed repeatedly every time either one of them looked his way.

The captain watched the young woman and smiled, she had been a fine guest onboard his ship, and if anything brought the ship some luck rather than bad luck. He turned to his surgeon and kicked the deck thoughtfully. 'Well, New Orleans is out of the question now, that's a French port still. Perhaps we could try.' He frowned to himself, the lost chance to trade at New Orleans was a blow and no doubt the news would be out about the small British ship that made a French captain of a man-o-war look foolish. Not that it was likely any captain would admit to such a beating. All the same, from Jamaica they would have to put to port on the mainland at some point. The captain looked at the surgeon and his young wife and smiled enviously, he leaned upon the rail of the ship and looked out to sea with an eagerness to reach their destination safely.

The rest of the day the crew made ready for land and trading with the port of Jamaica, most of what they carried would be traded in return for sugar, cotton and tobacco. All were easy to store and trade, provided everything was kept dry, they could make allot of money and profit on this trip. Other cargos were less profitable, but it made sense to diversify sometimes, besides, the captain liked the idea of a plentiful supply of tobacco. It might even be possible to pick up some white rum for the men. That afternoon, most of the crew reflected on their journey, the end of their outward trip was nearly over. The quartermaster would trade, and the ship would return back to England with a full cargo hold. The old admiral was still unsure where to put Daydan ashore with his precious cargo. The last thing he wanted was to deliver him straight into the hands of the French or some upstart Spaniard. Sofia was a fine young woman who in just six weeks really came out of her shell. She was a new woman, so full of confidence. She hung on her new husband's arm adoring him fondly, her smile was always welcome around the ship and her polite friendly manner was good for the men. She too began to learn new skills from the crew, especially the china man who could turn any kind of cloth into something useful. She was quiet and attentive, but with a razor-sharp intelligence and wit that her husband found fascinating. Sometimes, with little more than a look they knew what each other was thinking.

The ship sailed a good line as the captain instructed and with some strong winds, they made a steady passage through the Atlantic, between the many islands of the Caribbean. Just as the evening light was beginning to darken ahead and the brightest stars were starting to appear in the night sky, a shout from above broke the silence onboard the sleek beautiful ship as it sailed onward. 'Capitan, capitan, Land'o land'o.' The captain visibly shrunk down in his elaborate coat with relief as he looked up to his lookout, he cupped his hand and directed his shout up to his lookout. 'Jamaica.' The captain yelled. His lookout pointed with a wide happy smile nodding enthusiastically. 'Jamaica.'

As the light faded that evening, the Mary May was anchored just off Jamaica's coast a short sail away. The night sky in the distance was a multi coloured spectacle of yellow orange turquoise and mauve. Tonight, the sunset from west in the night sky over the ocean was magical, bright stars twinkled overhead, the moon dipped in the sky and looked larger and brighter than ever before. He stood behind Sofia at the very front of the ship looking over the bow holding her in his arms as they watched the sunset together. As they watched the sunset together, as they did on so many evenings. His young wife moved in close to him watching the horizon. He held her from behind holding her tightly in his arms shielding her from the cold. She turned and looked up into his eyes content and smiling happily to him enjoying the comfort of his embrace.

The crew and the captain were all staring at the magical sunset. He held her bare arm in his hand and turned to face her, giving her a small smile, he leaned down to her and kissed her soft lips tenderly. As they kissed, she moaned softly as their lips touched, he breathed in deeply closing his eyes enjoying the perfect moment with her and the sunset, his hand reached down and found hers, interlacing their fingers together he held her close. She turned and watched the sunset and leaned her cheek against his strong arms, her hand reached down slowly to herself and she smiled. For now, this was living, this was perfect, tomorrow they could begin their greatest adventure together.

CONTENTS

1.	A grave undertaking	2
2.	Am I dead	14
3.	It is time	24
4.	The shame	32
5.	The push	43
6.	The road to Bedlam	49
7.	Bedlam prison	56
8.	The bath house	70
9.	The Alchemist	79
10.	Parlour tricks	87
11.	Time for change	98
12.	No turning back	110
13.	The lecture	115
14.	The grand escape	124
15.	Out to sea	131
16.	Nothing is as it seems	139
17.	Ship of ghosts	144
18.	The Canaries	150
19.	Buts & barrels	160
20.	Sofia	175
21.	Land ahoy	186
	Contents	194
	Afterword	195

Afterword

A very special thankyou to everyone who has supported and encouraged me. Thank you for giving me the chance to do something I absolutely love doing. I only wish I had taken that leap sooner. Perhaps there is a lesson there. Please forgive my writing, it will improve, of that you can be sure.

Writing a book is no easy task, it takes time, it grows, it evolves, and it bites back. I really enjoy writing and letting my imagination run wild, letting my mind go to places that others dare not. All I can say is, this book has joined me on a journey. A journey of self-belief. When I started this book, it was an escape, now that it is finished, it feels like my way ahead is clear.

Do not let anyone tell you that you are not good enough. Do not let anyone stop you from chasing after your dreams. My dreams are tightly woven in the pages of this book, my future is in the stars.

"When you look to her, and her eyes sparkle, and she smiles, you know she's the one."

She is out there somewhere, waiting faithfully, my lovely lady, smart, passionate, sophisticated and full of life, waiting for a second chance.

XVX

"We are here to laugh at the odds and live our lives so well that Death will tremble to take us."

Charles Bukowski

To contact the author about this series: daydantaboo@yahoo.co.uk

Printed in Poland
by Amazon Fulfillment
Poland Sp. z o.o., Wrocław